SNC

SNOW

Book 1 of The Happily Never After Series

By

HP Mallory

10 Chosen Ones:
When a pall is cast upon the land,
Despair not, mortals,
For come forth heroes ten.
One in oceans deep,
One the flame shall keep,
One a fae,
One a cheat,
One shall poison grow,
One for death,
One for chaos,
One for control,
One shall pay a magic toll.

Snow White:
The shadows form a bloodless face
a shapeless girl lacking grace
on midnight wings her fate is found
and puts a djinn into the ground

ONE
Neva

Air escapes me in an undignified wheeze as I hit the unfinished hardwood floor, and I curl onto my side to minimize the pain of what's coming next.

The toe of Darius' boot catches me in the ribs, just below my sternum, where he knows the bruises won't show. Bruises don't make money. And that's what Darius is after. Even so, no man who's entered the Wicked Lyre Tavern has ever had the chance to get a good look at my tits. No one except Darius, that is.

But that's the price of sharing the attic space above the tavern with him. I'm given three meals a day, and a hit of the only thing that makes living in this miserable place remotely tolerable.

The force of his kick flips me onto my back and I turn my head sharply to the side, hiding my face behind the sable fall of my hair. I'm not giving him the satisfaction of seeing the tears that squeeze from the corners of my eyes.

"I said get up, slag. Are you deaf as well as stupid?"

I choke on my response, producing only a few inarticulate coughs instead of an answer. I do manage to prop myself up on one elbow, peeking up from beneath a fringe of hair to ascertain just how pissed he is. He wakes me like this most mornings, and I have to say, I prefer it to the mornings when he tries a gentler approach. Namely, when he prods me awake with his cock and demands I satisfy him. Somehow, the beatings seem a little more dignified.

"Maybe, if you hadn't kept me up all night," I grumble under my breath, crawling onto all fours. I keep my voice

1

low, though. I'm sore enough as it is. Besides, push Darius too hard and he'll decide to teach me a lesson. One I don't want to learn.

"What was that, slag?" he demands.

Yes. Definitely pissed. I'm not sure what I've done to earn his ire this early in the morning, but it doesn't bode well for the rest of the day.

I manage to get my shaking legs beneath me and climb to my feet, leaning against the opposite wall for balance. I hug the wall, feeling like the most wretched creature in the entire city of Ascor. I doubt there's a soul between here and the Forest of No Return that feels as shitty as I do at the moment.

When I manage to stop shaking, I turn in a slow half-circle to face the man who's both my tormentor and my savior. Darius leans against the vanity, careful not to disrupt the glass bottles and creams on its surface.

He watches me struggle, a cruel glint of amusement in his dark eyes. I wish he didn't look so much like his father. It makes it harder for me to hate him as much as I should.

Gregory was the only man who ever showed me an ounce of kindness, and it chafes me that this little bastard wears Gregory's face. It's not an especially handsome countenance: too boxy to be traditionally handsome, the eyes too deep-set and far apart, nose too large and teeth not large enough. But where Gregory's eyes were kind, Darius' always have the mean, rangy look of a feral cat. And he has the temper to match. He's also shorter and thinner than his father ever was.

"You're dancing in the back room tonight," Darius informs me, flicking the closet door open to reveal the small selection of gowns he's procured for my act.

All are made of silky or sheer fabrics and would easily cost a year of my wages. They've more than paid for Darius' tavern in the last few years. More accurately, *I* have more than paid for this tavern. After all, it's *my* body men are flocking to see.

"Please." The ragged entreaty is all I can force from my shaking lips.

He knows what I'm asking for.

Darius has kept *it* from me for three days. He can't honestly expect me to dance while my stomach tosses like a ship at sea. I need a bump if I'm going to be able to make it on stage sometime tonight.

I can read the answer on his face before he ever opens his mouth. That hateful smirk tics up a few degrees; he's clearly enjoying my distress. It's a rare treat for him to hear me beg like this. The last time he got the satisfaction, I literally came crawling back on hands and knees, begging for another dose.

Hopefully I won't have to do that again this morning.

He toys with the small, leather pouch at his waist, jiggling it in my direction as a taunt before flipping the material of his coat over his front to hide it from view.

"You'll get it when you've earned it, slag." Then he chuckles as he sneers down at me. "A group of merchants are selling their wares along Gendar Street for the next fortnight before moving north. At least half of 'em will be downstairs tonight. You please them and then I'll give you that bump you're so desperate for." His lips curl into a viper's grin, dripping insincerity like cloying venom. "And if you please *me* tonight, I'll give you another."

With his toe, he nudges a bowl across the floor, and a portion of my daily slop oozes over one corner and onto the hardwood. For just an instant, I imagine scooping the bowl off the floor and grinding his nose into the congealed mass of tasteless slop. Let *him* feel the indignity of being fed and put through his paces like a fucking show pony.

But my fingers only perform an ineffectual flex at my side, instead of the suicidally stupid action I've just contemplated. This place isn't palatial, my role is demeaning, my jailer is an arrogant prick, but I'm under no illusions. I'm better off here than I would be on the streets. That's the only reason I've stayed as long as I have. Because, as shitty as this life is, it's still better than being homeless in Ascor. I'll put up with Darius until I can squirrel away enough gold pieces to buy myself a way out of Ascor and a way in to some other city. Any other city, where my face isn't instantly recognizable as the salacious Snow White.

Darius selects a gauzy, multi-hued dress and tosses it lightly on the bed we share. I stare at it, mouth popping open in indignant surprise. I've worn this dress only once before, performing for Prince Achmed, who hailed from a place far, far away. A place called Agrabah in the Anoka Desert. The prince painted a hazy picture of Agrabah while I danced for him that night, dropping each layer of my gauzy drapings, one by one, until I lay mostly bare before him on stage. On the rare occasions I've dreamed of escaping, I've thought about traveling to Agrabah to find the prince again.

"The Dance of the Seven Veils?" I breathe, too tired to summon true outrage. "You can't be serious."

Damn Darius to the blackest regions of the nether realm! I've only done this dance once in front of an audience and that was a long time ago. Now he expects me to do it again without any practice, with barely a cup full of oats in my stomach and the fatigue of withdrawal threatening to drag me sideways to the floor? I'll make a fool of myself and then Darius will punish me for it later.

Darius worms a hand into his coat and dips one finger lightly into the pouch at his belt. It comes away dusted in white, like a baker's confection. He steps closer to me, offering the digit. I don't normally like to take it this way, but he's not leaving me much choice. This is all I'm going to get.

4

So I take his finger, guide it reverently to my mouth, and slide my tongue along every contour, trying to catch every speck of the priceless powder I can find. The process is over quickly, and my mouth tingles pleasantly as relief swells through me.

"Perform well, and you'll get more," Darius promises. "But, if you don't..."

He lets the statement hang, a sword over my head, waiting to drop. The meaning is very clear.

Failure isn't an option.

***

I tangle my fingers in the velvet folds of the navy-blue curtain and drag it back a few inches to peer out at the crowd beyond. Male voices overlap, sounding like a rumble of distant thunder. The room is hazy with pipe smoke, the heavy fog of it pressing into my lungs and further tightening my chest.

The number of men who occupy the chairs that ring the small stage staggers me, and I can tell there are still more I can't make out clearly, arranged at the small tables or standing at the back. How many men are packed into this back room? Fifty? One hundred? I don't think I've ever seen so many men crowded into the Wicked Lyre at one time, even around the annual festival, when spirits run high and men pay their last coin to see the creamy flesh of a nubile, young thing.

Every man in the room is wealthy. If their clothing isn't a giveaway, their voices would be. Cultured speech, with accents that range from the clipped tones of Grimm, the airy sing-song of a Wonderland noble, or the lilting honeyed tones of a cove-dwelling merchant from the Sea of Delorood.

I let the velvet slide between my fingers, dread settling in the pit of my stomach like a heavy millstone. How the bloody hell am I supposed to pull this off? I'm dizzy already. I'm going to go out there, slide one veil off, and then trip and fall on my face. And that will be the end of poor Neva Valkoinen, the end of Snow White. They'll find my body in an alleyway, a patchwork of blooming blue and purple bruises, swarmed by the city's vermin.

Darius' voice issues from the other side of the curtain, an ugly common accent among the sea of more pleasant voices. The room goes silent when he begins to speak, introducing me to the crowd as he has for years now. Is it four? I think it must be. Gregory died when Darius and I were seventeen. I'm twenty-one now.

And I don't know what to make of those years. They're gone and I have nothing to show for them. But nevermind. Thinking about the past only depresses me and my life is depressing enough as it is.

"And now, the main event! The greatest beauty you'll find in Ascor. Perhaps in all of Fantasia! I give to you, the lovely Snow White!"

The curtains are drawn aside to the sounds of thunderous applause, revealing me in all my dubious glory. I'm bathed in the glow of a thousand twinkling faerie lights that illuminate the stage. The lights are another item that sets the Wicked Lyre apart from other taverns, besides the star attraction. Darius is the only man within the city able to afford to light the place with fae-spelled orbs, day or night.

The weight of a hundred gazes falls on me seconds later, tracing what little they can see of my silhouette through the veils. The one dangled above my head is taupe, and the colors grow increasingly bolder the closer they get to the center of my body. Light glints off every jewel and bangle adorning me. And there are many. They chime as my body moves to the beat of the sultry music.

6

It's too bright. My head spins and I choke on bile. I feel as if I'm going to faint dead away. My eyes sweep the crowd, searching for something. Rescue? Pity? Perhaps a man who can look at me and see a sick girl being paraded on stage, instead of an object of lust to be used and discarded?

Every face I meet is eager, drinking me in like I'm a draft of Sweetland Port. There's no one here who gives a damn about me, no one who…

My gaze settles on a man perched on a stool near the back. He was easy to miss at first, because he's not nearly as rotund as most the men I see. Many men in Ascor wear the evidence of their wealth around their belt buckles, where girth stretches the seams of their fine clothing. But this man is different.

He's as tall and lean as any farm hand, with a slightly golden cast to his skin that suggests he spends a great deal of time outdoors. His clothing is less elaborate than the rest of the men in the room—he wears a simple scarlet tunic draped over buckskin trousers. Only the gold buttons that stud both give away the fact that he didn't just stroll into the Wicked Lyre by accident.

The understated wardrobe makes the artistry of his face seem even more absurd in contrast. His jaw is slanted at an angle that appears sharp enough to cut glass. A layer of golden stubble ripples across that strong line, drawing my eye to a perfect bow-lipped mouth. His hair has been swept to the nape of his neck, the flyaway golden strands gathered together by a leather thong. But it's his eyes that strike me most. I expect them to be blue, like those of one of the savage Northmen. But they're not.

They're a perfect tawny color, like the piercing eyes of a hawk. He cocks his head in an almost bird-like motion, considering me with detached interest. There's no ardent desire in this man's gaze. He doesn't even appear mildly aroused by my dance or by me. I can't puzzle out what he's doing here. Why come to this show, if he isn't here to get a thrill by peeking at Snow White's tits and ass?

I don't know how long I stare at him, but the moment I realize I'm still swaying to the melancholic beat of the music, I snap back into myself. My body begins moving without conscious thought, like a snake before its charmer. I close my eyes, trying to block out the appreciative murmurs that run through the room as I sway this way and that, releasing my veils to the ground one at a time. Amethyst, sapphire, ruby, and topaz drop from my body, curling like colorful smoke before they fall to the floor.

I pretend I'm alone. Alone but for the curious stranger, with his odd eyes and his benign interest. I pretend I won't be what these men, with their avaricious appetites, will be envisioning when they tug their cocks tonight. In my mind, the curious stranger and I are alone and this is art, not a tawdry peep show.

And then… it's over. I find myself on the ground, bosom heaving, in the final pose of the dance, with my head bowed. I'm wearing only the shimmering and slightly diaphanous white material that makes up the undergarments Darius provides me.

I'm exhausted and I feel sick to my stomach. My ears ring and tears are already wetting my eyes. I can only hope I don't heave up the contents of my stomach right here. But, then I remember there isn't much in my stomach to heave up.

The applause is a dull roar in my ears. I climb unsteadily to my feet, gathering the veils I've abandoned as the stage is showered with coins. I take two of them—only two because they're all I can hide in my tight brazier. Any more and I risk Darius' wrath.

I spy him in the back, leaning against the bar, talking to the mysterious stranger in the buckskin trousers. I allow myself a curious flick down to the stranger's groin and I'm offended when it appears I've had little effect on him.

Darius and the stranger are in deep conversation, to the point that I wonder if they're arguing. About what, I don't know, but I imagine the subject must be money. At the moment, though, I don't really care. There's only one reward I want for this night's work, and it better damn well be waiting for me when I get backstage.

TWO
Neva

A dizzy sense of euphoria settles over me on the shaky inhale. My nose goes immediately numb on contact with the powdery white stuff, but it's worth the momentary discomfort for the blessed peace I find afterward.

I eye the baggie Darius has given me, and my hands tremble with the effort of not sniffing the lot of it. Do that and I'll just end up bloodying my nose and pissing off Darius. Better to tuck the baggie away and save it for another day. My employer's moods are mercurial at the best of times, so I don't want to chance being stuck without the cocaine when another bout of Darius' temper strikes.

I examine my face in the small vanity mirror. Darius likes to buy mirrors and place them in every room of the tavern, so I can't, for one second, forget the reason I'd been cast out of my parents' home. Most women would spit on me for saying the beauty of my face is a curse; but then, most women don't ever lay eyes on me. The Wicked Lyre tavern isn't a place that boasts patrons of the female persuasion.

I run my fingers lightly over one cheek. It takes me being run damn-near ragged to put any flush of color into my ivory skin. My skin might have been fetching, if I'd been born with cornflower blue eyes and blonde hair. But the braided coil that gathers at my neck is a black so deep, it shines blue in sunlight. My eyes are large and luminous amber brown, like light shone through a glass of thick liqueur. They shine from a face that's almost eerily symmetrical, like the crafted features of a porcelain doll, and I appear almost as lifeless.

My face has been described as off-putting almost as often as it's considered desirable. If my heart didn't thunder in my chest, most would have thought me a misbegotten beast from further north, one of the blood drinkers cursed for their part in what had been done to poor Princess Briar Rose.

The desire to shatter the glass of the mirror is potent, but I stay my hand. I've had enough bad luck to last me a lifetime. I don't need to add still more to the already badly weighted cosmic scales.

Yet, I hate my reflection, all the same.

A knock on the door drags my gaze away from the vanity and the spoils of my performance. I've pulled on one of Darius' heavy woolen coats to ward off the chill. The only remaining veil I wear is thin and offers little in the way of modesty or heat. I stuff the baggie away for safekeeping as two men enter.

Darius walks into the room first, just as agitated as I'd seen him last, running thick fingers through his dark hair. He flicks his angry gaze back to the doorway and then at me, completing that loop a few times before he heaves a sigh.

"Well, don't loiter there," he says to the man who stands behind him. "Come in, then."

A second man appears in the doorway, and I recognize him instantly. He's the man from before, the only one in the crowd who didn't appear to be slavering over me. My breath catches in my throat now that I'm able to get a glimpse of what he truly looks like. From a stance, he appeared quite handsome. Now that he's nearer, it's all I can do to keep myself from running a hand along his lightly tanned skin to see if it feels as warm as it looks.

The man is truly stunning. The most beautiful man I've ever seen.

11

His scarlet tunic bunches around a belt at his waist and gives me a hint of just how muscled he must be beneath. A strange stirring begins between my legs, warmth pooling in my belly and every muscle within my body clenches tight. I'm actually shocked at myself.

Is this... Desire?

It must be! It feels exactly the way men have described the feelings I create in them. It's also the first time I've felt this way in the presence of a man. Usually I try to imagine I'm anywhere other than this rotten tavern. I try to busy my mind as ugly and lecherous men stare at me and attempt to touch me.

And though I've known the feel of a man inside me—I've only ever known Darius. Yes, he's been offered incredible amounts of coin by numerous men in return for my body but Darius always denies those requests. Why? Because he's selfish and he's greedy and he's never wanted another man to know me as intimately as he does.

Not that I've minded—all the men who have asked to pay for my privileges have been ugly, usually as ugly as Darius, himself.

Regardless, Darius, as my only lover, has never been able to bring me to that final, shuddering point where women supposedly find their pleasure.

I can't put my finger on why, but I have the impression this stranger's hands could handle a woman's body deftly. I find myself fixated on those hands, wondering if they're as rough as the rest of him appears, or if they're uncalloused from living a soft life of leisure.

I disregard the last thought as idiotic—to look at this man, one would immediately realize he's never lived a day of leisure in his life.

Darius regards him with a scowl and the sullen air of a child who's had his favorite toy stolen. The man only smiles back benignly, but even that touch of humor brightens his entire face, making him more lovely, more compelling.

"This man has just offered to pay for a night with you, Snow," Darius informs me, turning his glower in my direction, as though it's somehow my fault.

My eyes bug. Surely this is a joke? Because there's no way this man, with his simple spun clothing and his unassuming demeanor, can afford the price Darius asks for such a thing. Even the exotic and incredibly wealthy Prince Achmed could only afford to monopolize one of my nights with private dances, wine, and conversation. An heir to the throne of an entire nation still couldn't pay the sum Darius asks for me. An exorbitant sum because Darius knows no man will ever pay it. It's his failsafe, his assurance that he'll continue to be the only man who has even known the inside of Snow White.

Yet this man says he can pay that sum and will. Who in blazes is he?

"I'll send in wine and food," Darius continues in a sullen monotone. "When you're finished supping, ring if you need me."

With that, he turns, seizes the doorknob in a fist already shaking with rage, and exits, slamming the door behind him. I will pay for this later. And I'm afraid I'll pay for it in ways I never have before.

Why did Darius ever agree to this when it's clear he doesn't want to? Clearly, there is a price for everything...

I turn my attention back to the stranger. He actually smiles at me, and it's like watching day break against the sky. His smile makes me absurdly hopeful. For what? I'm unsure.

"What an unpleasant little man," he murmurs, almost to himself. When he turns those piercing tawny eyes on me, the air batters around in my lungs again as my mind scrambles to remember just how to breathe. The man tilts his head curiously at me, observing me with no more than casual interest.

"Yes," I say, unsure of what more I should say. If anything.

"Why do you stay with him?"

It's my turn to lift a curious brow. It seems as though the stranger genuinely doesn't understand. He waits in silence for me to respond, as if this question is an important one to him. Can't he see just how helpless Darius has rendered me? Can't he see that I rely on Darius for everything? For my very life?

But that's going to change soon, or so I've promised myself. One of these days, when I save enough coins, I'm going to leave this wretched place. I'm going to steal away into the dark and I'm never going to look back. Without a drug to sustain me, I'll have a wretched few weeks while I go through withdrawals. And, presuming I survive those withdrawals, I won't have any other option but to flee Ascor. Too many people know my face here. Too many people know to whom I belong. All it would take is one lech to come after me and any gainful employment I'm able to accept would be stripped away. Staying with Darius isn't a good option, but it's the only one I have… at present.

I allow the stranger a shaky smile in lieu of a response. Scooping out a small portion of my precious winnings, I offer him a bump. "Would you like some?" I hope he'll say no.

The man stares at the powder with a vaguely disgusted expression. That would be a 'no', then. Unthinking hurt flashes through me, though it's completely ludicrous for me to care what this stranger thinks of me. He's paid for one night, after all. I'm now his whore and in the morning, he'll be gone and I'll never see him again. I should probably just be grateful he's even bothering to try to make conversation.

We stand in strained silence for a few minutes until Darius returns. I discreetly take the bump of coke, not looking up to see what this stranger thinks of it. In the background, I hear Darius as he drapes a table. I turn to see him smoothing the bumps of a linen cloth and then he places two glasses onto the table, alongside a platter of grapes, melon, figs, crackers and cheeses. My stomach does a joyful little pirouette at the sight of the fare being laid out. A growing part of me doesn't care what this man does to me, so long as I'm allowed some of the meal. It'll be the best thing I've eaten in weeks, maybe even months.

"Enjoy," Darius bites out before backing out of the room again. He glares at me in a way that promises punishment when this man leaves tomorrow. I feel my stomach drop down to my toes.

When the stranger and I are alone again, the man gestures at the two chairs beside the table. "Sit and eat. You look famished." As if to lead by example, he sits down and smiles up at me.

I hesitate, even as my stomach yearns toward the food and growls audibly, embarrassing me. The man offers me an understanding smile and waves toward the food once more.

What if he's baiting me like a dog, and intends to hurt me the second I lay a finger on the meal? After all, I haven't done anything to earn such a reward yet. Perhaps, if I sat on his lap? If I pretended to be more interested in his cock than I was in the food? Yes. That would entitle me to a bit at least, wouldn't it?

He watches with concern as I stumble away from the vanity, still unsteady from the morning's withdrawal. I'm already feeling miles better than I was, but it appears I'm a few apples short of a full cart.

The man inhales in what appears to be surprise as I sink onto his lap. His tawny eyes fly open wide as he stares down at me, even as those strong hands settle at the small of my back, keeping me from sliding off his lap.

"What are you doing?" His voice is a low, melodic murmur. I blink coquettishly up at him, forcing my lips to twist into a playful smile the way Darius has instructed me. Not only do I dance, but I have to pretend all my visitors… arouse me. And Darius has taught me how to wear such an expression.

"I'm sitting on your lap," I purr. "Unless you want me to move?"

There's a glint of dark humor in those fathomless eyes for a just a moment before his hands slide beneath my ass. They don't curl around my flesh and squeeze, the way I expect. He just lifts me carefully and deposits me on the chair beside him. It's all done so effortlessly and with such amusement, that I don't feel the sting of rejection as strongly as I expect. He selects a piece of cheese from the platter and offers it to me.

I don't understand what I've done to offend him. I looked at him the way Darius taught me to and I tried to show my interest by sitting on his lap. Yes, I've earned a reward in the form of a piece of cheese, but I feel like I've done the wrong thing, all the same.

"As lovely as you are, I prefer to keep this… arrangement professional, for the time being."

Professional?

"You really should eat," he continues. "You're dreadfully pale."

At last, a genuine smile stretches my lips, even as I'm offended by his words. "Eating won't help that, I'm afraid. I'm as pale as a fucking shade and always have been."

He chuckles at this. "Good thing a Shepherd hasn't come for you yet."

I'm fairly sure Darius would beat off any Shepherd or Shepherdess that came to the door with their gilded lantern hung from a crook, priest in tow, with the intent to take my soul. The bastard would still try to sell me even if I died. But I'm not counting on meeting my end with the grim-faced reapers of souls just yet.

I should be so lucky.

"Darius wouldn't even let a Shepherd take me without paying."

The man snorts once in amusement and pops a grape into his mouth, chewing to disguise the distinct sound of his laughter. I take a tentative nibble on my piece of cheese and close my eyes when the sharp bite of cheddar washes across my tongue.

Gods above, it's been so long since I had a decent meal.

We sit in silence for another minute or so.

I'm most of the way through the wedge of cheese when he finally speaks again.

"My name is Herrick. Herrick Vorst." He watches my face for any flicker of recognition, as if he's accustomed to people knowing who he is. I bob my head once, hoping he's not going to grow angry when he realizes just how ignorant I really am. But I haven't heard much other than whispers of gossip and rumors at the tavern since I came to live here at sixteen.

"It's a pleasure to meet you," I say honestly, even if I'm surprised and confused he hasn't even tried to touch me yet. But I'm also grateful. Even if I end up fucking him at the end of the night (which is assuredly going to happen, considering he paid for me), this meal is still a kindness I hadn't expected to enjoy.

Herrick cocks his head to the side, eyes narrowing on me again. I honestly don't understand what he's trying to puzzle out when he looks at me like that.

"What's your name?" he asks, finally.

"Snow," I start, figuring that's the answer he wants—the thrill of hearing it repeated to him—that he will be the first man, outside of Darius, to bed the famous Snow White. As that realization hits me, I can't hide the anxiety that flows through me.

What if I disappoint him? What if I'm as terrible at fucking as Darius tells me? What if I get yet another beating at this man's hands?

"No," he interrupts, shaking his head. "Don't give me your stage name, please."

"I don't understand," I start. What does this man want from me? Every time I try to give him what I think he's asking of me, I'm wrong!

"Some of those simpletons might believe you're really called Snow White, but we both know better." He takes a breath as my heart starts pounding. "What's your name?"

I swallow the last of the cheese thickly. I don't know why he's asking me this?

It's just your name! I think to myself.

But, somehow, telling him my name feels more intimate than having sex with him. Thousands of men have seen me in the last few years, but only one of them knows my given name. Darius. If I tell this man my name, it would make him privy to a secret only Darius knows.

And it's that last thought that spurs me to give Herrick Vorst an honest answer, because I dislike the thought of dying one day with only Darius knowing my true name.

"Neva Valkoinen."

"Neva," he repeats, wrapping his tongue around the contours of my name as though it tastes sweet. Then he laughs a little to himself. "So, perhaps I'm the simpleton, eh?"

"Simpleton?" I ask, frowning at him.

He nods. "Your name really does mean White Snow."

I grin, despite my trepidation. This man is far smarter than a casual observer would be led to believe. "Yes."

"How did you arrive with a name like that?"

"Well, my parents came up with it," I answer.

"I meant how did you get your stage name?"

"Oh," I answer. "Darius spent days poring over books, trying to come up with a stage name for me that sounded appropriate. He thought it would be clever to play off my actual name."

"A clever thought for an idiot," Herrick responds.

I immediately feel the smile on my lips. "You should watch what you say," I whisper to him, confidentially. "You never know who could be listening."

He nods and smiles fully, making me realize he has a dimple on one side of his mouth.

"Point taken," he says.

I drop my gaze to the plate of food as my stomach growls again. He motions to it and this time, I stand up and help myself to each type of fruit, five crackers and another few wedges of cheese.

I return to the chair he set me in and face him again, only to find his eyes already focused on me. "You must be very well-traveled to know what my name meant."

His eyes grow a touch more guarded, though his amused smile doesn't fade. "You could say that, I suppose. I'm a merchant, after all."

A merchant? Interesting. "And what is it that you peddle, Mr. Vorst?"

What could he possibly sell that would allow him the means to buy me? This man is strange. Then it occurs to me he must have stolen his way into my bed. Not that I care.

"I didn't come here to discuss the mundane details of my business, Neva," he says, rather hurriedly and I realize he's ready to claim his prize. My anxiety increases tenfold and I nod as I put the plate of untouched food on the side table, next to the chair.

"Okay," I say as I face him expectantly.

But he doesn't move from his seated position. "Sit."

"Okay," I say again and sit, completely unsure of what to say or do. This Herrick Vorst is the most confusing man I've ever met. And he makes me nervous.

"I came because you pulled me here," he says.

"More like the sign outside pulled you here," I amend, taking a brave stab at humor now that he doesn't appear too volatile.

He shakes his head slowly, and a few strands of that perfect golden hair escape the leather thong at the base of his neck. It's distractingly touchable, and I fold my hands primly in my lap to keep myself from touching him.

Somehow my hunger is forgotten for the time being.

"No. *You* pulled me here," he insists.

"I don't understand."

"I was trying to find the concentrated mass of magic that was hiding in this seemingly unremarkable tavern."

"Concentrated mass of magic?" I repeat, shaking my head. What is he talking about?

He nods. "Yes. It felt familiar, and I was expecting to find an old friend within these walls. Imagine my surprise when I found a little witchling on stage instead."

My brow creases as I try to make sense of these bizarre words. Magic? Witchling? What in the name of Avernus is he talking about? There hasn't been a witch in any of the seven principalities of Fantasia for over a decade. Everyone knows that!

All the noble houses signed off on the decree in the only show of solidarity they've been able to display in a hundred years. The only magic users still around are the Shepherds, and they only remain because souls have to go *somewhere* after death. Not even the royals want spooks hanging around their cities.

I shake my head. "I don't understand."

He sits forward and reaches out, seizing my hand with enough suddenness to draw a startled yelp from me. He smooths his fingers over the back of my palm in a soft apology before he returns his gaze to mine and clasps my hands tightly in his, earnestness in those unnatural eyes.

"What… what are you doing?" I ask, suddenly afraid for the first time since he walked into my room.

"I won't hurt you, Neva," he says in a soft voice. "I just need to know *what* you are. It's important that Guild members are hidden away in these troubled times."

"Guild members?"

He nods. "It's clear you have a connection to Tenebris. I just don't understand why she'd leave you exposed like this."

I draw my hands away, and smile up at him sadly as I take a deep breath. He's clearly mistaken me for someone else. Hopefully he won't be angry he's paid so much money for me when he thinks I'm someone else. I'm not sure if I should break the news to him or if Darius should.

"I don't know what you're talking about, sir," I say and then inhale deeply. "Clearly you've mistaken me for someone else."

"No," he starts but I shake my head.

Hmm… this could cause quite the ruckus because I'm more than sure Darius won't give Herrick his money back. And since that's the case, Herrick might as well have his chance to enjoy me, given he spent an ungodly amount of money to spend the night in my bed. I stand and walk to him. I might as well get this over with.

"Unfortunately, Darius isn't the type of man to refund you your money." I take another deep breath as I approach him, placing each of my hands on the chair arms on either side of him. "I apologize for that, but I would like to try to make it up to you. If you'd kindly let me do my job, I'll…"

Herrick stops me before I can sling a leg over his lap. His broad, calloused hands brace my waist and I come to a stop with my face inches away from his. I'm sitting on his

lap and he's close enough that the warmth of his breath
tickles the loose strands of hair near my ear. My gaze dips
unwillingly to that perfect bow-lipped mouth, and I wonder
what it would be like to feel that mouth on mine.

"I should go," he murmurs quietly. "I've upset you."

"Go?" I repeat, suddenly disappointed even though I
can't fathom why. "You haven't even kissed me," I remind
him.

"It's okay," he starts.

"But," I say. "You paid enough gold for that
privilege… and more."

His gaze dips to my mouth just briefly and I see hunger
in his eyes. When I blink again, his eyes are unreadable, his
smile enigmatic.

"Gold is abundant and something I can easily find,
Neva. A kiss must be earned, not bought."

He finally smiles widely enough to flash teeth as he lifts
me off his lap and sets me on my feet, and I take a wary step
away. His canines are sharp enough to unnerve me. He can't
be a vampire, surely. His skin is sun-kissed and his eyes are
too bright. Still, there's something inhuman there.

"You ought to be careful about offering things like
kisses to men like me," he says and there's a warning in his
eyes.

"Why?"

He leans in just enough to tease my cheek with those
soft lips. The whisper that traces the shell of my ear makes
every part of me go warm and shivery.

"Because men like me are selfish and would steal you
away."

In the next breath, he pulls away and is halfway to the
door, throwing me a cheery, "Have a pleasant evening, Ms.
Valkoinen."

"But," I start again.

He motions to the plate of uneaten food. "Do eat the rest of your supper before that odious man returns."

The door closes behind him with a barely audible click and I sink into his abandoned chair, my heart beating wildly in my chest.

Only one thought haunts my mind as I absentmindedly finish everything on the plate.

Who in blazes is Herrick Vorst?

THREE
Neva

I'm beginning to wonder if Herrick Vorst doesn't regret his hasty decision to abandon me seven days ago, because he's become a near-constant fixture in the Wicked Lyre ever since.

From the moment Darius throws the doors open, near sunset, until last call in the wee hours of morning, Herrick is there. He sits in the back, consuming enough ale to poison an average man and, seemingly, I'm one of the few to notice him doing it.

He's the most attractive man to grace Ascor's streets in an age, and even drunken men can't fail to notice it. Perhaps it's because his trademark clothing makes him appear almost painfully common? If so, he must be even more intelligent than I first assumed. No enterprising thief is going to think to lift Herrick's coin purse, though I'm convinced he's got enough money to buy the tavern and everyone inside it three or four times over.

Why am I convinced? Because every time he's here, he spends a small fortune.

Every night, it's the same. I dance. He watches. At the end of the night, he'll ask me the same questions, irritated when I refuse to give him the answers he wants. I wish I knew who the fuck this *Tenebris* was, because I'd point Herrick in her direction immediately. For as beautiful as Herrick Vorst is, I'm convinced he's completely insane.

Why else would he continue to return here, spouting these ridiculous stories about witchlings and magic and

24

Guild members and Tenebris? He's clearly out of his mind.
Such a shame, too.

All the attention from Herrick has Darius more riled
than ever, the jealous streak he harbors growing wider with
every passing day that Herrick visits.

***

Darius stops moving inside me with a harsh grunt, and
my stomach turns at the feeling of warm liquid that drips out
of me, and down one thigh. I cast my eyes downward as he
proceeds to button his trousers. I'm going to need to change
my clothing again. He tore the blue and yellow satin dress
I'd been wearing in his haste to fuck me. Somehow, he'll
find a way to blame me for that, too. I need to sneak upstairs
to mend the dress before he takes notice.

"Go clean yourself, slag," he pants, body hunching over
mine in exhaustion. Funny how he can be so winded by
something that lasts mere minutes.

"*Neva*," I whisper. "Can't you have the decency to call
me by my name after you've fucked me?"

His dark eyes burn into the side of my face before his
fist catches me beneath the ribs. I wheeze, folding over his
arm like a limp rag as the air explodes from my lungs.

I shouldn't have taunted him—I know better. I don't
know why I did.

"Don't talk back to me, slag," he snaps. "Go upstairs
an' clean up before I strip ya bare an' parade ya around the
tavern like the whore you are."

Eyes watering, I fumble for the knob and exit the
storeroom, still slightly hunched over the fresh, throbbing
bruise that's beginning to form. A few eyes trail me with
interest as I make my way slowly toward the stairs. I don't
even have a chance to set my foot on the bottommost step
before a familiar hand closes around my wrist. It's not the

crushing grip of Darius—the only reason I don't rip my hand away at once.

Herrick Vorst is standing just below me, staring up at me in concern.

"You're hurt."

It's a statement, not a question. I lean my weight on the banister and ease my hand from his grip. To his credit, he lets me go, instead of hurting me further.

"It doesn't matter," I tell him quietly.

"Of course it matters," he stresses, a muscle jumping in his jaw. It's almost endearing to see how much he seems to care, though I can't fathom why he's bothering with me at all. Ah-yes, he thinks I'm someone else.

"I can help you, if you let me," Herrick continues. "Just duck into the back room and..."

"No," I say shortly, taking another step away from him. I'm not that stupid—the second I step into the back room with him, he'll force himself into me. Without paying. And that will irate Darius. If Herrick wants to stop me, he's going to have to make a scene. "I'm sorry, but you had your chance, Mr. Vorst."

"For the sake of all of Fantasia, girl. I'm not trying to fuck you!"

I'm surprised, but a second later, I realize he's lying to me. Of course, he's trying to fuck me! Every man tries to fuck me! "Well, whatever you are doing, you're making things worse for me. So, I'd appreciate it if you'd leave."

"I can't leave, Neva."

Anxiety worms its way through me. If Darius sees us standing here together...

"Things were fine before you got here," I snap at Herrick. "And since you've been here, they've gotten so much worse!"

"I worried that would be the case," he says.

26

I shake my head. "You need to leave, Mr. Vorst and never return. I can't help you. I'm not the person you think I am."

I turn to leave but he won't release my hand. "That brute hit you."

"He constantly hits me," I throw the truth back in his face, angry with him for pretending to care.

He gestures to my chest, and I have just a second to wonder how he knows Darius hit me and where. Darius never does so in public.

"I can help… heal you, Neva," Herrick says.

I exhale sharply through my nose, deciding he needs to go and he needs to do so immediately. "I don't care what you can do, Mr. Vorst."

"Call me Herrick."

"Herrick," I say on a sigh. "If Darius sees us standing here, together, he'll punish me more than he already has. So, could you do me a favor and please leave? I don't want to deal with another bout of his temper tonight." I pause for a moment. "Please."

Herrick's gaze stays intent on mine and I almost want to weep. His eyes are unguarded and kind. It's the latter that almost slays, because kindness is the one thing that can penetrate the careful barriers I use to keep myself untouchable. The stone barricade of Snow White threatens to tumble and leave Neva Valkoinen achingly vulnerable. I can't afford that.

Gregory was also kind, and he ended up leaving me in the hands of a monster after his passing. What wreckage will this man leave when he's through selling his wares in the city? Best I never get the chance to find out.

"Neva…"

"Please," I whisper. "Just, please go."

I turn on my heel and race up the stairs as fast as this newest injury will allow, putting distance between Herrick and myself. Once safely inside my bedchamber, I slump over in a chair, curling myself around my injury until the throbbing of my heart aches less keenly behind the bruising.

But, I can't tarry long. There's always something to be done. So, I stand up and doff my dress, hiding it in the back of the closet until I have a chance to take needle and thread to it.

When I return to the tavern's ground floor, I'm wearing a simple blue shift dress and a band to hold back the mass of my hair. I breathe a sigh of relief when I can't spy Herrick anywhere in the interior. There is, however, a man waiting for me at the bottom of the stairs, with Darius crouched like a gargoyle at his elbow. The sour look on Darius' face is familiar.

This can't be fucking happening. Again. How have two men managed to scrape together enough coin to buy me with less than a fortnight between them? And this man is nowhere near as attractive as Herrick.

Darius almost spits the words I'm dreading, and I know the bruise I'm already nursing won't be the last I suffer today. As if it's my fault, he's agreed to sell my body.

"Go back upstairs and disrobe, Snow," he instructs me coldly. "Mr. Anon will be up shortly after we've settled payment."

I squeeze my eyes shut until the stinging behind them stops threatening to spill tears and ruin the whole façade. I'm going to find Mr. Vorst and slap him for disarming me so thoroughly with his abrupt kindness.

When I open my eyes, the lump in my throat is all I have left to contend with.

"Yes, sir," I breathe.

And for the second time in as many minutes, I stalk back upstairs and prepare to steel myself for the worst that's yet to come.

FOUR
Neva

I'm sitting at my vanity, lips half-painted with tinted gloss, when I hear steps climbing the stairs. I expected negotiation to take several minutes, perhaps even an hour, given how reluctant Darius has been to share me. But, apparently such isn't the case. The steps stop at the head of the stairs, and then I hear the sound of my door opening. I turn to see Mr. Anon standing in the doorway.

"Hello," I offer with a polite smile.

He doesn't say anything but allows his eyes to sweep over the sparsely furnished room and my mostly bare body. I haven't quite gotten down to bare skin, but I'm as close as I can get. The undergarments are made from finely spun lace that Darius grumbles are expensive, and yet still buys every time he rips them from me.

Anon has also caught me with a small pouch of coke tucked between my breasts. I was preparing to take a bump before he came up. This certainly isn't my most flattering moment.

"Erm... I'm sorry, sir," I say as I turn to face him. "I didn't expect you so soon. Darius tends to haggle longer."

"I made him an offer he couldn't refuse," Anon says gruffly.

He fingers something at his side, and unease slithers through me. The large man hulks into the room and closes the door behind him. He locks it.

Much like Herrick Vorsk, Anon isn't dressed in fine fabrics that flout his wealth. The only piece of finery I can spy on him is a signet ring on his left pinkie, which appears to depict a large bird in flight. I pick through my limited knowledge, trying to find a house sigil that matches a giant bird, but I come up blank.

Mr. Anon doesn't look at me with avid lust the way so many men do, which makes me wonder if something is wrong.

I'm not an imbecile, no matter how many times Darius makes claims to the contrary. Fortune is a fickle thing, and I'm not stupid enough to think I'll be granted mercy twice. This man intends to have me and have me he will. I suddenly wish Herrick had been more interested in bedding me. At least then I might know what sex is like with a man to whom I'm attracted.

I am most definitely NOT attracted to Mr. Anon.

I begin to approach him when I catch something in his eye—a certain expression that instantly causes the hair on the back of my neck to rise. This man hasn't said or done anything to cause this strange reaction, but I'm suddenly terrified of him, all the same.

What's wrong with me?

I press my back to the wall, cursing myself for being caught wearing so little. Sharp blue eyes stare at me, freezing me in place for a second, like the hare who's been caught in the gaze of a hawk.

"Get on the bed." The command is cold and clipped, and my heart kicks into a higher tempo when he continues to stare me down.

"I want to speak to Darius," I croak, suddenly worried something is very wrong. Darius would never have allowed this man up the stairs by himself, I suddenly realize. Darius would have followed him to make sure he didn't take a detour and steal something. Darius is the most untrustworthy person I've ever met.

"Why?"

"To make sure you've paid for me," I lie, but it's the only thought that comes to me. All I know is I want to get away from this man, though I don't know why.

A chilly smile comes to rest on his thin lips and he fingers something at his side again. "Believe me, he's been paid what he's due, little girl. Now, on the bed."

I only inch further along the wall, my every instinct telling me to distance myself from Anon as quickly as possible. I reach behind my back, trying to be as unobtrusive as possible, to seize the handle of a broom that's been propped against the wall. Mrs. Potts must have been in to clean this evening while I performed.

"On the bed," he orders again, and the loud bark makes me jump.

"You undress first," I wheedle, trying to buy myself time. I need to get away from him, to find out where Darius is…

Anon's gaze travels from my face to my almost nude body for the first time since he entered, as if he's taking note of something. A smirk ghosts his lips, but his gaze doesn't linger overlong on most men's favorite parts.

Instead, that finger performs an almost sensual stroke over the thing at his side. He pulls the object into the light to reveal his grip has been on the glimmering silver handle of a dagger, emblazoned with an absurdly large bird. I have a choked second of horror when I realize the blade is already bloodied.

Darius had been paid what he'd been due, all right—catching a dagger to the heart. And now I'm going to be next.

"Fuck," I hiss, scrambling backward and almost losing the grip on the broom in my panic. My heart is hammering and I feel lightheaded. I've never been this close to death and now that I am, I'm petrified.

Anon's smirk grows when I brandish my improvised weapon. It's a twig broom, barely enough to sweep dust from the floor. It's ridiculous, but it's also the only thing I have with which to protect myself. Yet, what good is it trying to protect myself against…

"Are you an assassin?" I ask, because I'm not entirely sure.

"What gave it away?" he responds.

But the question remains as to what type of assassin. And who sent him? His weapons are too fine for an average thug for hire. He dispatched Darius quickly and quietly and now he's far too calm for my liking.

"I did try to make this easier," he starts.

"Easier?"

He cocks his head to the side. "You could have just gotten on the bed and died like a good little girl. One thrust and it would have all been over." He laughs. "Though I suppose one thrust is what you're used to, eh? The bloke downstairs didn't seem like he'd have much stamina."

"Then you've killed him?" I ask, just to be sure.

"Aye," the man answers without hesitation.

I swallow hard. I can't say I'm sorry to know Darius is dead. I'm not. And were I in a different situation, I would probably be relieved. But now, all I can think about is the fact that I'm next.

Anon whips back his dark cloak to reveal still more weapons hidden on his person, as if he's giving me a preview of the smorgasbord of death he intends to unleash on me. There's a shortsword, a small crossbow, and even a small mace hidden among an army of knives. My mouth is an arid wasteland and my knees shake so hard, it's difficult to stay upright.

"Whatever you've been paid, I can pay you more," I say, immediately thinking of Herrick. He'd pay to keep me alive, I'm convinced. Well, that is, if I hadn't insisted he leave. Fuck my cursed luck!

Anon laughs. "You can't afford that type of money," he says.

"Yes, I can," I insist, now trying to stall. "You don't know the caliber of my clientele."

He takes a few steps closer, but says nothing, just continues brandishing that fucking smirk that makes my stomach turn.

"Stay back," I croak, taking a swing at him. He easily bats away the ineffectual strike, nearly wrenching the broom from my hands.

"No more talking," he says as he rushes me, knife at the ready, and I barely manage to deflect him with the broom.

His next swat sends the broom flying from my hands and sends me toppling backward onto the bed. Rolling away, I barely escape the thrust of the dagger. It impacts the mattress, spilling stuffing when he wrenches the blade out.

There's no way I can make it to the stairs in time, and the only man who might have come running at the sound of my screams has vacated the building. Damn my own foolish lack of foresight! I really could use Herrick's help now but, clearly, I'm not going to get it. And that means I'm going to have to rely on myself.

I glance at Anon and the rest of the room, realizing there's not a damned thing I can do to protect myself. I glance to the side and from the corner of my eye, I spot the window just behind me.

It's my only option.

Turning around, I hurl myself at the window, jumping forward with as much strength as I can muster. I shield my head and face with my arms and shriek as the glass explodes outward in a shower of shards and fragments.

I can feel the shards slicing into me all over my body, peeling ribbons of skin from me before I even enter freefall.

But then I feel the sting of the wind as I fall. I look up and see Anon's shocked expression as he leans out the window and watches me fall.

My sudden weightlessness catapults my stomach straight into my throat, scalding acid coming to rest behind my teeth as I struggle not to scream again.

My last desperate thought is that I might be able to slow my fall when I hit the neighboring shop's awning which is just below me. The cloth is thin but if it slows me even a fraction, maybe I won't split my head open like a gourd when I hit the ground. I windmill my arms, angling my body so I can land horizontally on the billowing cloth...

And I completely overshoot my target. There's one sickening moment when this realization hits before I'm slamming down hard. The impact isn't as catastrophically painful as I think it should be, but it still manages to jar my bones and my head. My vision swirls and my mind is foggy.

How the hell am I still alive? I ask myself. But I don't have time to answer.

"What the bloody hell?" I hear the words and turn around, realizing I've landed on someone!

"Oh no!" I yell as I feel the truth of the warmth beneath my back and head. I've crushed some unfortunate victim flat beneath my weight!

I force myself upright even as my vision continues to blur and my head aches something fierce. But at the realization I've probably just paralyzed someone with my own brainless stunt, I have to ensure he or she is okay.

I feel strong arms wrapping around me as the person I've landed on pulls us both upright. I look down at the hands wrapped around my arms and at first, all I can see is the blood covering us both. My blood. Then I realize the hands are large and male.

"Oh, Gods, I'm so sorry," I start, not even recognizing my own voice, as I turn around. "I didn't mean..." But I cut myself off mid-ramble when the man straightens, looking perturbed but relatively uninjured.

Herrick's tawny eyes narrow on me, examining my face like I've lost my mind. "What in Avernus are you doing, Neva?"

"Herrick," I breathe, amazed at my luck. Stupid tears spring to my eyes as I drink him in. He barely looks ruffled, even though I've just crushed him flat to the cobblestone street in my attempt to escape my attacker.

"Neva, what's…"

His sentence stops abruptly when I remember.

I gasp and turn to face the window and spy my would-be killer as he balances on the window ledge, before vaulting off in a graceful swan dive, like he's some carnival tumbler.

Just when I think he's about to crack his head on the stones below, he tucks his body and rolls to his feet, taking the brunt of the move on his broad shoulders. He comes up with the knife still in hand, eyes zeroing in on me.

"Fuck!" I shriek.

Herrick's gaze cuts from the man's face to the dagger clutched in his hand. The fucker isn't nearly as cut up as I am, owing to the fact that I took most the brunt of the glass. Meanwhile, I'm dripping scarlet to the pavement, drawing the shocked gazes of everyone currently on the street. At half-past two, that's thankfully a small number.

Herrick's eyes narrow again, and this time, all his ire is focused on the man stalking toward us. He takes a deliberate step to the right, putting his lean body in front of mine.

"Stay behind me," he instructs in a voice that's barely above a whisper. He raises the pitch when he turns to face the assassin, who has almost closed the distance between us. "And you don't take another fucking step, Acolyte of Gryphus."

What did Herrick just call him? I'm not even sure. My heart is pounding through my ears and it's disrupting my hearing or maybe that's owing to the headache that feels like it's ripping up my brain. I still feel sick to my stomach, but now I'm also getting lightheaded.

Anon pauses when he's barely a foot away from us, his gaze flicking from Herrick to me for the first time, blank shock stealing across his face.

"How the hell did you know who I am?" Anon mutters, more to himself than to us.

"This isn't a sanctioned kill, huntsman, or your signet ring would be active," Herrick sneers at him. "I'll give you a chance to back down now, before I'm forced to hurt you."

I sway on my feet as vertigo crashes into me. I'm losing too much blood, my world has been flipped upside down in a matter of minutes, and my silent and insane voyeur somehow knows the man who's trying to kill me.

"Step aside and I won't flay you open like a haddock," Anon counters, though he doesn't sound as composed as before. Herrick seems to have shaken him, but Anon recovers quickly, closing the distance when Herrick refuses to move aside.

"I warned you," Herrick says.

"Back off, stranger, this isn't your fight," Anon responds from where he stands maybe five feet from me. "The girl is a whore. She's worth nothing to you other than a fuck. She isn't worth your life."

"She's no whore," Herrick responds as I wonder if he still thinks I'm this Tenebris character. Well, let him for the time being, if it means I can get away from Anon!

Anon has the speed and focus of a viper when he leaps at me and then strikes, driving the dagger down hard toward me. I let out a small shriek, screwing my eyes shut as though my voice can somehow cushion the pain that's coming. Yet, no pain comes. Instead, I feel myself falling backwards as Herrick pushes me. My eyes are jerked open again when Anon yowls in pain. I land hard on the ground and focus just in time to see Herrick's knee disappear into the man's gut before he thrusts Anon backwards. As I watch in fascination, Anon flies into a nearby building. My eyes go even wider when he actually sails right *through* the stone wall and into some poor sap's home, dust from the pulverized rock rising in his wake.

Herrick seizes my wrist and begins dragging me down the street, pointedly ignoring the stares and shouts that follow us.

"Can you run?" he demands, eyes sweeping over me quickly, assessing my injuries with a clinical eye.

I try to move faster but I don't get very far. I'm exhausted and there's blood covering me from head to foot. I list to the side and Herrick spits a curse, as he scoops me into his arms, before I can collide with the stone pathway.

"I'll take that as a no," he mutters to himself. "Get a grip on my neck and hold on tight. I don't want you falling."

The lightheadedness is growing worse by the minute and I'm having a hell of a time keeping my eyes open. "Why should I trust you?" I manage to rasp. My vision is beginning to dim and I cling to my last scrap of consciousness with white-knuckled hands. If I go under now, I might not wake up again.

Herrick's tawny eyes soften for just an instant as he stares down at me, and an amused smile alights on those bow lips. "You don't really have much choice now, do you? It's me or the huntsman."

"The huntsman?" I repeat.

He nods. "Don't be fooled, he'll be getting back up. They're harder to kill than fucking roaches."

I nod and reach up with the last of my strength, twining my arms around Herrick's neck as blackness slops across my vision like spilled ink, blotting out the star-spangled night above us.

FIVE
Herrick

I suck in a deep breath, holding it for as long as I dare. The chase, combined with the rich iron tang of her blood, is awakening all my worst instincts. I won't lose control here. If I unleash my beast in the streets of Ascor, it's inevitably going to reach the ears of Queen Salome and there will be no stopping the redress that action would bring. So, I breathe as sparingly as possible, even as the huntsman tracks us through the back alleys of Ascor at a dead sprint.

My legs burn with the effort of keeping us both moving forward at a steady clip. I'm faster than the huntsman, but only just.

Malvolo would find this situation hysterical if he were by my side right now. After all, he's the only one of us who remains combat-ready even after the war, ever the dedicated soldier, even when there's no enemy left to fight. His daily drills have seemed farcical to me for years. Now, I'm regretting letting myself get so out of shape.

I long for four legs instead of two. I don't even need the full use of my beast. I could stay on the ground and keep Neva just as safe. Anything has to be better than this inferior two-legged shape.

The huntsman grunts with effort and his footsteps slap the ground further behind us than before. He's slowed, and I figure out why a few seconds later when the bolt of a crossbow spears an apple of the cart I bypassed seconds before. The apple goes tumbling off the cart, pulling several of its fellows with it, nearly tripping me in the process. I'm sure that wasn't the huntsman's intent, but it almost accomplishes his goal as I barely manage to vault over the line of tumbling fruit and land on the balls of my feet on the other side. I have three seconds or less before he reloads another bolt and gets me in his sights again.

And this time I might not be so lucky.

The five huntsman houses that serve beneath the Order of Aves are almost as far removed from humanity as I am. They simply have the misfortune of being slightly smaller monsters. I, once again, long to shift and crush this huntsman underfoot like the gnat he is.

I cast one yearning look at the sky before I juke to the right, avoiding the hissing crossbow bolt. It sinks an inch deep into the mortar between the cobblestones. If Neva is struck by one of those enchanted weapons, she's as good as dead. Even powerful little witchlings like the one in my arms are still heartbreakingly mortal, and it's clear she has no idea how to use the powers she's been given.

I continue in a straight line for as long as the jumbled city blocks will allow. Turning will only slow my momentum and give the implacable huntsman time to catch up. I'm under no illusions that the crossbow is the only long-range weapon he has on his person. Eventually, though, I do have to turn, as a stream of muck makes the street impassable.

The smell of shit, piss, and blood is so thick here, it makes my eyes cross. I forget sometimes why my brothers and I avoid cities. The waste of humanity is too difficult to handle in such concentrated doses.

Disgusting.

I stick as close to the stream of excrement as I can stand, knowing it'll throw the huntsman off our combined scent for a time. Neva's honeysuckle sweetness would tickle even the least acute of inhuman noses, and overlapped with my own aroma, it's damn distinctive.

Speaking of the witchling, she's getting clammy to the touch and growing even clammier by the time we reach the city limits of Ascor. There's a ten-mile stretch between Ascor and the Forest of No Return. That will be the most daunting challenge yet. No buildings to shield us, and I'll still be too close to the city to shift form.

I glance down at Neva and curse under my breath. I don't like how quickly she's fading. I need to get her to a safe location so I can examine her wounds. All this will be for naught if she dies the moment we reach the forest.

I dive into the tall prairie grasses and begin wading through them, cursing the location of that damned tavern. If it had been located toward the north, we could have slipped between the cornstalks and been lost from view. This grass is long enough to impede my stride, but too short to offer much cover.

The scream of air displacement is the only warning I get before the huntsman's chakkar enters and then explodes through my left shoulder in nearly the same instant. My entire arm goes numb and Neva sags as the support goes out from beneath her legs. It's fortunate her arms remain locked around my neck, because I come close to dropping her as fire licks away the numbness.

The huntsman missed his mark, which makes me the luckiest monster in all of Fantasia. Only a few inches lower and my arm would be severed and on the ground. Chakkar are not something to fuck with, and the fact he's willing to use them shows just how desperate he is. This huntsman has been paid by someone very influential to see the job gets done, no matter how barbaric the means.

A grim little smile plays out on my mouth, even as I adjust Neva, holding her awkwardly against my chest in a quasi-embrace. I knew there was something special about her. And, if we both make it out of this alive, I'm going to figure out just what that something special is.

The huntsman has finally entered the tall grass as well, which is as much of an impediment to him as it is to me. At least I'm out of his throwing range.

The Forest of No Return is just up ahead, the gnarled branches of the black oaks reaching for the night sky with twisted fingers. I have no idea what sort of damage I'm about to inflict on her unconscious mind by dragging her through the cursed tract of land, especially when she's in such a state. But, at this point, we have no other choice.

I step into the first grove of trees, shuddering when the wind claws at my face and tosses Neva's hair around her slack, pale face. I spare one glance at the huntsman, who's almost a mile up the hill. His eyes burn into me, his hatred almost matching his fear. He reeks of it and I know I've won this battle, at the very least. The huntsman isn't going to follow me past this point.

It turns out there are things that even huntsmen fear. And I'm dragging Neva right through one of them. Gods above help us.

I shoot one poisonous glance over my shoulder, giving the man the briefest glimpse of the luminous gold of my inhuman eyes. Even the disgraced Acolyte of Gryphus has the good sense to blanch when he realizes the fate that could have awaited him, if I'd been willing to shift. He stumbles to a halt, and his final chakkar lands woefully short of its mark.

I stoop, pick it up, and toss it back to its owner at twice his speed and strength, sweeping into the cursed forest without checking to see if it hits its mark.

SIX
Neva

A scream bubbles up in my throat, but the heavy weight of darkness presses me down, crushing all air from my lungs, denying me the chance to give voice to the terror streaking through me.

There's no sound, but for the screaming of the wind and the thud of blood behind my ears. Thick, dark strands of ivy form a leafy choker around my throat, tightening like a noose with every second. The cold flays me open, leaving my insides exposed and vulnerable as a thousand carrion crows descend on me from the inky, starless sky.

I choke, tasting blood in my mouth, thrashing futilely as more ivy traps my wrists. I can't even loose a cry when the first crow plucks a stringy gray intestine from my middle and tears away a gobbet of flesh.

A young woman sits idly by, watching with interest as I struggle. She's cross-legged on the muddy turf, gray eyes assessing me from beneath a cloak that matches them exactly. A fringe of wavy, deep-red hair peeks out from the hood. Her lips are nearly as red as my own, and her skin is the same translucent ivory. It looks more natural on her. Her wrists weep ruby droplets and a pair of crows alight on her arms, attracted to the scent of her blood.

I know this phantom shape.

I've seen her a thousand times in dreams, when my fevered mind seeks respite from the barrage of daily cruelty. But this isn't the usual dream, where we, as mere girls, played on a grassy knoll or braided flowers into one another's hair. Here, she's a woman, tall and heartrendingly

beautiful. I can't tear my eyes away from her, even as
infernal crows devour my insides.

"You have to wake, Neva," she says, her voice a
hypnotic contralto. "Wake and remember."

Remember what? I want to scream. This pain seems to
stretch to infinity. There was a life before this pain, wasn't
there? A horrid, depressing life of degradation and
deprivation, but a life, nonetheless. Though I strain, nothing
outside this cursed existence seems real.

"Remember who you are. Remember your purpose,"
she urges, even as the crows bite more deeply into her
wrists. "Remember and wake up, Neva. Wake up!"

Fresh pain ripples through the side of my face and I
moan. My middle is a bloody ruin, only so much slurry at
this point. But tree branches curl toward me, branches
pelting my face with sharp, nubby appendages.

"No," I groan. Why won't the pain stop? What have I
done to deserve this? "No, please!"

"Neva!" The bellow that issues from the girl I know so
well doesn't match her willowy body. It has a low, almost
melodic lilt. And it's... familiar.

Wrenching my eyes open feels like shouldering a
boulder and heaving with all my might. But I manage to
force them open just a sliver. Enough to see sunlight canting
in from the east, the rising sun spilling color onto the sky
like paint from an artist's palette.

I suck in air with the keen desperation of the recently
drowned, attempting to spring upright at once. My head
spins dangerously and I nearly collapse all over again, only
saved from the side of a grassy hillock by a pair of strong
arms.

"Easy there," a man soothes, sweeping my hair away
from my shoulder as my stomach heaves violently.

"Herrick?" I ask, shocked to see him.

I choke on bile and taste the weak tang of blood in the back of my mouth. My tongue aches. I must have bitten it when I was in that nightmare.

"Yes, it's me," he says in a soft tone.

I clench my eyes against the pain.

"I'm sorry," he murmurs as I open my eyes again and turn to retch.

"I knew the forest would be hard on your unconscious mind. Still, it was going to take a week to walk around it, and the huntsman would have caught up to us on the road. It was the only way."

"The huntsman," I repeat as I remember Anon in my bedroom and then I jumped out the window and...

I take a moment to compose myself so I don't shriek. Whatever Herrick just put me through was a thousand times worse than catching a knife to the gut. But I can't deny that I'm grateful to be alive. The phantom pains are fading quickly, leaving behind only the cold memory of the fear they evoked.

"What's happened," I start but Herrick shakes his head.

"I will explain to you, I promise," he says with a sweet smile. "But now is not the time."

It isn't until my breathing has leveled out that I notice Herrick has doffed his tunic, leaving him in only a soft pair of buckskin trousers. His physique is even more impressive than I'd imagined. Every inch of him is chiseled perfection, a stretch of golden skin over rippling muscle. His nipples are a dusky brown against all that gold, and I entertain the thought of tracing one briefly with my tongue.

"Where is your tunic?" I say thickly when I've managed to recover my wits somewhat.

Herrick gently plucks at something on my front. "You're wearing it, Neva. You weren't dressed for the elements. Bad enough I had to drag you through the forest. I didn't want you to freeze to death."

I glance down and see the truth in his statement. "Thank you," I whisper, still feeling out of sorts.

I lift myself onto my elbows, noting with some confusion that my arms are swathed in bandages. I'm not sure where he found the material to make them.

I cautiously test my balance. When I don't list sideways or heave my guts out my mouth, I feel safe enough to stand. Herrick keeps a gentle grip on my elbow, ready to steady me if I need it. Only then do I get a good look at my surroundings, and I'm quietly floored at just how far we've managed to travel.

We're cradled between the bases of two very tall mountains, with only a thin stretch of green valley to separate the twin peaks. The craggy stone is a deep gray that tends toward plum, with a dusting of snow at its zenith that completes the candied impression. Dandelions dot the green hillocks, and a lightly worn path winds like a beige ribbon up to the mouth of a small thatched cottage. It's a tiny thing, standing barely taller than Herrick himself. Yet, Herrick isn't exactly small—he must stand nearly seven feet!

The cottage is still at least a mile off, and I feel about as steady on my legs as a newborn foal. The tunic only hits me at mid-thigh and a light breeze ruffles the hem. I shiver violently. Well, now I know just where the cold was coming from in my dream.

"How are you feeling, Neva?" Herrick asks.

I take a deep breath and assess the condition I'm in. "Better," I say and it's the truth. I'm not sure how or why, but I feel better now than I did before I passed out.

Herrick must sense how unsteady I am, because he links his arm with mine, placing my hand on his forearm like some courtly gentleman. My fingers brush across an odd sigil etched into his skin with light blue ink. It's the oddest shape—what seems to be a snake coiled tightly around a staff.

45

"What's this?" I murmur.

Herrick glances down, as if only just noticing my preoccupation. A smile lightly traces the corners of his mouth, though it never quite reaches his eyes.

"It's the Rod of Asclepius."

"What's that?"

"The symbol for a deity lost to antiquity."

"Who was Aslepius?" I ask, feeling the need to make conversation, though I'm not sure why.

"The only thing we truly know about him was that he was associated with healing. That's why guild medics and healers had the sigil etched into their skin during the war. It helped us sort out who served what function."

"Then you're a healer and you healed me?" I ask as I look up at him.

He smiles at me warmly. "As much as I could, given our circumstances."

"That's why I feel better?"

"Probably but you still need to rest and you'll soon be able to do that."

"The Rod of Aslepius," I repeat, like the sound of the words on my tongue. "So, I should call you Doc?"

His answering smile is genuine this time and lights his whole face. Ye Gods, is this man beautiful! That grin threatens to knock the breath from me all over again.

"You wouldn't be the first," he says quietly.

He drops his hand to his waist, drawing my eyes to another tattoo, this one done in shimmering gold that barely stands out from his skin. The raised edges almost look like a brand. It depicts a shield pierced by both a broadsword and a wand, encircled by twinkling stars.

"What's that one?" I ask.

He glances down and taps the tattoo lightly.

"This is a Guild tattoo."

"What is that?"

46

He shakes his head. "You know even less than I imagined."

I give him a frown and he smiles again.

"I half expected to find a Guild tattoo on you," he says.

"Why?"

He shrugs. "You'd almost have to be one of us for the Acolyte of Gryphus to come after you."

I realize he's talking about Anon.

"What's a Gryphus?" I ask, stumbling a little as he guides me down the worn path toward the cottage.

Smoke curls lightly from the chimney and I want to be inside the warm confines of its walls as soon as humanly possible. It's only the furnace-like heat rolling off Herrick that's keeping my teeth from knocking together. I don't understand how he can be this warm when the air is so frigid.

"*Who* are the Acolytes of Gryphus?" he corrects me. "They're one of the five houses under the Order of Aves. Accipitrine, Corvid, Cathartidae, Strigiform, and Gryphus."

"That means nothing to me," I say.

He nods. "You have much to learn."

"I guess." I still haven't decided if he's sane.

"The Order of Aves is a league of aviary shifters, able to turn into birds many times their natural size, and they're bred for one thing: the hunt."

"And the man who attacked me was one of them?"

Herrick nods. "The acolytes of House Gryphus turned on their fellows during the war and sided with the great evil."

The dizziness is fast returning, though this time it has less to do with the aftershock of traveling unconscious through cursed forest, and more to do with the feeling that a woodpecker is trying to slowly drill a hole into my head.

"Forgive me for being obtuse, but what is *the great evil*, exactly?"

His gaze cuts to me in surprise, thin, perfectly sculpted brows coming together as he just stares.

"You're having me on, aren't you?"

"No!" I insist. "In case you didn't notice, I led a fairly sheltered life, in as much as Darius wouldn't let me leave the tavern."

He nods. "I apologize."

"Darius," I repeat the word and at Herrick's questioning gaze, I explain. "I'm pretty sure the Gryphus huntsman killed him."

"Is that such a great loss?"

I smile. "No, but it's almost unbelievable, all the same." I grow quiet for a few seconds. "I've prayed for the death of Darius so many times and now that he's gone, it almost feels like I merely dreamed it."

"Well, for your sake, I think it's a good thing."

"Yes," I say with a nod.

"But, going back to the subject of just what you do know about… any of this…"

Heat floods my cheeks and my eyes prick. I hate feeling stupid, especially in this man's presence. "I really don't know anything," I say.

He shakes his head, gaze sweeping over me again, assessing. "The Great War only ended a decade ago, Neva," he says, frowning down at me. "You would have been eleven or so when the fighting ceased. You have to remember something, even if it's vague?"

"I don't."

The past is a big, blank nothing for me. I don't remember much before coming to Gregory at the age of twelve. I'd been struck in the head by a horse, or so I'd been told. I lay in a coma for weeks, and my family had found it too difficult to care for me, leaving me for dead in a pile of potato peelings outside a tavern. That was where Gregory found me.

Herrick still seems incredulous. "You don't remember anything at all? Lycaon's hellhounds were particularly vicious during the sack of Ascor."

I shake my head, shame burning hot beneath my skin. I can feel the flush creeping down my neck steadily. Before long, I'll be as red as his tunic.

"I've told you I don't remember anything. Could you please stop gawping at me and just explain?"

Herrick snaps his jaw shut and purses his lips, mulling over his words for several long moments as we continue down the path.

"It's a long, drawn-out, and very bloody story. But to give you the bare bones, fifteen years ago, beings emerged from one of the nether realms and began to walk among the people of Fantasia. They possessed great beauty and charm, and within a year, they'd managed to enthrall the majority of the seven principalities. Well, aside from the Wonderland folk—that lot is too mad to be convinced by anything but their own convoluted logic, I suppose."

He lets out a dark chuckle and shakes his head. Why, I'm not sure. I don't know much of Wonderland folk because they don't get out this far south very often.

"Morningstar and his people managed to turn the heads of most of the nation before the Guild could even fathom the threat we now faced. They rallied millions of our own people against us. We were facing overwhelming odds, even without the creatures they had at their beck and call. We managed to convince most of the monarchies of the threat in time to put up a fight. It was prophesied ten chosen ones would rise to face the challenge, but ultimately, the nations tired of waiting for these saviors to arrive. Instead, they sacrificed ten witches to seal Morningstar and the others away."

"And sacrificing the witches worked?"

Herrick's face darkens, and I get the first true look at the war-hardened man that lay beneath his genial exterior.

"It will only continue working for a time."

"But not forever," I add, venturing a guess. "And these saviors still haven't turned up?"

"The Guild is still searching, or so I'm told. We've lost contact with them, though. My brothers and I retired to a quiet life of mining after the war ended. Malvolo simply couldn't be bothered to do anything else."

The wind is picking up, tossing my hair around my face. It came unbound sometime during our journey here. I curl reflexively into Herrick's side, pressing into his bare chest in hopes of leaching some of that precious heat from his torso. Despite being half-naked in the glacial wind, he doesn't seem too uncomfortable.

"What is Red Rose?" he asks.

The change in topic is so abrupt, it almost gives me whiplash. His tone shifts from grim to curious, his face smoothing out into the handsome and benign mask he wore when we first met.

"What?"

"Red Rose. You kept saying 'Red Rose' in your sleep. I wasn't sure what the significance was or if you were merely spouting gibberish."

"Red Rose is a who, not a what," I correct him, feeling a little better now that I can patiently explain something to him for a change.

"Okay," he says with a smile. "Then *who* is Red Rose?"

I shrug. "She's just a girl I imagined when I was little. A daydream of a friend who got me through the hard times. I dreamed of her again during our misadventure in the forest." I pause. "Which is probably why I called her name."

I don't mention the crows, the strangling vines, or the bloodied woman. It was probably the effects of the forest that skewed my dreams so badly.

50

"I see."

He sounds like he wants to say more, but he holds his tongue as we reach the rounded door of the cottage. Herrick releases his grip on my elbow for just long enough to jerk the door open. It swings outward with a creak of protesting hinges, coming part of the way off. Herrick sweeps me up in his arms like a bride and carries me over the threshold. We pass an oak table outfitted with three sturdy chairs on our way to a back room. With his foot, Herrick nudges this door open to reveal a large master bedroom with three beds shoved against one wall. One of them already appears to be occupied.

A blast of hot air buffets us as we step inside the room. A large fireplace dominates the wall across from the beds and I frown at it. This is unlike any bedroom I've ever seen. Don't fireplaces normally go in kitchens?

My numbed skin comes alive in little prickles as the warmth envelops us.

Herrick deposits me on the bed nearest the door and wags a finger at me before crossing back to it. "Stay here and get some rest. I have an errand to run, but I'll return shortly."

"Where are you going?" I ask immediately, worried about being left alone. That assassin is still out there…

"I have to go to the mines for just a moment," he answers. "And don't come looking for me! It's very dangerous out there," he says as he glances back at the door. "But, you're safe here."

I don't really have the will to argue with him at this point. Though I've only walked a mile today, I'm still exhausted from the loss of blood and everything else I've experienced. Yes, Herrick was able to somewhat heal me but he's right—I need my rest. Something I'm absolutely looking forward to.

All I want to do is curl up in front of the fire and luxuriate in the warmth like a spoiled cat. I nod and squeeze my eyes shut tight. Immediately, I begin spiraling downward toward unconsciousness. The last thing I feel before I'm sucked under is the fullness of Herrick's mouth brushing my cheek.

"Sleep well, little witchling."

SEVEN
Malvolo

Herrick was supposed to be back two days ago. If he's not returned by evening, I'm going to drag him back from Ascor and beat his ass soundly into the ground for having the gall to worry me.

I use the mouth of rough-hewn stone tunnel to heave myself out into the open, blinking in the harsh light of the mid-day sun. I really have been in my cave for too long if spots are dancing across my eyes at the influx of light. The precious seconds it takes for my eyes to adjust make me uneasy. Enemies are everywhere, and erstwhile Guild members are Salome's favorite quarry these days.

Whispers have reached us, even in this far-flung mountain range, that the kings are quietly targeting the lesser among us, capturing and hanging them on trumped-up charges.

My lip curls. For five years, we held the Great Evil at bay with blood and steel, accruing greater casualties with each passing month. And how did they repay us for our sacrifices? By taking the coward's way out, butchering ten witches to put a bandage on the problem, slaughtering the people who defended them so ardently.

Humans really are deplorable creatures.

Apprehension tingles at the base of my skull, irritatingly persistent and growing with every day that passes without word from Herrick. It was supposed to be a simple journey—Herrick was supposed to go to Ascor and exchange gold and rubies for provisions we'll need when winter seals the passes. A simple journey, yes, but not without its dangers. It's extremely foolhardy to wander into

Ascor, when the castle is situated at the far edge. All it would take is one soldier to recognize Herrick from his days in the army and Salome's attack dogs would be after him in an instant.

If Herrick's dead, I will storm the castle and end every worthless life inside its walls, consequences be damned. I've lost too many brothers to human cowardice already. Nouille. Veseo. Maug. Choro. I won't lose Herrick or Reve. At the very least, I won't let their deaths go unavenged.

My lips tug into a feral little smile. It's been a long time since I've had the chance to let loose and enjoy a little bloodshed. Reve simply can't spar with me, and Herrick so rarely has the patience for it anymore. Tearing into Salome's pale throat would be enormously satisfying. Facing off with her guard afterward, even more so.

So where the fuck is Herrick?

The subterranean tunnels of the mine emerge onto a sloping hill, and the grass crunches lightly beneath my feet as I make my way toward the small cottage that shelters at the mountain's base. It's high time I checked on Reve. The long-burning fire I set will be dying to embers after three or four days, now that the potion-coated wood has lost its potency. Even if I weren't waiting for Herrick, I would have needed to make this journey today. Someone has to look after Reve. If the frost is sticking, winter has come to depose autumn from its short-lived reign.

Smoke curls lightly from the chimney and I pause when I notice the door hangs slightly ajar, broken off its hinges. The apprehension I've been wrestling with for days blossoms into outright fear, and I sprint the remaining half-mile, arriving at the door in minutes.

An unfamiliar scent permeates the house, augmented by the heated air of the cabin. I press my back against the outside wall, trying to gather what information I can about the intruder or intruders before I enter and tear them limb from limb. Sometimes, that moment of foresight is what tips the scales when the difference between life and death balances on a knife's edge.

The scent permeating the house rests somewhere between sweet and spicy, and is utterly alluring. Cloves, perhaps. It's also distinctly female. Unexpected, but not to be discounted out of hand. Many of the fiercest Guild warriors I've met have been female. Salome prefers her guard to be male, but it's entirely possible she's sent a female huntsman, hoping to lower our guards before the dagger is plunged into our backs.

No sounds issue from the door except the crackle of the fire in the grate. The tangy scent of blood also hangs heavy in the air, driving my pulse into a frenetic pace. Someone inside is injured, but at this distance, it's impossible to tell who. It's likely Reve. He's as helpless as a lamb in his current state. I can't stand here any longer, a mute observer while he could be dying. Or maybe he's already dead. Yet, the blood doesn't smell like his.

I shove the door the rest of the way open and wince when the hinges loudly herald my entrance. So much for stealth. I'll have to rely on speed and strength. The scent of blood is strongly concentrated in the back room and I stalk forward, drawing the short sword strapped to my belt from its scabbard.

Sword at the ready, I step inside, fully expecting to find an attacker looming over a bloodied Reve.

If someone has killed my brother…

Instead, I find a woman sprawled on my bed, her limbs loose and pliant in sleep. She's not even clutching a weapon, and I doubt she'd have any place to hide one on her person. She's wearing only a scarlet tunic that rides up around her hips, revealing scandalously thin lace undergarments beneath.

What the bloody hell?

It's a struggle to pull my gaze away from the curve of her pale, slender legs, but I do, following the line of her body up to an equally stunning face. Her mouth is lightly parted, and she looks as though she fell asleep with a question perched on those petal lips.

I'm so caught off-guard by the appearance of this girl, it takes me several seconds to realize the scent of blood rolls off the bandages that wind down her arms. She's bled through in places, hinting at deep lacerations beneath the crudely wrapped bandages.

That's when I remember my brother.

I glance up and notice he sleeps peacefully on the bed closest to the wall, completely unharmed. A small smile tugs at the corners of his pale mouth, as though he's pleased to have a companion at last.

I look back at the sleeping woman and shake my head.

Who is she? What is she doing here? And why in the name of Avernus did she choose my bed to bleed on?

I don't relax my guard, still unsure if this is a trick. Better to be cautious than dead.

The girl stirs, arms stretching above her head as her mouth opens in a yawn. Her eyes open languidly, and I'm struck once again by her beauty. The color of her eyes is almost resinous, caught between amber and burnished gold. They fly open wide at the sight of me, looming like a dangerous shadow at the foot of the bed. It's little wonder when she lets out a soft yelp and raises her hands to shield herself.

Energy crackles in the air around her and my spine immediately stiffens as the wash of magic touches me. The residue is familiar and unwelcome.

Tenebris.

If the girl was sent here by Tenebris, it doesn't bode well for her. The power is thick and buzzes like a swarm of bees on my skin. She's untrained, if she's allowing the power to flow so freely.

Even worse. An untrained little witch has found her way into my house, and she's gathering her magic for an attack. I near her and lean over her, scowling at her beautiful face.

"Stop drawing on your power, witchling, or I'll cut your throat where you lay."

She goes very still, but the power abates only a fraction.

"I told you to drop it," I snarl.

Her eyes are glassy and she bites that full lower lip, struggling to keep the tears from falling. "I don't know how."

"Don't fuck with me, witch…"

"I'm not a witch!" she protests, voice strained.

"Don't fucking lie to me," I growl.

She shakes her head and her eyes go wider. "I swear. I'm… I'm just a girl from Ascor."

"What are you doing here?"

"Herr… Herrick brought me here."

I snort when she mentions Herrick's name. Of course, this little waif's presence is his doing. She's a lure he can't resist. Beautiful. Young. Relatively pure of spirit, if not in body. A wounded little dove he can rescue. Acting the part of a gallant knight, as always. I should have seen it the moment I stepped in. His scent saturates both the tunic and the bandages crafted from his undershirt.

Hmm and that's a curious subject all its own. Herrick must really like her, if he's scent-marking her already.

Well, regardless, he can't keep her. We don't need another mouth to feed, and harboring a witchling in these times, with Salome on the prowl, is just asking for trouble.

As if my thoughts have summoned him, the clodpole comes swaggering into the cottage, donning another tunic, this one a less-favored ocher shade. A pair of hares dangle from one fist and a bushel of greens in the other, but he almost drops them both when he sees me looming above the girl, weapon still at the ready.

"Malvolo, it isn't what you think," he begins in a low, wheedling tone.

I arch a brow at him, a sneer curling my lip. He's been in the cottage all of a minute and I'm already reminded why I prefer solitude to his company. The fool has more compassion than common sense.

"So, you *didn't* drag a forbidden witchling into our home and put her to sleep in my bed?"

Herrick grimaces. "All right, it's exactly what it looks like. But put the sword away. You're scaring her."

I don't budge. I ought to just kill the girl. One quick nick in the artery and she's dealt with. It won't be as drawn out as the noose or immolation she'd surely face if caught in Ascor.

"Explain yourself. Now," I growl at my brother.

"Fine. Outside. Let Neva get her rest." He glances at her and his expression softens. "She's wounded and she needs to heal."

I cut another glance at the girl, who's still doe-eyed and trembling. She looks ready to bolt. She'll definitely not return to sleep after this.

Grumbling under my breath, I follow the bloody idiot into the sitting room, past the kitchen and out the door, into the cool air outside. My temper doesn't abate, but I do sheathe my weapon, admitting, if only to myself, that it was perhaps an overreaction.

The witchling doesn't appear to be a match for me. Yet. It would be somewhat unsportsmanlike to fight her in the state she's in.

As soon as he's mostly settled the lopsided door, I round on Herrick. "Explain."

He leans heavily against the wall, retrieving his pipe from the pouch at his waist. He stalls, packing in snuff before lighting it and puffing thoughtfully. He blows a perfect ring and watches as the wind whips it away.

"I was heading back here when I happened by a tavern in Ascor."

"You usually aren't one for drink or women," I point out. "So why bother stopping at a tavern?"

He nods. "The tavern was emitting a strong magical signature. I thought perhaps it was a Guild artefact someone had happened upon. Regardless, the signature bore the distinct feel of Tenebris, which meant it was dangerous beyond imagining."

"Stick to the story."

"I sought to buy or steal whatever this artifact was from the owner. Imagine my surprise when I find the source is a slip of a girl, not a weapon or artifact, at all."

I incline my head towards the cottage. "That same slip of a girl?"

Herrick nods. "The greedy little bastard who owned the tavern clearly didn't know what he had, or he would never have paraded her in public."

"So why the fuck did you bring her here?"

"It wasn't my intention… at first," Herrick admits. "But someone hired a Gryphus huntsman to kill her. And when she leapt from her bedroom window, cutting herself up to hell in the process, I couldn't just let her bleed to death on the street."

"I thought the huntsman was after her?"

Herrick glares at me. "I couldn't just let the huntsman murder her while she bled to death in the street."

"So you thought to bring her here?" I demand.

He nods. "She's something special, Malvolo."

"And how the fuck do you know that?"

"I can feel it."

I shake my head at his stupidity. "She's trouble, that's what she is," I shoot back. "And I won't have you bringing that trouble down on our heads, Herrick. I don't care how pretty or magical she is."

"What are you saying?"

"I'm saying she has to go. Now."

"No fucking way," Herrick responds, his jaw tight.

"You're putting all of us in danger and no fucking woman is worth that."

"If I put her out on her own now, she'll die. You know that huntsman will find her."

"I don't care."

"Even you aren't that cold-hearted," he argues.

I consider his point for a moment and feel irritated that I have to concede it. "You're sending her away when the snow begins to stick to the ground, do you understand?"

Herrick regards me soberly, disappointment tightening the lines around his eyes. "I knew you were jaded, Mal. But I never thought you callous. She's injured and woefully underprepared for the world out there. Would you really send her away to die?"

I fucking hate it when he makes me feel guilty for having the barest hint of self-preservation.

"Humans took everything from me, let's not forget," I ground out. "I'll not let her lead them here to plunder what we have left."

"And why do you think she would?"

"You have a month to nurse your little dove back to health, Herrick. Then I want her gone."

I stalk away before he can formulate a response. I don't want to hear him champion the little witchling. We've worked too hard to ruin it all now. One way or the other, she's going.

Even if I have to drag her away by that thick sable hair.

EIGHT
Herrick

"Grumpy, isn't he?" a dry female voice inquires from the doorway.

I turn to find Neva leaning out from the gap between the door and the frame. She's glaring daggers at Malvolo's retreating back, lips pursed in dislike. Despite myself, I find her ire amusing, in as much as it surprises me. In the last few hours of her company, I've begun to realize she has quite a spark beneath that stoic exterior.

"He's always been a bit of a malcontent, yes. That wasn't the worst reaction he could have had, honestly," I tell her, with a shrug.

I'm genuinely proud of Mal's restraint, under the circumstances. I meant to spring the news on him over supper, once I had time to collect my thoughts and make a reasoned argument for Neva's sojourn here. There was a time when my brother would have slit her throat the moment he detected her power. The fearsome Malvolo has a reputation for a reason, and mercy isn't one of his virtues.

"He wants me to leave, doesn't he?" she asks, her expression conveying her worry.

"Yes," I answer honestly, seeing no reason to lie.

"I don't have to stay," she starts.

"Yes, you do. You need to heal and if we leave you out there on your own now, you'll most surely die."

She's distractingly feminine, posed as she is with one hip bumping the doorjamb and a hand behind her head, framing all that ebony hair around her face. I've tried to maintain a clinical air around her, regarding her as an injured girl in need of help and not as a woman with more raw sex appeal than is good for her. But she's becoming increasingly hard to ignore. She's flush with power that grows by the day.

Her beauty disarmed even Malvolo, a feat which I'd begun to believe impossible. He's not had a woman in fifteen years, since before the war began.

I can't deny that she's a siren's call for my beastly half. I want to drag her back to the caves and see just how good that creamy skin tastes. But, alas, I'm too civilized to do so.

"Why does he hate me?" she asks, her voice sounding like it belongs to a little girl.

"He doesn't hate you," I start.

"Well, he certainly didn't welcome me with open arms!" she says, a smile playing with her lips. "Is he your brother by blood?"

"Yes."

"And yet you are both so dissimilar."

"How so?"

She shrugs. "You're kind and thoughtful and he's... a... a cock."

I choke on a lungful of smoke and cough on my laugh. I would pay a third of the gold I possess to see the look on Malvolo's face if she'd uttered that sentiment in his presence.

I'd imagined she'd need time to regain her spirit. But she's sprung back quickly in the wake of the tavern owner's death, as resilient and flexible as a sapling.

"Malvolo's history is... complicated."

"Does it have something to do with the war?" She cuts quickly to the heart of the matter, surprising me with her perceptiveness.

"Yes."

"What happened?"

I shake my head. "I can't explain it all, because parts of it are deeply personal and those parts are his to tell. But the crux of it is that Malvolo tends to mistrust humans."

"Why?"

"When we needed their support the most, they took the coward's way out and sealed the Great Evil away, choosing to, instead, inflict it on a future generation when the seals break."

"When the seals break?"

I nod. "The Great Evil will return. The death of the witches won't be enough to keep it sealed away forever." I sigh as I turn to the rest of Malvolo's story. At least, the part I'm willing to tell. "Malvolo, Reve and I lost four of our brothers during the war. And their sacrifice was essentially rendered moot, because we didn't prevail."

"I'm sorry," she says, her voice soft.

I just nod. I don't like to think of the deaths of my brothers and I make it a general rule not to.

"The seals keeping the Great Evil at bay are simply forestalling the inevitable, at this point. Morningstar will break free. And if our champions don't rise in the meantime, we're all truly fucked."

"Morningstar?" she repeats.

I nod. "He is the greatest of all evils."

My voice threatens to shake as I recount the deaths of my brothers. My nightmares seem less potent than Malvolo's, because I was in the second wave when our brothers fell, tending to the wounded brought behind the line. But seeing their bodies, crumpled and tossed away like spare parchment, bodies blotted with dark spots of blood…

Our kind are damn near indestructible so I can only imagine the force needed to twist my brothers into such shapes, and the pain that accompanied it.

I clear my throat, trying to dislodge the tight knot of grief.

"Malvolo blames Tenebris and himself for the state Reve's in."

"What state is Reve in?" she asks.

"He's cursed with a sleep like death. He's been frozen for a decade now, and there's no hope for a cure."

"How? What happened to him?"

"The spelled spear was aimed for him, wielded by a Gryphus huntsman. It was of Tenebris' design originally, and purloined when the Gryphus sect defected to the enemy. It wasn't truly her fault."

"Who is Tenebris?"

"She's a might sorceress." I take a breath. "And the residue she's left on you is unmistakable. It was bound to provoke Malvolo."

In all honesty, it provoked me, as well when I'd ventured past the tavern. And when I entered, the pull only grew stronger. I half-expected to find that thrice-damned spear in Darius' possession. I'd have traded all the wealth in our mines to find and destroy that fucking spear.

Instead, I found her—a girl with seemingly no idea what she is. She's a beautiful enigma, a puzzle I don't have long to figure out. I'll have to make the month we have count.

Neva raises her arm and discreetly sniffs her wrist, as though she could actually smell the magic on her skin. It's oddly charming and I hide a smile by taking another long drag on my pipe.

"I don't understand any of this," she finally admits. "And I think you're wrong about my power. I've never shown a spark of magic or anything before. Doesn't this sort of thing tend to manifest when you're young?"

"Generally, but misery can squash magic out of people. And you seemed to have misery in spades."

She's quiet for a long moment, before she crosses to my side. "I guess I never thought of myself as miserable, but I was." She clears her throat. "I mean, I hated Darius but I just tried to make the best of a terrible situation."

She looks up at me and smiles and her eyes reveal her gratitude. I'm caught off-guard when she drapes her slender arms around my chest and pulls herself in tight against my body. She's chilled from standing mostly bare in the doorway. I berate myself for not offering her a pair of trousers. They'd be too big, of course, but at least the buckskin would be warm.

"You're chilled," I say, rubbing my hands along her arms, trying to create enough friction to ease the gooseflesh popping along her forearms. "You should go back inside. I'll put more wood on the fire."

She doesn't say anything to that, just curls a little closer, tucking her head in the hollow of my throat. The scent of her is more potent like this, teasing my nose. I like it that my tunic covers her in my scent. It wasn't my intent to mark her, but I'm grateful for it, all the same.

Before I can reconsider, I've ducked my head, pressing my face into her hair, surrounding myself with her enticing aroma. She's so damned close. Despite her profession, I truly believe she has no idea what she's doing to me.

I find it difficult to believe she's only experienced that repugnant little barkeep, though he was sure to tell me he'd been her only, in order to up his fee, to be sure. But I find myself wondering if such was really the case? I don't understand how it could be. I remember all those men in the tavern, watching her with lust dancing in their eyes. Most of them were well off—maybe even wealthy enough to afford her and if they could, they certainly would. Yet, that little ogre of a man had insisted she was his only in body. He'd explained the ridiculous claim by the fact that he was greedy and possessive. I could not have argued with either.

With any other maiden pressed to me like this, I'd have had her bodice unlaced and her body pressed up to the wall of the cabin, using my hand to orchestrate her pleasure until she was ready for me.

But not this woman. Neva is resilient, but not indestructible. Her body is still healing, and there's no assessing just how much damage has been inflicted on her heart. So I content myself with pressing a light kiss to her hair. I am a patient beast. And hopefully there will come a day that she will not flinch away from me, a day when I'm able to teach her the way an honorable man truly worships a woman's body.

"I'm so sorry," she murmurs against my throat. The feeling of those soft lips on my skin sends a jolt of pleasure straight to my groin. Gods, she's too tempting for her own good.

"For what?"

"For your loss—the loss of your brothers," she murmurs. "I can tell how much you and Malvolo loved your family, even if Malvolo has an unpleasant way of showing it. I really don't mean to be trouble."

"Don't treat yourself like a burden, Neva."

She sniffles, and warm, salty tears slide down my throat before soaking into my tunic. "I am though. You didn't complete your business in town because of me. If we'd never met, you wouldn't have put yourself in the sights of a Gryphus huntsman. And you wouldn't be in an argument with your brother."

"I made choices and I still stand behind them."

"Choices?"

"Once I saw you and felt your power, I wasn't going to leave you."

She runs those slim, trembling fingers over my shoulder, as though she can see the wound left by the chakkar. It's a fading pink mark, after days of travel, but still visible. Neva is more sharp-sighted than I gave her credit for, if she spotted it while I was shirtless.

"You were hurt. I'm not worth that."

A growl builds in my chest, my beast affronted by this contradiction. We know treasure when we spot it. And this woman is shaping up to be a rare gem, something definitely worth our interest.

"You're worthy if I say you're worthy," I tell her sternly.

She lets out a hiccup and a barely audible sob. "I'm not, Herrick. Don't you see how silly this is? You never hear of the whore being saved by the dashing gentleman in the ballads. No one ever goes to battle for a whore."

"You are not a whore," I ground the words out. And a growl spills out from between my teeth. I wish for a way to kill Darius twice for the damage he's done to this girl. The severed artery he no doubt suffered was too merciful a death.

"Close enough," she says on a sigh.

"Purity isn't found here, Neva," I say, sliding my hands from her arms down to her waist, memorizing the feel of her beneath my hands. Even though I still wonder how many men she has been with, I will never ask. It isn't my business and the answer doesn't change my feelings for and towards her.

I stop at the inner curve of her hip, tracing the line of her thigh just before her sex. Her scent grows a little muskier, perfumed with desire. Is she even aware of what she's feeling?

I move my hand away before I get any ideas, laying my palm flat against her chest. "Purity is found here. An untouched maid can be the vilest of monsters, and a prostitute can be damn close to a saint." Then I pause. "And you are not a prostitute, nor are you a whore," I say with stern resolution. "And if I ever hear you referring to yourself as such again, you will have my temper to deal with." She looks up at me then and I nod down at her. "And let me tell you, my temper is an ugly bastard." She laughs at that.

"Thank you, Herrick," she says softly. "For everything you've done for me and everything you continue to do for me. No one has ever treated me with such kindness and yet expected nothing in return."

"You are worth that and so much more, Neva," I say as I smile down at her. "Now let me deal with the huntsman. You focus on healing. We'll figure out the rest later."

She raises her head as she nods and I suddenly find her face inches away from mine, tilted at an appealing angle. Her eyes are more luminous with their sheen of tears. Scarlet lips part invitingly.

"Neva..." My voice holds an unspoken plea. *Stop me.*

But she only stares at me, surrendering with a small sound when I cup her cheek and kiss her. It's a brief, tender press of lips, certainly the most chaste I've ever experienced. It becomes decidedly less so when her small tongue darts out to test the seam of my mouth, breath quickening. Her bosom heaves against my chest, her spine shifting into a more supple position as I press a hand to the small of her back. I shouldn't be doing this. Not when she's so damaged, not when she's only known a monster's touch. I need to take my time with her—to teach her that not all men are as bad as she must think them.

My lips part, permitting the increasingly bold woman to explore at her own pace. She tastes exceptional: spicy, with a note of unexpected sweetness at the tail end. She groans into my mouth.

And that's when I lose control of myself. I grip her around the waist and move her back a step, pressing the line of her back against the cottage, entirely lost in her scent, her taste, the sensation of her. I push myself against her, so she can feel the proof of my excitement. I want to be inside of her, right here and right now.

And then it's over.

The moment her back hits the wall, she springs free of my hands with a cry of surprise. The tears spill over once more, streaking down her pale cheeks. A dagger of sharp guilt twists in my gut.

Wrong.

I knew it was wrong before I did it and, selfish creature that I am, I couldn't resist once she gave me a taste.

"Neva..." I begin again, this time the words are laced with desperation.

But it's too late. Far too late.

"I need to…"

She ducks beneath my arm, still barefoot and mostly nude, and darts away, as fleet-footed and silent as any deer. I stare after her, debating whether or not to follow her. Doing so would only make her more frightened of me. So I watch her retreating figure until she disappears from sight. All the while, I wonder what in the name of Avernus I've just done to the poor girl's psyche.

NINE
Neva

I'm forced to stop after a few miles because the burning in my feet is almost unbearable. Between the cold and the bracken underfoot, my soles feel as cut up as the rest of me. I stumble to a stop at the edge of The Forest of No Return. No amount of fear will compel me to go into that place alone. I know what sort of nightmares wait for me in the trees. But I have to keep away from Herrick. I *have* to.

Stupid, naïve Neva, thinking Herrick was any different from the rest of them. He seemed detached during the week he observed me in the tavern, but all that objective calm stripped away when he put his hands on me. Stupid me for encouraging it.

I bring a trembling hand to my lips. The ghostly imprint of his mouth still burns against mine, and I sink to my knees near a steaming pool. I allowed myself to be swayed by the tenderness of his mouth and his kind words. Let myself be drunk on the taste of him, like bitter chocolate on my tongue. And then he'd jerked me into the wall and pushed himself against me and I'd felt his hardness. That one small act shattered the stirring curiosity within me, the blossoming desire I'd never known before. Smited with that small act of brute force.

I squeeze my eyes shut, shudders racking my body. Kneading my temples, I try to ward off the memories that begin swimming to the surface. Darius clutching my arms above my head as he hiked my skirt that first time. The tangle of sheets that trapped my legs, the crushing pressure of him on top of me, the pain, shocking in its intensity. The ache that remained days afterward to remind me of exactly what he'd done.

How filthy I felt afterwards.

I swing my aching feet over the lip of the pool, letting out a half-sob when the heat manages to assuage the worst of the pain. It can't remedy the burn in my eyes or the pit of shame that's lodged itself in my gut. I sink in further, relishing how the steam clings to my skin. And finally, I decide to throw caution to the wind and remove the tunic and undergarments so I can sink fully into the pool. I can always submerge if Herrick happens by.

But the chances of that are rare. I'm far away from the cottage. Far away from the one man who rescued me from the worst of circumstances, only to prove he was no different than any other man.

Men only want what's between my legs. That's all they think about and the sooner I learn that lesson, the better off I'll be.

I set aside the baggie of cocaine I brought with me. I'd had it in my bra from the moment the huntsman broke into my room and I'd managed to hide it from Herrick this entire time.

Now, I pile a pinch onto the back of my hand and snort it within seconds. I need the blissful sense of numbness that comes seconds later.

But the desire to scrub myself raw doesn't fade. Neither does the ache between my thighs that blossomed when Herrick touched me there. I tend to shy away from most touch, but there is something steady and non-threatening about Herrick. He's got the hands of a doctor, and before today, I would have trusted them not to hurt me.

Tears squeeze from my eyes.

My back pressing to the cottage, Herrick's hands curling tighter around me, caging me in. My head hits the siding too hard, knocking me from my daze, and everything

slides from dream to nightmare in seconds. He's touching
me, hand hovering inches above my mostly bare ass. It will
take no effort at all for him to hoist the tunic and tear my
undergarments. Then he'll hike me up and shove himself into
me. He feels big. Much larger than Darius. Yes, Herrick will
tear me in two.

I choke on another sob. I hate this. I hate Darius for
doing this to me. Hate that he's reduced me to a shivering
little girl, afraid of the most basic touch.

I seize the baggie, squeezing it tight in my fingers. I
ought to just upend it and let the powder melt into the water
of this hot spring. But I can't. It's too important to me.
Instead, I rip it open, tapping out line after line on my palm,
inhaling each as quickly as I can. There have to be several
grams in this bag and, suddenly, I want to snort them all—if
it means I won't have to remember, won't have to feel and
won't have to think any longer, it's worth it.

The only other time I've taken this much, I'd spent a
day laid out on Darius' bed having a waking dream about
Red Rose and a misadventure through a dungeon, running
and giggling as we fled a dragon. Somehow, I'd known the
beast wouldn't harm us and so I was unafraid.

That dream sounds pretty damn nice at the moment.
Anything to escape the painful reality that Darius has left me
a broken doll, unable to play with anyone, even if I wanted
to.

I sink lower and lower into the water, resting my head
against the side of the pool. The steam strokes its fingers
against my cheek, and my body floats weightlessly. I never
had this at the Wicked Lyre. Darius never drew my baths
with warm water, and I was lucky if I could bathe twice a
week. This is almost like being wrapped in an embrace, the
gentle motion of the water threatening to lull me to sleep.

I prop my head on my arms, leaning my forehead
against the browning grass, sighing when a feeling of airy

detachment finally settles over me. My skin prickles, but not with fear. My heart beats like a hummingbird's wings and I feel as though I might actually lift off the ground.

"Damn Darius straight to Avernus," I mumble.

He deserves it. The only way I can find peace is to snort it or shoot it straight into my veins. I'm just a sad little whore, no matter how vehemently Herrick protests it.

My eyes slide shut and I tip sideways, barely registering the dull splash and the drag of water pulling me down. It's not such a bad way to go. One influx of air and I'll find myself greeting a Shepherd, my soul carried off in a gilded lantern to wherever witching whores go after death.

Just one breath.

I hear the creature's voice in my head as it encourages me to open my mouth, to drag in the thick glug of water, and...

I do.

I find myself stepping out of a thick mist onto a battlefield. Not far off stands a young man, elbow propped against a tree. I almost don't see him, draped in the shadow of an oak. His burgundy hair blends almost seamlessly with the Byzantine shadows that stretch over the field. The sun itself seems smudged with darkness, and the sky is tinged almost red. Figures are frozen in place in the valley below, where the reek of blood hangs heavy in the air. Bodies are trampled underfoot. Creatures of every shape and color are amassed on both sides of the line.

The man watches the immobile figures spread out on the ground with impassive, hazel eyes. His lips part after a moment of thought, and then he speaks.

"Pawn to F4."

73

TEN
Reve

This is the 6,072,043rd game of chess I've played.

To say I'm bored is an understatement of the highest order.

I think I'd prefer the blackest pits of Avernus to the nightmarish dreamscape that is my half-life. At least the scenery might change, for once. If I ever escape this curse, I'll track down the Gryphus huntsman who lobbed the spear at me, and I'll tear him to pieces over the course of many years.

I've had a decade to plan his demise. But even planning his grisly end has become tiresome.

Occasionally, I can project the essence of myself into Herrick's dreams or Malvolo's, if they're near enough. But they avoid the cottage now, for the most part. I try not to judge them too harshly for that. Had it been Herrick laid out in my place, I know I couldn't stare at his corpse-like body for long. Too painful. Better to stay active and distracted than locked forever in place, just like your brother.

So this is all I can do. Shuffle through a parade of endless games, until I'm finally woken by the chosen one— or, until I mercifully perish. The final battle is my backdrop, its participants the many players in my endless cycle of banal entertainments. Chess is the easiest way to spend the hours. It takes time and thought, though I never allow the Guild to lose, so the outcome is a foregone conclusion. I am growing weary. Maybe I'll keep the battle short.

"Pawn to F4," I instruct one of Morningstar's infantrymen, and he obligingly shuffles forward. I can

command most everyone on the battlefield, bending their avatars to my will with ease.

The man's armet obscures most of his face. The jingling of his chain mail is almost too merry a sound for my current mood. I'll kill him quickly. This is a fool's opening. A two-move checkmate, if played right. I open my mouth to issue the next move...

And someone else speaks instead.

"Pawn to E6."

I startle, turning in time to see a young woman step onto the ridge that overlooks the field. She's as pale as a shade. Her hair is a midnight curtain that falls to her mid-waist, stopping above the curve of her hips. Aside from bloody bandages, she's not wearing a stitch of clothing. At first, I believe this may be a figment of my fevered imagination. But I know better.

The only players in my dreams are those who were present at the battle. After ten years, I know every face on this accursed field. And this woman wasn't one of them.

She reeks of Tenebris' magic. I squint at her, bemused. She doesn't look like Tenebris. Too pale, for one. And too tall. The sorceress, Tenebris, is below average height, even for a human woman. Her hair falls in loose chestnut curls to her shoulders and never budges past that point.

Too unmanageable, she used to say. Easy to light on fire in the event of a potions accident.

"That was a foolish move," the girl murmurs. "You're leaving your king open."

She gestures toward the field, where Morningstar looms, larger than life, ready to bat a fucking war elephant aside with his mace. I snort. As if I'm invested in protecting the enemy king. I'm far more intrigued by the enigma this girl presents.

"Who are you?" I ask, not quite angry, but still disturbed by her presence here.

Is this an attack? A succubus sent from the nether realm by Morningstar to finish what the Gryphus huntsman could not?

She doesn't look dangerous. And it's not Morningstar's scent on her skin. But if she truly has been sent by Tenebris, I doubt she'd appear bare as the day she was born. Powerful, Tenebris might be, but concerned with little but her studies. I doubt a man has been able to get so much as a peek beneath Tenebris' cloak the entirety of her life. As virginal as an abbess, that one.

No, this girl could not have been sent by Tenebris.

As I watch her, she turns her body toward me a fraction so I can spy just the hint of a rosy nipple beneath the fall of her hair. I can't tell if she truly is this mesmerizing or if I'm simply hard up after so many years of forced celibacy.

Whoever she is, I want her. What a pleasant change it would be to lay her out on the ground and settle between her thighs, sampling her quim until an entirely different scream echoes over the battlefield.

The woman raises a slender brow at me. "Who am I? Isn't that supposed to be my line?" she asks with a smile. "This is my dream. Or is it my death?"

"What are you talking about?" I demand.

She frowns. "I was drowning."

"And you did nothing to stop yourself from drowning?"

"No," she answers. "I was quite willing to go."

"Well, regardless, I don't believe you're dead."

"Why?"

I shrug. "Because you've somehow ended up in my dream and I'm certainly not dead, though most times I wish I were." I grin, taking the bite out of the words. Her thighs rub together subtly as she moves forward and she darts a glance down at the ground, even as her desire saturates the muggy air. I've forgotten just how gratifying it is to be wanted by a comely stranger.

"Not that I mind visitors," I add thoughtfully. "I haven't seen anyone in ages. Herrick is in the cottage more than Malvolo, but only just. They're both anti-social these days."

Her eyes skim over me again and light in understanding. "You're Reve?" she asks.

I bow at the waist with a ridiculous little flourish. "At your service, my lady. And you are?"

"Neva." She just stares at me with that incredible mouth pursed, brow a mass of lines. "This can't be possible. You're... stuck in dreamland."

"And it would appear so are you."

"No," she insists. "I saw the Shepherd and it told me to inhale the water and so I did."

"You wanted to die?"

"How many times do I have to answer that question?" she barks.

"Why would you want to die?"

"If you lived my life, you'd understand," she answers, sounding put out.

"It's been my dream for longer than I can remember to be able to live at least one day of real life again," I say as her expression softens.

"I'm sorry."

"Apology accepted," I answer.

"Are you cursed to relive this place?" she asks as she looks around herself.

I nod. "I can't escape this day when inside my own head. And it takes effort to step into the minds of others. That's why it makes no sense for you to be here. No one has ever entered my mind before, whether dead or alive." I pause and study her with narrowed eyes. "Must be the Tenebris magic tainting you. Did she send you here?"

She throws up her hands. "There's that name again!" she says. "How many times do I have to tell you lot I don't know Tenebris? I didn't even know I was a witchling until recently," her voice begins to fade. "If I really am a witchling... I have yet to prove to myself that I possess any sort of magic."

Interesting. That must be why Herrick and Malvolo have taken her in. She has to be at least within proximity to my body, or this two-way link wouldn't be possible. Of course, that wouldn't explain why she believes she's killed herself.

But, nevermind.

For the first time in ages, I move from the shadow of the oak. I reach for her and pause when she shrinks back, as though I were preparing to strike. She curls in on herself, shielding that tempting body from view. The acrid stench of her fear burns my nose, and I let my hand drop at once.

"Sorry. I didn't mean to frighten you."

She looks at me with suspicious eyes.

"I won't hurt you, Neva,"

"Right," she grumbles. "I've heard that before."

What a jaded little girl. Barely bloomed and already her petals are bruised.

Hit by a sudden stroke of inspiration, I trudge down the hill, away from her, until I reach the rear line. I stoop to retrieve one of the fallen banners. The pierced shield, wand, and stars of our sigil glitter gold in the dusky light of the sun, laid out on a field of royal blue. Draping it over one arm, I return to the top of the hill. Warily, she watches me approach and flinches when I extend my arm to her.

"What are you doing?" she demands.

"I thought you might feel more comfortable and less... vulnerable if you were dressed," I explain, offering her the banner. She eyes it for another second before snatching it from my hand. She drapes it awkwardly around herself. It's too short to cover much, but at least it hides her curves from

78

*view. She does seem calmer when I can't see the planes of
her tight, little body.*

"Thank you," she murmurs.

*"May I touch your face? I promise, my hands will not
stray."*

Neva's eyes are guarded. "Why?"

*"I'd like to know what sort of sorcery you possess that
allows you to visit me… here. It should be impossible. The
spear was made to cage the god of dreams within his own
imagination. No one should be able to broach it. Yet you can
and did."*

"You think you'll be able to feel my magic?"

*"Any creature with enough power will be able to sense
your magic. But few can actually tell you what it means." I
waggle my fingers at her playfully, eliciting a small smile.
"Don't you want to know?"*

*She eyes my proffered fingers, hesitating a few
additional seconds. Then she steps closer, taking my hand
and pressing it to her cheek. Power swarms like ants across
my skin. I lean my forehead into hers and peel away that
first tingling layer of energy, stepping into her mindscape.*

*That magic belongs to Tenebris, no doubt about it. But
it's simply artifice, a ruse to draw the unwary eye away from
the true power that lies within.*

*The immensity of it is staggering. It batters against steel
bars, seeking any escape. How the fuck did Tenebris manage
to contain this? I circle the mental construct and watch the
eyes of a shadowy figure follow my every move. The edges of
it are amorphous, shifting constantly like smoke.*

I stagger back a step when the pieces fall into place.

The shadows form a bloodless face,

A shapeless girl, lacking grace;

On midnight wings, her fate is found,

and puts a djinn into the ground.

"Gods," I breathe. "It's you!"

Neva draws back, amber eyes reflecting the color of the dying sun. Her gaze almost seems made of fire.

"What's me?" she demands. "What do you mean?"

But I never have the chance to say more, because she pops out of existence in the next instant, as though she'd never been.

Strained silence. Three beats of my heart. And then I begin to laugh.

ELEVEN
Malvolo

"Son of a whore," I snarl. Herrick leaves her for fifteen minutes, and already she's trying to get herself killed.

Not that I care. I really don't.

In fact, I almost ignored Herrick's demands that we search for her. What do I care if the stupid witchling gets lost in the Forest of No Return? It means less effort in the long run if I don't have to run her off our land. I told him as much.

And now he's on the opposite end of the valley, searching the northern borders of the forest while I'm stuck with this mess.

The girl bobs facedown like a cork at the surface of the hot spring, sodden hair fanned around her head. Her skin is tinged lightly pink, which is more color than I've seen in her to date. Herrick will flay me alive if I just leave her as she is.

But, if I did just leave her as she is, doing so would make my life significantly easier. The girl is trouble. Obviously.

But, fuck me. I won't let my brother down. And fuck me further, but I don't think my conscience (what little still remains) will allow me to just leave her to die here.

Punctuating my hasty descent down the hill with several more curse words, I reach the edge of the pool within thirty seconds and wade into the scalding water after her. It would have been much easier to fish her out if she'd been considerate enough to keep her clothing on before her suicide attempt. As it is, there's nothing to hold onto but the mass of her dark hair, and I doubt she'll appreciate it being yanked out by the roots.

I slide an arm beneath her waist and flip her, so she's face-up. My heart stutters for a beat. Her face is slack, eyes open and slightly glazed.

Dead? She looks dead. Yet, this pool is maybe three feet deep! Not only that, but she's been gone for fifteen sodding minutes! And she's magical to boot! Bloody hell. Herrick is going to kill me if I don't try to do something about it, even though it's his own bloody fault she got scared off.

I won't stand for it! I'm not having him castigate me because the girl was idiotic enough to drown in a pool this shallow.

There's no time for care, so I toss her onto the bank none-too-gently, before clambering out after her. My shirt is soaked, my jerkin clings unpleasantly, and strands of dark hair flop into my eyes because the damn stuff won't stay in place when it's wet.

"You'd better be fucking worth all of this," I warn her, jabbing a finger at her lifeless face before I run through the basic first-aid steps Herrick taught me.

Hand over hand, compress the chest one hundred times a minute. Pause. Tilt chin. Two breaths. Repeat.

Her skin is hot, pink and nearly boiled, from the looks of it. Even if I can somehow restart the daft girl's heart, she could still die of heat stroke.

I curse Herrick to the blackest pits of Avernus as I scramble to preserve her life. Why did he have to bring her here? What had possessed him? Tenebris has caused us nothing but misery. And Tenebris is still written all over this girl. Yes, she's trouble! And haven't we had enough trouble in our fucking lives?

I knock something small and soft sideways with my elbow as I shift to breathe for her. My gaze flicks to it and I snarl another curse. White powder spills into the browning grass like a dusting of snow. But from the scent, it's nothing so innocuous. Some sort of human drug. Probably an opiate or amphetamine.

Something hard to come across in this region, so whoever gave it to her had deep pockets. Most drugs and potions are smuggled out of Wonderland, which numbers among the many reasons I despise the place. Nothing comes from Wonderland but madness and misery. Both in equal measure.

I hook a finger into the pouch and drag it nearer, abandoning her for a moment to check the contents. Ye Gods, the bag is half empty! No wonder she collapsed. An amount that large can stop a heart. That is, if she took it all in one sitting.

I glance up at her and frown.

"Stupid girl," I mutter before tipping her chin up, parting her lips slightly, and pressing my mouth to hers. Even slack as they are, her lips are distractingly lush. I'm able to temper my reaction to it by the bitter grit that coats her mouth. Her chest rises with my breath and her breasts brush my chest in a soft press of flesh.

Damn it, Malvolo, focus.

I need Herrick here, with his irritatingly calm demeanor. Even if I get her heart going again, she's going to need to cool off immediately, or we'll be stuck with a permanently addled woman. And that's another thing I don't want to deal with. It's bad enough I have to deal with Reve in such a condition.

I stop thinking and reprimand myself.

I didn't mean that. I love my brother, no matter the fact that he's lost to dreams.

I'm on my fourth round of compressions when her body bucks to life. She turns her head sharply and vomits, bringing up water and the remains of her breakfast. For several minutes, she splutters, and I sit back to watch her. I'm surprised to see her alive again. I didn't imagine my ministrations would make a damn of difference and yet, here she is.

Groaning, she clutches her middle as her stomach tries futilely to empty itself once more, when it's clear there's nothing left to expel.

"Ugh," she groans as she shifts her gaze from the ground to the view just in front of her. She has yet to see me.

"Serves you right," I grumble.

She blinks rapidly, lips parting in confusion as she drinks in the sight of me.

"What a brainless thing to do! If you were going to snort enough to collapse, you should have had the good sense to do it *out* of the water!"

"Malvolo?" she rasps, volume stolen from her question by the ache in her throat, no doubt. She glances around herself and me, as if she expects to see someone else here with us.

I cut my eyes away from her. I shouldn't find her as compelling as I do. She's a liability. She's wounded and just came back from the brink of death. She clearly has a death wish. And she's linked inescapably to Tenebris.

But… it's been so long since I heard a woman say my name.

Weak, sentimental fool, I chide myself. *One pretty face doesn't make up for the trouble she'll bring down on our heads.*

"Come on," I half-snarl. "You're not out of trouble yet."

I scoop her from the ground, balancing her weight easily in my arms. She's feather-light and molds perfectly into my sodden chest, laying her head into the crook of my elbow with the most trusting expression I've seen in someone outside my family. It makes my heart twinge in the oddest way and I clutch her a little tighter.

She's too damn warm. The temperature of her skin almost matches mine. Not a good sign. I need to cool her off quickly. There's a stream nearby, fed by snowmelt in the spring and a dozen smaller tributaries.

I break into a brisk jog, as she winds her slender arms around my neck, hauling herself up to cradle my throat. Her lips inadvertently brush my skin and I jerk in surprise, a trickle of warm arousal seeping into my veins. What the fuck is she doing?

I wade into the stream, wincing when the cool water envelops me. The stream is especially frigid this time of year. All the better to cool her, but the stab of cold is almost physically painful to my newly roused cock. Gritting my teeth, I sink onto a boulder submerged in the shallows and arrange her on my lap, bracketing one arm around her waist to keep her steady. Her head lolls back, settling against my shoulder. Her body shudders, appreciating the change in temperature about as much as mine.

"It's cold," she whines.

"You need it," I counter with a scowl.

"Why?"

Why? Why the blasted hell is she questioning me? Fuck, I don't have time for this! "Because you nearly cooked yourself in the hot spring, daft girl! Clearly, I have to bring your temperature down."

"Oh."

"What the fuck were you doing anyway?"

"I just wanted to forget," she sighs.

"Forget what?"

"It doesn't matter," she murmurs. "It's over now."

The cryptic answer infuriates me even more than the brainless stunt she pulled earlier. Women. Why can't they ever talk sense? I'll drag the answer out of her when she's well. She owes me that much for saving her. "Is that why you took the whole contents of the white stuff in the baggie?" I ask.

She looks up at me. "Cocaine," she corrects.

"Did you take it all in one sitting?"

She simply nods. Then a thought occurs to her and she looks up at me again. "Is it…"

"It's gone," I interrupt, though it's a lie.

She swallows hard but drops her gaze back down again and I wish I could read her thoughts. Why would one as beautiful as she try to end it all?

"No matter what you're running from, it's not worth your life," I tell her sternly, gripping her chin firmly and forcing her to meet my gaze.

Those luminous eyes threaten to knock the breath from me all over again. They'd be stunning enough to appeal to any man all on their own—paired with that face and the hum of magic that charges the air around her, they're damn riveting. Even the flush in her cheeks only adds to her beauty. Was this what drew Herrick in? I can't see any other reason. She's a bumbling simpleton, otherwise.

Her full lips press together in a scowl and her brows knit as she glares up at me, those resinous eyes going as cool and solid as a block of amber. "What would you know about it?"

"More than you will ever know, witchling. Now, be quiet and soak for a while. If we get your body temperature down, you *may* survive to nightfall."

She shifts on my lap, and despite the cold temperature, my cock twitches with interest. I breathe out sharply through my nose, ruffling the wispy hairs that curl around her ear. I'm too old and too experienced to let a girl influence me like this. I'm acting like a youngling, compelled by the first pretty, defenseless maiden I see. If I allowed my instincts to take over, I'd drag her back to my cave and act on selfish impulse to horde her away like treasure. Good thing for both of us that I'm adept at keeping my instincts at bay.

She's quiet for a few blessed minutes and I manage to steel myself against her unthinking charm. Her eyelids are at half-mast, a drowsy sort of calm settling over her now that the initial cold has stopped stabbing needles into our skin. I once more find myself wishing Herrick was here. I know how to twist a body into pieces, not how to mend it. Do I allow her to fall asleep, or would such a thing be catastrophic in her condition? My lack of knowledge chafes.

I smack her cheek lightly, deciding it might be best to keep her awake. "Hey!" I say in a gruff voice as I smack her cheek again, just as lightly but it still would be quite vexing. "Wake up!"

She blinks awake and glowers at me again. Her ire is almost amusing as much as it is surprising. It would almost be worth it to scare her into submission. One look at my beast and she'd be running and screaming into the Forest of No Return.

Hmm, not a bad plan.

"You're a deeply unpleasant man."

I snort. She doesn't employ much tact, does she? No pretty flattery or carefully considered words with this female. No words of gratitude for pulling her away from the brink of death. No tears. Instead, I get anger and a barbed tongue. Her abruptness is almost refreshing.

"I'm well aware."

She can't even muster the energy to roll her eyes, though I think she wants to. "Why do you hate me so much?"

Her question takes me aback for a moment or two. "I don't hate you," I reply dryly. "I just don't trust you. There's a difference." I pause. "And I don't particularly like you, either. But, hate? Hate is a very strong word. There's only one person I hate."

"And who is that?"

"No one for you to concern yourself with."

She wiggles her firm bottom, twisting in my arms until she can face me. The action brings her in even tighter against my manhood, which strains against the front of my pants, ignoring all of my reasoned arguments. It's a simple creature, unconcerned with things like consequences. All it wants is to slide into her warm pussy and rut her until she cries my name. Truth be told, I'm surprised she hasn't noticed it yet.

"I don't like this any more than you do, Malvolo," she says, breasts rubbing firmly against my chest but she doesn't seem to notice. In fact, she hasn't seemed to even give two fucking damns about the fact that she's entirely naked!

I must be mad as a fucking hatter, because I ache to slide my hands up her lithe little body and cup those breasts. Her nipples are tight and hard against me. From the cold of the water or desire? Impossible to tell, with the water stifling any scent of her arousal.

"I think of the three of you, I like Reve the best," she mutters. "At least he's got manners."

"Reve?" I repeat, glaring down at her. "What the bloody hell are you talking about?"

She shrugs. "He was trying to find answers for me, before you rudely yanked me out of the dream."

I freeze beneath her light touch, processing her words. No longer is my cock the first thought on my mind.

Reve spoke to her?

Reve hasn't bothered to contact Herrick or me in five years. It's a drain on his already limited reserves. So why did he waste energy to project his consciousness into hers? What is it about this little witchling that's drawn both Herrick and Reve to risk everything for her?

"I don't understand," I grind out, glancing sharply at her. I don't understand what I'm missing, but clearly, I've overlooked something crucial. "Explain."

"You don't understand what?" she snaps, some life creeping back into her voice and limbs. Her hands curl into fists where they rest on my shoulders. Clearly, she dislikes me as much as I dislike her.

"No one can communicate with Reve," I start.

"Well, that's bullshit," she argues.

I sigh in frustration. She's certainly a trying one. "And at best, if he's able to communicate with you, you must be in close proximity to him. Not miles away in a fucking hot spring!"

"Well, you're wrong on both counts."

"Then fucking explain to me why I'm wrong."

She shrugs. "I was in the hot spring and I imagine it was probably at the moment the Shepherd took me that I found myself on a battlefield where I met your brother."

She explains the whole story of the battlefield and her supposed conversation with my brother. I would not have believed her—would have imagined her story simply one concocted after the immense amount of 'cocaine' she fed herself, but her description of the battlefield and the words Reve spoke to her strike me as genuine.

Then how in blazes was she able to make it so? Truly, the witchling has even more power than I supposed and now I'm beginning to think I should most definitely have left her to die in the hot spring.

"What is it about you?" I ask, more to myself, as I shake my head.

"What is what about me?"

"It's certainly not your intelligence or self-preservation instinct, as you appear to have little of both."

She bristles, straightening to her full height in my arms. It puts her at eye-level with me, seated as she is in my lap. Those luminous eyes narrow into dangerous slits.

"What are you trying to say?"

I shrug. "You're clearly a fool."

"I am not a fool!"

"Yet you're turning to a drug to get you through life, a drug that nearly killed you."

"Maybe I wanted to die, asshole!"

"Take it from someone who's suffered a thousand times more than you can imagine, numbing yourself is the coward's way out. You face the pain and push through it, or you don't deserve the life you've been given."

"I don't want the life I've been given!"

"Then you're only proving my point," I continue with another shrug and frown. "You're a fool."

A furious crackle of energy hazes the air between us and, for a second, I'm absolutely certain she's about to send a bolt from the heavens to strike me dead. I gasp and pull myself away from her.

But not before her face crumples and she scrambles off my lap, dragging herself onto the bank with weak, trembling limbs.

"What the bloody fuck was that?" I insist as I stand up and try to snatch her ankle and drag her back, but she dances away before I can get a proper grip on her. She gives a great sniff and kicks at my outstretched hand. It connects with enough force to break my middle finger. I pull back and hiss out a pained sound between my teeth as I shake my offended hand. She's much much stronger than she looks.

"Go fuck yourself in your sanctimonious ass," she snarls and tries to stalk away. She's still not stable enough to make the move impressive; it's more of a staggering march. And she's stark naked which makes the whole show even more awkward.

I should follow her, but I'm only able to stare raptly at her lovely ass as she makes her escape.

Who is this Neva Valkoinen?

Herrick braves exposure for her. Reve communicates with her—the first time he's taken notice of someone in years. And I'm left in a freezing stream, cock hard and arms empty, feeling bereft, wanting a woman in a way I haven't in years.

What in the name of all the Gods is she?

And how do I stop myself from caring so goddamn much about the answer?

TWELVE
Neva

I want to beat in Malvolo Vorst's infuriatingly attractive face.

It had almost been pleasant, waking in his arms. He's just as attractive as either of his brothers. Even though he's the most unfriendly and hostile person I've ever come into contact with.

Actually, that's not true. Darius took that title… but Darius is now dead so maybe it's a title I can return to Malvolo.

Regardless, it's shocking how different the Vorst brothers are, given they all share the same father. Reve's features border on pretty, with an air of permanent boyishness framed by wavy burgundy hair. He has a smile that's infectious and the air of a prankster—someone who doesn't take himself too seriously. From what I can remember of my dream, or my bout with death, Reve is slim and tall with large, broad shoulders that taper into a narrow waist and long legs. He's not quite as big or broad as his older brothers, but he's impressive, all the same.

Herrick's beauty is polished and controlled, and he almost appears innocuous until one gets close enough to spot the smoldering intensity that lurks beneath his benign exterior.

And Malvolo? He's the most overtly sexual of the three, even though he tries to deny his nature. And he's also the most feral and unpredictable. His dark hair is as long as Herrick's, but wild, as though he simply can't be bothered to do anything to tame it. His eyes are dark, with just the edge of red-orange tracing the outside of his iris, making them

resemble the dying embers in the grate I'm currently staring
at.

Malvolo Vorst might be stunningly handsome but I hate
him!

I poke unhappily at the ashes while ugly thoughts of
Malvolo haunt my mind. I can't stop thinking about him and
I hate it. The bastard insults me and destroys the rest of my
cocaine, and I find myself day-dreaming about his hands on
me? It's utterly absurd.

He didn't destroy your cocaine, I suddenly tell myself.
The thought is followed by the absolute conviction that
Malvolo has the remainder of my cocaine hidden away in his
cave.

I'm not sure how I know this, but I do.

Not that it matters, I think to myself. *Malvolo will never
give it back to me.*

There are better things to think about. Like Reve's
puzzling situation. Like Herrick's absence, as he makes the
trek through the forest, looking for something to ease my
pain.

Nausea and fatigue have kept me in bed for days, and
the clawing pain of withdrawal worsens with each passing
day. Herrick wants to try poppy juice, the new favorite
narcotic bandied about in the wealthier circles of Ascor. It
ought to be a less addictive alternative to satisfy the
cravings. But he's not due back for another two days, at
least.

I'm not sure I can make it that long.

Not to mention the fact that I'm beginning to doubt my
misgivings about Herrick. He's certainly trying to dull and
numb my pain. He's going out of his way to make a long
and perilous journey to find something to help me.

*Yet, he would have forced himself on you the other
night,* I remind myself.

I don't know if that's true. Yes, he was dominant with me. Yes, he made his intentions known—he wanted me and had I allowed him, he would have taken me. Of that I'm sure.

Had I allowed him…

The words play through my head as realization dawns on me.

I pulled away from Herrick in the heat of the moment and he *didn't* force himself on me! And that means something.

How many times had I tried to shy away from Darius? How many times had I pretended to be ill? Even the moments when I was ill with headache or something else, it never mattered to him. My *feelings* never mattered to Darius. All that did was the warm wetness between my thighs. And, even that is an exaggeration—my sex was never wet when Darius forced himself inside me…

I've been wrong about Herrick…

Maybe, I correct myself. *You don't know him well enough yet to make that decision. It could be that he's just as bad as all the rest, but he hasn't yet revealed his true colors.*

I struggle with my drooping eyelids, forcing myself to keep going. Tending the house is hard, tedious work, but it keeps me busy and it gives me something to think about other than the wretched situation I find myself.

If I settle in front of the fire, I'll fall asleep, and the nightmares will hold me captive for hours until I scream myself awake again. I don't know if they're caused by the unfortunate trip through the Forest of No Return, or simply a symptom of my withdrawals. I've never actually felt this poorly before. And it's all Malvolo's fault. If he'd left me even a small dose, I could have eased off by degrees, instead of being tossed roughly onto the sobriety wagon against my will.

At least I know Reve will be there if I do lapse into dream. Since that night when I met him on the dream battlefield, he's come to visit me in my own dreams, a silent observer who cradles me when the nightmares finally cease. Without his soft hands and the comfort of his hard body, I'm not sure I'll make it through another night.

I knuckle my eyes and yawn hugely, pushing myself up from the grate. Ash coats the front of Herrick's tunic, turning the red fabric a dusky rose beneath the filth. I can't find it in myself to care. It's completely uncharitable but in this instant, I hate him, too, for being unable to remedy things quicker. I hate him for not confronting Malvolo and returning the cocaine to me. Hate him for being gone when I need him.

Dizziness crashes over me in a wave and I brace my hands against the wall to keep from tipping over. Damn Malvolo! Damn him to Avernus! Let Lycaon's hellhounds strip the meat from his bones and Sol's fire burn his remains to ash!

With the fire stoked, the floors swept, dinner prepared, and everything dusted within an inch of its life, there's not much else I can do to distract myself from the fatigue. Reve nearly overflows his small bed, or I would climb in with him. His brothers have him arranged sideways, one hand thrown out to the side while the other cradles his head. A flush tints his pale cheeks, and long lashes brush the high sweep of his cheekbones. I can only see the similarity to his brothers in that full, bow-lipped mouth—the only feature the three share. His mouth is parted slightly and I wonder, for just a second, what it might be like to feel those lips against mine. Would he feel warm? Or is he cold, poised as he is between life and death?

I cross over to him, kneeling by his bedside. This seems like a gross invasion of his privacy, but my curiosity prickles, demanding to be sated.

Extending a trembling hand, I brush it over his cheek. I inhale sharply, surprised at just how warm he feels. It's as if he's just fallen asleep. I expect his eyes to flutter open any moment and for him to greet me with a sleepy smile. It's no wonder Herrick keeps the covers draped over him when he's home. His brother is alive and aware and there's absolutely no waking him from this half-life.

Poor Herrick. Poor Reve.

My thumb brushes idly across those lips. Slightly chapped but nonetheless soft beneath my touch. The desire to kiss that gentle mouth rises in me again, and before I can think too deeply about it, I find myself hovering mere inches above those gorgeous bow lips.

Just once, I reason, just so I know what it would feel like. Reve can't hurt me like this. And he's so starved for sensation, this distraction wouldn't bother him, would it? I lean in a little closer...

A crack of sound has me bolting upright with a shriek and I whip around, half-expecting the beastly Malvolo to come charging in. But it's just the shutters—they've come unlatched, battering about in the gale that sweeps down the mountain. Cold scrapes my face as I stalk over and slam them shut, bolting them more securely this time.

I'm annoyed by my own impulsiveness. God, I'd nearly kissed a comatose man! It's just as bad as kissing a drunk or a corpse! Well, maybe not   quite as bad as the latter. But, still, what in the bloody hell am I thinking? I'm clearly going insane from lack of sleep.

I curl up on Malvolo's bed, clutching my knees to my chest, burying my face in his pillow. It smells sharp and clean, like a snow-laden pine. It's Malvolo's scent, and I absolutely loathe that it stirs something inside me that Herrick or Reve's touch haven't yet.

Malvolo looks at me as though he can't decide whether to twist my head off or devour me whole. And for some bizarre reason, his absolute feral unpredictability stokes something deep inside me. Yes, I can't stand him! Yes, he makes me so angry, I want to cry! And, yes, I want to feel him penetrating me. I want to see the expression in his eyes when he shoves his cock (which I could tell from the cold spring was incredibly large) into me.

I don't know what I'm doing but my hand moves of its own accord as images of Malvolo race through my mind. I shove my hand between my thighs and I feel the wetness covering my fingers instantly. I find that sensitive nub and I begin rubbing it as a groan steals from my mouth. I squeeze my eyes shut, willing the throbbing to go away and seconds later, I explode in fiery ecstasy. My eyes fly open as I pant and realize I've just brought myself to that release I've heard so much about. Darius could never do it and yet, I possessed the capability all along. It simply took… thoughts of Malvolo to bring me there? I don't want to face the truth in that statement so I, instead, surrender to sleep.

Reve stands by, as he has for days, back pressed against a stone wall as another nightmare plays out. I'm little again, legs stubby, my hands small and pudgy as they extend toward the prone figure on the ground.

With a whimper, I back up a few steps as the ever-widening pool of red touches the tip of my pretty white shoes. The smell of metal coats the inside of my nose, a horrid, sharp scent that turns my stomach. My father's face is pale and bloodless. His hand scrambles to find purchase on the wall, but he can't find a handhold deep enough to haul himself upright.

"Papa!" The word comes out a half-sob.

His middle looks funny, with meaty furrows showing under his torn clothes. Something pulsates beneath them and I tear my eyes away, bile creeping up the back of my throat.

"Run, Neva," he rasps, pointing a shaking finger toward the end of the corridor. I quail. I don't want to go

*there. The dungeons are where the bad people live. It's dark
and cold, and I need my papa with me.*

"I can't go without you."

*"Find Draven," he orders, voice as firm as it can be,
with more and more red seeping out of him. There's so much
red, eating up the gray flagstones and staining them. My
shoes are dyed crimson with the stuff, though the white bows
remain mockingly pristine.*

"But, Papa—"

*A snarl echoes down the hall and we both flinch away
from the sound. It bounces and booms off the stone,
amplifying the noise tenfold. It sounds like a dozen hounds,
when I know there are only three. Three is already too many.
I can't fight them. I can't hope to outrun them.*

*My heart begins a frantic sprint. I want to run. But I
can't leave Papa behind.*

"Go!" he roars.

*My father never shouts. The shock is enough to work
my chubby little legs into motion, buckling when I reach the
dark end of the hall. I tumble down the first three steps
before catching myself on a metal banister bolted into the
wall.*

*The cold bites at me as I descend, and tears leak from
my eyes as my father's shouts follow me down into the
depths. They've found him! Those hideous beasts are hurting
him! I need to go back and do* something!

*The click of claws on stone sounds behind me and I
start taking the stairs two at a time. The eager pants of a
hellhound follow me down and down and I find myself
running as fast as I can. If I should trip and fall, I'll be just
like Papa, screaming and screaming with no one to hear.*

*"Draven!" I screech, hoping my father's faithful friend
can hear me. "Draven, where are you?"*

*I reach the first floor of cells seconds later and stumble,
expecting another step down. I catch myself on the crude*

stone bars. The space is dimly lit by torchlight, which illuminates a narrow path between the walls of cells. There's no Draven in sight.

I begin to weep openly now.

I don't want to die, I don't want to die, I don't want to die…

A growl sounds behind me and I spin, heart stuttering to a brief stop when I behold the creature there.

The hellhound is a shadowy mass of black fur. Flame crackles off its back and tail as it stalks toward me, sparks shooting off its fur like static charge. Singed paw prints mark its progress across the stone. Even at this distance, the heat rolling off its massive frame makes my eyes water and the hairs on my arms curl.

"Hold still, little girl, and I'll make this quick," it warns. The voice is too distorted to guess whether it's a boy or a girl hound. It barely sounds like the common tongue at all, like its throat can't even wrap around the idea of human speech.

I close my eyes, hands coming up to cover my face, as the hellhound lunges for me.

When the thing lets out a caterwaul that shakes the stones all around me, I open my eyes and what I see startles me. Draven stands, straight-backed and impossibly tall, with the hellhound skewered on his broadsword. His dark hair shines with blue highlights under the torchlight, and his handsome face is disdainful as he flicks the massive creature away, as if it weighs nothing at all.

Papa always said huntsmen were strong.

The beast's spine cracks when it impacts the iron bars. I wait for it to get up, but the creature doesn't stir. The creature is dead. Draven's contempt bleeds away and concern washes across his face instead when he sees the state of my dress and shoes.

"Are you hurt, Neva?"

99

"N-no. Is my papa...?"

Draven's expression shutters, and it's all the answer I need. Tears stream down my cheeks harder than before as he bends and scoops me up from the ground.

"We need to go," he says softly.

He steals away into the shadow, and I'm left in the minutes-long gap between dreams and lucidity.

"Poor Leon," Reve mutters. "I knew they'd lied, but not quite this egregiously."

I turn to him, face going slack in surprise. "Leon? You knew my father?"

"Not well. But we fought together in the war. I respected him and his commitment to the cause. I always guessed such was what got him killed, but I didn't realize just how much treachery must have gone on to orchestrate his death. We told him not to marry the night hag, but he didn't listen to us."

Reve's grimace mars his otherwise perfect face. I step toward him, yearning blossoming like a flower in my chest. Everything in my mind, all my memories prior to age ten are a blank. Reve holds the key to answers I've only dreamed of.

Answers to so many questions!

Who were my parents? Why would they give me up to Gregory? What did any of this have to do with Tenebris?

"Tell me who he is, Reve. I need to know... please."

He shakes his head, amber eyes somber. "I'm afraid whatever spell is controlling your memories will have to be broken on its own."

"But why?" I insist.

"If I tamper with it while it's still this potent, it will only damage you, Neva."

Wrong answer. Desperately, I grip the front of his light green tunic. "Tell me, Reve, please! I'll give you anything."

The hint of a smile touches his lips. "Give me a kiss, and then maybe I'll talk."

I cross my arms. I'm not in the mood to play with him. All my earlier fascination with that gentle mouth is gone, now that its owner is so blatantly extorting me. It feels too much like Darius' games, baiting me with the simplest of things. Well, I'm not going to dance at the end of a string to entertain him.

"I thought you were different," *I grumble, trying to force back tears that threaten to overtake me. The disappointment coursing through me is almost impossible to face.*

"You don't understand, Neva," *he starts but I shake my head.*

I stalk toward the growing light, pressure building in my chest. Screaming myself awake is growing tiresome.

Find Malvolo! I suddenly think to myself. This is all his fault! And he needs to make it right!

My throat is hoarse when I bolt upright, cry dying off as soon as I'm fully cognizant. The wind has died to a dull roar, and a brief peek out the shutters shows the bruise-like shade of nightfall hanging over the valley. I've slept for at least a few hours. It eases the misery by only a few degrees.

I'm fairly sure Malvolo is in the mines, the caves. It's the only place Herrick and Malvolo go when they "work" as they both refer to it. And whenever they return, they're covered in soot from head to toe.

I need to find those mines. I need to find Malvolo.

Herrick's warnings not to enter the caves ring dully in my ears, but I push them aside. I don't care if I get lost in the labyrinthine mines. I'll map out every crevice, if that's what it takes.

I'm going to find Malvolo. I'll take back what's mine or I'll die trying.

THIRTEEN
Neva

Herrick's boots are too big, and I'm tripping all over the damn place as I stagger through the caves. The tunnels are massive. Big enough to smuggle a company of men or trolls through, with space to spare. How long have the Vorst brothers been working to clear this space? None of them appeared to be much over thirty, if that. But, running the sums quickly through my head, I know they have to be at least that.

The war ceased fifteen years ago, and they'd all been old enough to fight. That would mean they were all at least thirty-six, perhaps older. Gregory had looked much older approaching his forties than any of these men do...

The improvised torch I hold above my head illuminates seams of silver, gold, and copper striating the rocks. Here and there, glittering gems stud the wall. Now I understand how Herrick was able to purchase me so easily that night—there's enough wealth here to fund a kingdom for decades. And this is only one tunnel in one mine! The wealth here is truly staggering. If any of the surrounding principalities knew this place existed, they'd descend like crows to pick it clean.

I expect the air to grow colder as I descend into the bowels of the mine. Instead, the air heats to an almost uncomfortable temperature, and dragging in each breath becomes a challenge. The memory of heat and a hellhound's bared teeth flashes through my mind for a few seconds, rooting me to the spot in terror. I clutch the jagged edges of a diamond until blood runs between my fingers and my heart stops trying to thunder out of my chest.

The heat must be coming from Malvolo's cave. Herrick says Malvolo prefers his solitude and sleeps here the majority of the time—the reason why I don't see him in the cottage very much. It follows, then, that the heat has to be coming from some sort of furnace that keeps this place from being bitterly cold.

I think I've been staggering around for about an hour, but it's impossible to tell without the moon or stars to track my progress. My ankle twists, yet again, and I drop to my knees, giving my tortured body a rest. It's only when I pause that I realize there's something echoing through the tunnels that I didn't register before. The sound is almost that of the wind sighing. Except, it can't be. The sound is soft and rhythmic, a cadence so soothing, one could easily fall asleep to it.

And that's when it clicks.

Breathing.

The soft sound, and the warm updraft that's been raising the hair off my neck, is… someone or *something's* breath. My heart squeezes painfully in my chest. How massive must a creature be to produce breath so loud and strong? The savage northmen who rule the lands above Grimm and Wonderland believe in a serpent that nibbles at the roots of a world tree. My mind conjures up unpleasant images of a serpent, lipless mouth open wide as it prepares to slide me down its gullet.

Trembling, I back my way along the wall. Now I understand why Herrick warned me away from the caves. There's something enormous living here, and if I'm not careful, I'll find myself its next meal. Does Malvolo know about this creature? Perhaps he's just too much of a misanthrope to care if he's eaten…

The support against my back suddenly gives way and then I'm tumbling downward, yelping in fright as I slide steeply down a tunnel I didn't notice until it was too late. The tunnel corkscrews violently, whipping my head around before I'm in freefall, arms windmilling to slow my descent. It doesn't help much, and I end up impacting something hard, face-first.

For the second time in a fortnight, I'm left curled on my side, wheezing, as I try to recapture some of my escaped air. When I try to lift my head, I find stars dancing in my vision. I shake the dizziness from my head and notice my torch, where it lies a few feet away. That's not the only thing I notice—the air here moves rhythmically throughout the cave. Sickening realization slams into me and I struggle not to bring up my meager supper.

Fuck, fuck, fuck.

I've just crashed into the lair of whatever resides in these caves—and in my state, it'll be damn close to impossible to climb the steep exit. Maybe I can hide here until Herrick comes looking for me? No, that's no good. Who knows how long I'll survive? If that thing, whatever it is, finds me, I'll be gone in a few swallows.

When I stoop to retrieve my torch, the small circle of light lands on a pile of minted gold coins. I lift the torch up to eye-level and discover still more gold. The shifting surface beneath my feet is a mountain of gold coins! I pick one from the pile, testing my teeth against it the way I've seen merchants do. There's a slight give. It's real! I look out over the vast pile once more as I swallow hard. I've never seen a treasure this large. I doubt any person has!

I've never considered myself an especially materialistic woman, but staring at all this wealth now makes me wonder just how different my life could have been if I'd had even a fraction of this wealth.

Hazy memories of Prince Agrabah surface again, though this time they seem more hopeful. If I took a few handfuls of this gold and made it out of the cave alive, I could board a ship and sail away from this accursed place forever.

I could start a new life.

I could go east and find Prince Agrabah in the Anoka Desert and tell him of my new financial situation. Maybe then he'd consider me worth… worth what?

He'll always remember what you are, I tell myself.

Nevermind that, I think in response. *I'm going to take as many coins as I can and I'm going to start a new life! A life far from this one!*

I reach down and using my tunic as a hammock, I pile as many of the gold coins into the tunic as I can.

Maybe I'll go west to Sweetland, a place rumored to grow confections from the earth with rivers and streams made of chocolate. Or maybe I could go north and settle in the village of The Hollows, perched on the edges of the Enchanted Forest?

Screw it! Go as far west as the Edge of the World, past the waterfall, and make a new life in the Neverland Islands!

Regardless of where I *could* go, there's still the pressing issue of that monster.

It takes a few seconds to realize the cadence of the wind has changed. No longer a gentle in and out, the breath huffs in, like a wine connoisseur getting the aroma of a glass before drinking.

Oh, fuck.

It's awake.

The thing has scented me and is now trying to sniff me out—I can hear it. I'm sure anything with keen enough senses would pinpoint the stench of my fear in seconds. I hold the hammock of my tunic tightly in one hand, so none of the coins will drop free. Then I whip my head to one side and find the mouth of the tunnel jutting out several feet above my head.

A blast of air, as hot as a furnace, ruffles the hem of the back of my tunic, the part I'm not gripping in my hand. My legs lock like a colt's and I have to force myself to look down.

My torch casts a weak circle of light, but it's enough to make out what exactly it is I'm facing. My heart crowds my throat, blocking out my scream. A giant, reptilian face hovers above mine, teeth bared and a vast, brassy sound building in its chest.

It's a dragon.

It's a huge, motherfucking dragon, and I've just invaded its horde. I've got its gold in my tunic.

I'm dead. I'm so, so dead.

I immediately loosen the hand holding my tunic closed and the gold coins fall back where they came from, taking with them my dreams of Sweetland, The Hollows and Neverland. Not that any of those places will matter to me when I'm dead.

I raise my hands in the air to show the monster I'm no longer trying to make off with its treasure. Hopefully the thing will have a streak of mercy.

An enormous clawed hand shoots out and seizes me, whipping me into the air with no effort at all. I shriek as I'm lifted ten, fifteen, thirty feet in the air, and the dragon drags me close enough that I can inspect the artistry of its face.

"Please don't eat me," I whisper.

I can admit the thing is beautiful, even if it's about to use my bones for toothpicks after it munches on my flesh.

The scales are as dark and smooth as obsidian and the nearest one cuts a furrow into my much-abused palms. A crown of horns tops its massive head, and just beyond those, I can spy one massive wing, flared out to its side, the foreclaw scraping the stone walls of the cave. Where the second wing should be, though, there's only a jut of bone and the leathery tatters of what must once have been the matching appendage.

I'm momentarily diverted by this realization. If it only has one wing, that means it can't fly. The missing wing doesn't look fresh and gaping, but still clearly pains the beast, because it rolls its shoulder as though soothing an ache.

"Someone hurt you?" I murmur, more to myself than to it, even as I wonder why in the hell I'm trying to converse with a dragon. Maybe I am as stupid as Malvolo said.

Regardless, the fact that this mighty beast has been wounded just seems wrong. It's a travesty of justice that this magnificent, deadly dragon should be deformed in such a way.

Its head tilts to the side, considering me with black eyes edged with the red-orange of dying embers. Then it presses me between its two front legs, cradling me like a babe against its chest, and it begins to move.

No... move is the wrong word. It's completely stationary, still towering over me. But, as I watch, it begins to shrink. The fine bones of its face shift and morph in a way that's almost grotesque. Hideous snaps and pops echo like shots around the cave, stone augmenting the sound just as it had in my dream.

It drops me.

I close my eyes, willing this all to be another nightmare, but when I dare to peek at the ground, I realize I'm still in the cavern. Gold still litters the ground at my feet and piles of it still line the walls of the cave.

But gone are the dragon's clawed feet. Instead, I see the bare, long-toed feet of a human man. Shocked, I follow the line of the legs, finding them equally bare. Nestled between those legs is the largest cock I've ever seen. I swallow audibly, forcing my eyes further upward to a bare, chiseled torso, and finally to a familiar, scowling face.

Malvolo glares down at me, more anger than I've ever seen in his ember eyes.

"What the fuck are you doing here, trying to steal my fucking treasure?"

FOURTEEN
Neva

"Y-You're a dragon!" I stammer as Malvolo glares at me.

Malvolo snorts and his voice drips with scorn when he speaks. "Well-spotted. I take back all my previous comments about your intelligence, witchling. Your deductive reasoning is astounding."

This is Malvolo, all right. I've only met him a few times and yet I'd know that prick's condescending tone anywhere.

"You don't have to be an asshole about it," I grumble. "Wasn't scaring the piss out of me enough?"

Malvolo arches a brow. "I can't tell if you're heartbreakingly naïve or too stupid to live."

My hands clench into fists at my side and something hard digs into my palm. "Talk to me plainly, you bastard. What's going on here? How is it even possible you're a dragon?"

And if he is a dragon, did that mean the others are, as well?

Of course it does!

Armed with this new information, a lot of things start to make more sense. I hadn't questioned how Herrick had managed to send the Gryphus huntsman through a wall, or how he'd managed to heal the huge gash in his shoulder. His teeth were sharp enough to unnerve me, even in human form. And the unflappable calm he's displayed must have been cultivated over many years.

These mines had been carved out over centuries, by three huge dragons, instead of a legion of miners. Yes, things were starting to make sense. But, that didn't mean I liked them any better.

"I've always been a dragon," he says dismissively. "It isn't my fault humans have forgotten how to properly spot one."

"Why didn't Herrick tell me?"

He shrugs. "Maybe because it's none of your fucking business?" he answers and then glares at me some more. "I don't try to fathom why my idiot brother does what he does most days. But even I thought he'd warn you against coming here."

"He did."

"But you didn't listen," he answers.

"Clearly."

"So, you're a fool and a thief."

I hold my chin up. "I'm not a thief."

One of his eyebrows arches. "Did you or did you not load a whole slew of my coins into the fabric of your tunic?"

"Yes, I did."

"Then that makes you a thief."

"I didn't know the coins belonged to you."

"But you knew these caves belonged to us."

Okay, clearly this line of argument isn't going to get me anywhere. I prop my hands on my hips. "I figured a few gold coins wouldn't put a dent in your wealth," I answer then motion to the area surrounding me. "Look how many you have! There must be hundreds of thousands of coins in here!"

"I've lost count."

"See?"

"What did you want the coins for?"

I frown, surprised he'd even ask this question. "I wanted to get away from here and start a new life for myself."

"Where?"

I shrug. "The Hollows or Sweetland or maybe Neverland."

He scoffs at me. "Neverland doesn't exist."

"You don't know that."

"Oh?" he asks as he plops his own hands on his hips, making me extremely aware of the immensely large appendage dangling between his legs. I accidentally look down at it and then immediately pull my attention back to his face. He smirks as he catches me.

"Oh," I respond and then shake my head. "I mean… yes. You… you don't know Neverland doesn't exist!"

"I've traveled all over Fantasia, to every principality and I've never seen Neverland."

"Have you been to the Waterfall at the Edge of the World?"

"Yes."

"And?"

"And nothing."

"Nothing?" I repeat, surprised.

"Yes, no archipelago of Neverland Islands. There's the waterfall, the cliff's edge beyond it and… nothing else."

"Well, that isn't why I came here," I answer, still completely thrown off by the fact that I can't keep myself from glancing down at his cock. It's just so… so big!

"I've killed men for less than what you've done."

"What I've done?" I echo, awash in my earlier confusion.

He nods and his cock swings back and forth but I fight not to look at it. I hold my head as high as I can and I'm sure I appear completely idiotic.

"You came into my horde and stole from me," Malvolo explains. "It's a killing offense."

I don't say anything but watch him as he turns around, giving me a great view of his taut and round ass. Then he crosses over to a gilt-backed chair and settles himself on it with the air of a spoiled prince presiding over court. He sits splay-legged, obviously not bothered by his nudity. It's a real effort to keep my eyes from his groin.

The cock had been impressive before; stirring with his interest, and now with his legs spread wide and his malehood on display, it's almost captivating. But I force my gaze down to his feet. The last thing I want to do while I'm being lectured for being a thief, and a stupid one at that, is stare at his naughty bits.

There's pile of tapestries near his feet. I stride forward and between my overlarge boots and shifting footing, the place is almost impossible to navigate. I pick one of the tapestries up and offer it to him without letting my gaze dip.

"Why are you handing me this?" he demands.

I keep my head held high. "So you can cover… yourself."

He chuckles and throws the tapestry to the side. "I'm rather enjoying the fact that you can't keep yourself from looking at it."

"Ugh, I hate you!" I yell at him as my hands become fists at my side.

"Regardless, what are you here for?" he asks and then clears his throat. "Stupid question. Did you know there was treasure here before you came?"

"No."

"Then?"

The truth seems very petty, in light of what's just happened—I came here to demand he replace or return my cocaine. I'm pretty sure the least he'll do is kick my shapely behind out of the cavern if I even suggest it. And as idiotic as it sounds, I still want it. When I scan the cavern again, I see a baggie of white in the mouth of an overturned vase that sits near the tapestries.

So he lied! He never destroyed the cocaine! He stole it!

"You call me a thief!" I yell at him, suddenly livid.

112

He glances in the direction of my gaze and spots the white stuff. Then he looks back at me with a shrug. "I'm not one to destroy things."

"And yet you told me you did."

He shrugs again. "That was for your own good."

It's then that I realize fighting him won't do any good. He's obviously much stronger than I am physically so I'll have no hope in hell of getting the cocaine past him. But, there's something I *do* have that he doesn't—feminine wiles.

Mind made up, I turn to him with my sultriest expression fixed in place. I take the steps that separate us and place each of my hands on the arms of his throne, leaning over him. My face is just inches from his.

"What… what are you doing?"

Getting my cocaine back, asshole.

He jerks in surprise when I wedge one thigh between his and straddle one of his broad legs. I lace my fingers at the nape of his neck, brushing his chest carefully with mine the way I always do during a lap dance. If there's one thing Darius taught me that I can be grateful for, it's how to snare a man's interest.

My lips hover only an inch above his and we're so close, our breaths mingle. "I'm here to finish what we started."

His gaze dips to my mouth and his lips part. A ragged snarl escapes. "Don't you fucking tempt me, witchling. I'm not in the mood for games."

"It's only a game, if you want to play," I purr.

I kiss him.

I intend for it to be a chaste press of lips, but that plan shatters like fine china as Malvolo gets a grip on my waist and hoists me up, so I'm forced to wrap my legs around his waist. His mouth is hot and devours mine with a single-minded intensity that consumes me. His cock drags along my sex, drawing a moan from me. His hand fists in my hair, tugging almost to the point of pain.

He's going to take control, Neva, I think to myself. *Pull away now, while you still can!*

But I can't. I expect myself to panic, because clearly I'm no longer in control, but Malvolo doesn't give me time to feel anything but the heat of his mouth and the crushing of his body on mine. All I can see, taste, or feel is him. His scent is sharp, that familiar snow and pine—a startling contrast to the burn of his skin. His mouth tastes like spice and his skin feels like the trace of velvet along mine. He drags his mouth away to trail burning kisses down my throat. The unexpected sharpness of his teeth sends a thrill of mixed terror and arousal riding straight to my core.

"Oh, fuck," I breathe.

"That's the idea," he all but growls against my throat.

Fucking Malvolo—that had been the plan. Fuck Malvolo and get my coveted prize. How exactly? I hadn't thought that far in advance. And now? Now fucking him sounds like the ends and not the means. It doesn't sound like a punishment at all.

Malvolo brings us to the ground, laying me out on the heavy tapestry he so carelessly flung earlier. His mouth never leaves my throat. He seems determined to sample the throb of my pulse. I wonder if he'll bite me and I'm a little distressed when the prospect doesn't alarm me the way it should. But then something else occurs to me.

"Are you going to turn into a dragon?"

He chuckles. "Do you want me to?"

"No," I answer immediately.

He chuckles again. "Okay then."

He proves that the gold buttons I've been fiddling with on my tunic are more than simply decorative, undoing them with small, deft flicks of his wrist, parting the fabric as soon

114

as he reaches the bottom. Warm air caresses my bared flesh, and he feels deliciously hot against me.

One hand still fisted in my hair, he licks a trail up to my ear, rolling the lobe between his teeth in a move so sensual, it drags another moan from my throat.

Another strong hand trails its way down my body, taking time to weigh each of my breasts, assessing them. He apparently doesn't find them lacking, a small hum of approval rumbling in his throat as he traces his thumb across one peaked nipple. It puckers still further at his touch, and my breath comes in shallow pants.

What is he doing to me? My only experience with men, aside from the very rare lap dances I've been allowed to give, has been Darius. And he handled me roughly, not caring if he left bruises, and usually encouraging them. Often, Darius just hiked my skirts and thrust inside me, even if I was dry. I'm used to gritting my teeth through the first several minutes.

But this is so different. I hesitate to even call it by the same name.

My core is aching, but not with the chafing feel of Darius fucking me raw. Slickness coats my thighs and my entire body craves touch. Malvolo is beautiful. Not even his trademark scowl can disguise that. With a square jaw lined with a day's stubble, those ember eyes burn with intensity as he examines me, watching the effect of his ministrations play out on my face.

I jerk upward in surprise when he traces the curve of one hipbone with his finger and then dips further down still, sliding two long digits through my slickness, his gaze fixed on my face as he slides them into me. The intrusion is shocking, but welcome, the fullness easing the ache somewhat. Not what I wanted, but still sweet relief.

A breathy sound escapes me, and he grins. Another wave of want spreads through me—it's the first time I've seen something approaching good humor on his face, even if the smile promises wicked things will follow.

"Fuck, it's good to hear that sound again," he says.

Masculine pride coats the words and absurd disappointment calms my ardor for a few seconds. Of course, it's stupid to expect to be his only. He and his brothers have existed for centuries, at least, if the elaborate network of caves is anything to go by. Hundreds of women have probably been where I am now, spread out and bared to his burning gaze and skillful hands.

The thought flies from my head as he presses the pad of his thumb against the aching bud above my entrance. Lightning zings through my veins and jolts of pure pleasure claw their way up my spine.

He pumps those fingers in and out of me and my hips jerk up in response, tilting my pelvis to give him better access to a place inside me that makes my toes curl.

All the while, that thumb keeps up a steady circular motion. My body tenses, the blissful feeling coiling like a spring within me. My skin feels unbearably tight and needy. I'm not as naïve as he seems to believe, because I know what this is.

That I'm finding it here, in this man's arms, laid like a treasure on a mountain of gold, is such an absurd notion that a laugh bubbles in my throat. I bite the inside of my cheek to keep it from escaping.

His fingers curl, stroking the spot just inside me, and the pressure builds to an almost intolerable level. Sensation balances on a razor's edge, wobbling precariously between pleasure and pain.

I pant. "Please..."

"Say my name," he commands huskily, voice taking on the raspy tones of the dragon. His eyes bleed into the dragon's slit-pupiled gaze. It should scare me, leave me cold at the realization that I'm being touched by one of the most violent, possessive, and ill-tempered races in existence. But the glint of that possessiveness in his eyes thrusts me over the edge.

My body bows, head arching back. I knock into a little pile of gold and send it cascading away, sliding in a shimmering avalanche to the bottom of our little dune. I drag the soft material of the tapestry between my fingers, trying to keep myself tethered to something. When I settle back onto it, my body feels boneless, and an intense sense of satiation settles over me like a cloak.

My cocaine lays only a few feet away and I can't summon even an ounce of desire for it. Holy fuck. No wonder people dedicated art and poetry to this act. I'll do just about anything to find that elusive feeling again; it's the closest to pure joy I've ever known.

Malvolo's wicked smile traces along the column of my throat.

And then the unthinkable happens.

Pain explodes at the base of my skull and I scream, hands clawing through the tapestry again, so I don't flay his hard biceps or back to ribbons. It feels like someone is jabbing the end of a pickaxe through me, trying to cleave me in two. Light and color explode before my eyes in a familiar rush.

I've never had one of these attacks while awake before.

Draven sprints through the woods, fleet-footed and nearly silent, as though his leather boots never actually touch the ground. I'm thrown over his shoulder to leave his hands free to dive into the knee-length black coat, ready to draw out the chain scythe or dirk—his favored weapons for close combat.

"Where is Carmine?" I whine. "We have to go back for her."

"Your sister is safe, Neva," he says, breath coming a little harder, but he isn't winded. "It's you we have to worry about."

"No," I start.

"It's only you Lycaon wants dead. Now hush."

"But where are we going?" I hiss, unable to follow his harsh command. Dozens of questions crowd my mind, messily queuing up to be the first out of my mouth.

Black oaks stretch high above us, their branches barren, though in spring they should be sporting green, palm-sized leaves. Nothing seems to grow here, wherever here is. It's black and desolate, and something about it causes the breath to freeze in my chest and my guts to slither uneasily. An amulet bounces off my collarbone with his every step. He said it would keep the worst of the wood's effects from me, but I hadn't understood what he meant until now.

Something crashes through the underbrush behind us and I drag my eyes from their contemplation of the scrubby brown plants that line our path. A figure, dark and huge, hurtles through the underbrush. A crescent of white reflects off sorrel eyes, the moon betraying the creature's position. It glints off sharp, inch-long teeth, and my breath shudders out of my chest with just a hint of a whine.

Draven doesn't slow, leaping over a fallen tree with the agility and speed of a gazelle. He lands on the other side and, without breaking stride, reaches into his coat, drawing out the polished mahogany handle of his chain scythe.

"Close your eyes, Neva," he orders in a voice stretched taut with worry. "And do not open them until it's over."

"When will I know it's over?" I whisper, squeezing my eyes shut.

I catch a grim little smile sliding across his fine mouth before he responds.

"It's over when the screaming stops."

118

FIFTEEN
Reve

*At some point, Neva must slip into unconsciousness,
because she strides through the thick veil of smoke that
borders my conscious mind and keeps me trapped in this
never-ending horror show. She strides through easily, as
though she belongs here. I half-expected her to avoid me
after my poorly worded request when I told her to kiss me.
But the magic of Tenebris' spell doesn't allow me to outright
ask for my freedom. It was meant to keep Hypnos from using
his myriad admirers from freeing him easily.*

*I've been drawn inexorably toward Neva's dreamscape,
trying to do what I can to ease her suffering. The breakdown
of Tenebris' spell is messy, a tapestry of intricate magic
fraying at the edges. Unlike my enchantment, the spell
placed on Neva was never intended to last forever—it will
last only as long as her power can be contained. With the
presence inside her growing ever stronger, it won't be long
before massive chunks of her memory return.*

*It's happening even now. She clutches her head, lovely
face scrunched in pain, those scarlet lips parted in a silent
scream as she relives some internal terror. I'm not privy to
whatever it is—not here, in my own mind. Perhaps that's
better. I can't affect her in her own dreams. But here? My
magic resides in my mind and I can use it to help her. The
memories crash down onto her like an avalanche, gathering
speed as the spell breaks down, piling onto her with a
suffocating weight. Too much too fast will drive her mad.
Why hadn't Tenebris foreseen this as a possible outcome?*

*"Come here, little dove," I say, meeting her halfway up
the slope and pulling her into my arms. Together we sink*

*onto the grass, her hands still clutching her head. I gently
bat them away, replacing her dainty hands with my much
broader ones. "Let me help you."*

*My fingers probe into the silky fall of her hair, pressing
into her temples. I have to stop this. But the only way I can
think to do so will require her total surrender.*

"Do you trust me?" I whisper.

*Her eyes crack open, clear agony playing out on her
face. She nods wordlessly, unable to speak.*

*I'm not sure if she truly does trust me or if she views it
as the only option left to her.*

*My hands slide from her temples down to the delicate
curve of her jaw and I tip her head up, slanting my mouth
over hers. Lush and lovely, her lips part in surprise, and a
small moan of relief escapes when I ease my magic into her,
coaxing it into her skin like a deep tissue massage. It's not
enough, but it's encouraging that she responds this well so
early in the process.*

*We tumble onto the grass, with me on top of her. My
knee presses between hers, easing her legs open. I keep my
weight off her, propped on my elbows. It would be so easy to
take this further than it needs to go. She's so damn tempting.
But she'd never forgive me. So I leave one hand curled
around her cheek while the other returns to her temple.*

*Though I push my magic into her as gently as I can, it's
still an intrusion. My magic wasn't meant to be inside her,
and her body can sense it. I'm open and achingly
vulnerable, our souls pressed together in an embrace that's
more intimate than sex could ever be.*

*Memory spills forth, a soothing distraction to keep her
from focusing on the hatchet job I'm sure to do of the spell.*

***

121

I watch silently from the opposite hill as Malvolo and Herrick squabble over the winnings from their race. Herrick insists he crossed the finish line first.

"Only because you tripped over it," Malvolo scoffs. "It doesn't count if your overlong nose went over first."

"Should we get Mother?" asks Nouille placidly from my other side. He's barely glancing up from his book.

I smile. The good-natured bickering will carry on for a half-hour or so before Herrick, ever the peacemaker, will admit defeat and hand the winnings over to Malvolo, who will stash them in his absurdly large horde. He's getting to be as bad as father, with all his adventuring and whoring. There's a reason all seven of us have different mothers. How many bastards will Malvolo have by the time he's a century old?

"No. Let them be."

While Neva watches with fascination as the childhood memory flashes by, I examine the cage she's built around the thing. It stares at me with fury glinting in its eyes, snarling when I stoop to examine the holes it's torn in its prison.

There's no way I can craft anything half as clever as Tenebris is capable. The magic I begin to patch over the hole is little better than chicken wire. It will only last a few weeks, if I'm lucky. But perhaps by then my idiot brothers will deduce what's happening and request Tenebris' help.

***

Herrick leans casually against the mast of the ship, staring out at the blue-green waves. The Sea of Delorood is just as beautiful as it's purported to be. It's a rare respite from the war and Herrick is taking advantage, basking in the summer sun. Malvolo is down below, practicing his bladework with Captain Carel. No time for relaxation for the fearsome General Malvolo.

The waves slap the sides of the 'Serpent's Bane' in a soothing rhythm. I could almost sleep, if I didn't know what was waiting for us in Delorood. We're approaching the coves now. We'll be in the City of Bridgeport by nightfall and on yet another battlefield by first light.

A craggy rock juts from the sea a mile out and I can see the shape of a siren soaking in the sun, her cerulean tail trailing into the sea. Her bare breasts point toward the sky, and a sweep of pink hair obscures half a pretty face.

"Beautiful, isn't it?" Herrick murmurs, not looking at her.

"Quite."

***

Pulling my magic away from her feels like ripping off a limb. We come apart with a groan of pain.

"What was that?" she whispers.

"A distraction," I murmur. Somehow, after the intimacy we shared, it doesn't feel right to speak at normal volume.

"From what?"

"I needed to repair the spell. It has to come apart slowly and I can't stop it. You need to find Tenebris."

"I don't know Tenebris, so I'd have no idea where to go to even start looking for her."

"Ask Herrick," I urge. The mist rolls forward, threatening to drag her away from me. She's regaining consciousness. "Herrick has Guild contacts. Tell him…"

Another blink and she's gone, leaving me kneeling on the hill, hands braced around the imprint of where she lay. I'm achingly lonely, my traitorous cock left hard and wanting, with the lingering imprint of her magic on my soul. I flop down into her vacated spot, trying to savor the fading warmth.

I miss her already.

SIXTEEN
Neva

"I think she's coming around."

Herrick's voice draws me unwillingly from the thick, cloying fog and into painful reality. My muscles ache, my stomach feels sour, and a headache is trying to cleave my skull in two. On top of all the physical discomfort is the nagging sense of emptiness that came after Reve pulled away from me. Whatever he just did makes what Malvolo did to my body feel incredibly base.

I felt Reve, felt what it was like to *be* him. He fed me pleasant memories and soothed the worst of my pain. I want to find and kiss that full, gorgeous mouth of his. He wants a kiss? I'll give him a hundred when I'm well.

"About fucking time," Malvolo grumbles, back to his surly self. "She's been seizing for a half-hour. I didn't think one orgasm was going to fucking kill her."

He tries to make it sound casual, but I can hear an undercurrent of worry in his voice. My lips quirk just a fraction. There's a heart beneath that gruff exterior, after all. And then I realize what he's just said.

I look up at Herrick and I can see the surprise registering. He doesn't say anything, but he doesn't need to. His jaw is tight and there's a pained expression in his eyes.

"Don't congratulate yourself too heartily, Mal," Herrick says at last. "This has nothing to do with you. The spell is coming apart too quickly. I can't figure out what stopped it."

"Reve," I croak.

"Reve?" they both say at the same time.

I nod. "It was Reve. He helped me."

Cracking my lids, I can make out the blurry shape of the two men, crouched at the foot of the bed. Both their heads whip toward me at the sound of my voice.

"Reve spoke to you?" Herrick asks, frowning down at me in disbelief and confusion.

"Shocked the fuck out of me too," Malvolo grumbles. "This makes twice."

I don't mention it's about the fifth time Reve has reached out to me. I scrub my face with both hands and sit up, refusing to open my mouth until my stomach settles. Reve was trying to tell me something before I was ripped away. What was it?

"Tenebris," I mumble. "Reve told me to find Tenebris."

The pair exchange a glance. "Why?" Herrick asks.

"He said if I remember too much too fast, it will kill me." The words come thickly, my brain moving as sluggishly as molasses.

"Remember what?" Herrick presses.

I scowl at him. "If I knew, do you really think I'd keep it from you? I'd like to know what I am as much as you do." I don't mean to snap at him but I feel awful.

"You could start by not snorting the pixie dust," Malvolo mutters.

"Pixie dust?" I ask, bemused. Herrick's eyes flash open wide.

"Pixie dust?" he echoes, his tone torn between outrage and disbelief.

"Pixie dust," Malvolo confirms. "The cocaine she's been chasing is cut with pixie dust."

"What does that mean?" I ask.

Malvolo shrugs. "The effects vary depending on the faerie. I'd say this stuff was from the Blue Faerie, for its memory-altering properties, given how keen you are to forget things." He arches one perfect eyebrow at me, daring me to contradict the statement. "You had to have known the pixie dust was in there."

"I didn't."

Memory-altering dust? How long have I been snorting it? And why had Darius wanted me to take it in the first place?

I knead my temples and close my eyes, trying to take comfort in the fluffy pillow beneath my head. I'm lying in Malvolo's bed with Herrick fussing over me. My head aches still more fiercely with every revelation, and I'm beginning to miss the simplicity of unconsciousness. At least then my nightmares aren't so confusing.

"Here," Herrick says at once, pressing a small glass vial into my hand.

It's filled to the stopper with a tangerine liquid that shimmers in the low light. I lick my lips, fighting the urge to tip the whole thing into my mouth straightaway. This is the poppy juice he's been after for the last few days.

I feel abruptly wretched. This stuff costs an exorbitant amount, and Herrick braved the forest to get it for me. What have I been doing in his absence? Skulking around, feeling sorry for myself, and seducing his brother in a vain attempt to get a dosed batch of cocaine that's only making me sicker.

"Place three drops under your tongue," Herrick instructs, pulling the stopper loose with a light pop. "Any more than that, and you risk another overdose. We'll start lowering the dosage to decrease dependence after a few days."

I dip my finger into the stuff. It has the smell and consistency of berry jam and forms a perfect dewdrop on my fingertip when I draw it out. I cautiously pop it into my mouth, expecting it to taste like the vile cough syrups Darius forced down my throat at the slightest sniffle. He never allowed me to lie in a sick bed for more than a few days, and he garnished my pay if he had to take me to a healer. I'd gotten used to taking daily tonics to keep sickness at bay.

I moan at the taste. It's exactly like a raspberry, a delicious tangy sweetness that coats my mouth even as a sense of euphoria settles over me. The poppy juice absorbs even faster than the cocaine ever did. My headache abates by degrees and my stomach settles. The low-level tremors that seized me every few minutes are gone. In their place, a honey torpor sweeps through me, and a dippy smile curls my lips. The fatigue still weighs heavily on my shoulders, but I place the next two drops under my tongue eagerly, staring longingly down at the bottle when I've taken the dose prescribed. It would be so easy to throw the rest back like a shot. It would be a very pleasant way to go.

I slap it into Herrick's palm as that thought chases around my mind. I can't quit now. Not when I'm finally starting to get the answers I've sought for half my life.

Herrick is still unsmiling when he pockets the vial. There's something stewing beneath that calm veneer, though I'm too exhausted to puzzle out what it might be.

"Thank you, Herrick," I murmur, taking the hand that rests lightly on my bed covers. "This helps me more than you can ever know."

That coolness in his tawny eyes recedes and he looks more like himself. He's got the soft soul of a healer. Even though he's angry with me for some undisclosed reason, knowing he's helped brings him satisfaction. I can see the truth in his expression.

128

A sound of derision comes from Malvolo's throat, and he's already striding out the door by the time we turn to face him.

"If you two are going to begin some saccharine interlude, I want no part of it. I'll be in my cave. *Don't* disturb me again, human." He turns to look at me. "And don't get too comfortable either. Your time here is ticking."

And the brief glimmer of humanity I'd spied in him is snuffed like a candle flame. Traitorous as it is, my body still yearns after him and I track him out the door, eyes firmly fixed on the corded muscle of his back and his admittedly impressive backside until he disappears from sight.

"I see you two have become better acquainted in my absence," Herrick says dryly.

I sink back into my pillows, hands dropping to the bed covers in shame. We've finally reached the crux of the matter. "I'm sorry." I don't know what more to say.

"You don't have to be sorry or explain yourself to me, Neva. We shared one kiss. It's not a binding commitment. You wouldn't be the first woman who preferred Malvolo; he's got a certain... gruff charm that women seem unable to resist."

"No, that's not it," I say immediately, but then lose my words.

I'm swimming through the poppy juice and it's difficult to pay attention to the conversation but I realize it's an important one.

"Then what is it?" Herrick asks.

I lift my hands to thread my fingers through my hair, nervously smoothing it to keep from meeting his eyes. "I *don't* like Malvolo."

"You could've fooled me."

"Let me finish," I nearly interrupt him. "I don't like him… at least, not in the way I like you or Reve. Malvolo is… he's an ass. An infuriatingly smug ass. I'm grateful to him for discovering the pixie dust, but…"

"Then why did he bring you to orgasm?"

"Because I thought seducing him was the best way to get my cocaine," I admit, not feeling especially good about the admission.

"Seducing him?" he insists. "To get your cocaine?"

So I tell him about going to the mines to find Malvolo and when getting there, how I spotted the cocaine in the cave and knowing I wouldn't be strong enough to defeat him with my physical strength, I resorted to using my feminine skill, the only thing I thought I possessed.

"And yet you never retrieved your cocaine and Malvolo was able to bring you to orgasm?"

I blow out a breath. "I don't know what to say, Herrick," I admit. "This is all so complicated."

"I don't think it's as complicated as you make it out to be." I look up at him and his eyes are hard as he continues, "That night when you and I kissed, I admit I got carried away. I pushed you perhaps too far and you pulled away from me."

"Yes."

He pauses for a moment. "I know my brother and I can well imagine he's hardly a tender lover."

I see his point. "It was different. I saw Malvolo as a means to an end."

He shakes his head. "Yet, he got the better of you. You meant to take the control from him but he took it from you as easily as he manipulated your body."

"I suppose that's one way of looking at it," I admit. Really, it's the only way of looking at it because it's entirely true.

"And, yet, you never allowed me the same," Herrick says and drops his eyes.

"I can't explain," I start but then lose my train of thought. It's so difficult to fight this high.

"You don't have to explain, Neva," Herrick responds. "You owe me nothing."

"I owe you everything," I argue. "You've done nothing but help me."

"And I would do it all again," he says quickly, a sad smile spreading across his mouth. "But it doesn't change the fact that intimacy isn't something to be bartered for favors."

"I've hurt you," I start, feeling the truth of my words deep inside me.

"You've got enough to contend with, Neva, don't concern yourself with my feelings. I'm centuries old. I'd like to think I'm well-adjusted enough to sort out a little rejection."

But he doesn't understand. It... this isn't rejection. "You don't understand, Herrick."

"I do," he says as he starts to stand up, but my voice stops him.

"No one has ever treated me tenderly," I explain. "Not Darius. Not any of the men who tried to buy me. Not even Malvolo. I... your kindness means so much to me, I don't want to take the chance of changing it."

"Changing it?" he repeats, shaking his head.

I nod. "Men take what they want and then that's it. They reveal their true colors." I take a breath. "With Malvolo, there's nothing to reveal. He is the same asshole he's always been. And Reve… he can't take anything from me because he only exists in the dream world. But, you…" I swallow hard. "You are the kindest person I've ever met and I'm scared of changing that."

"You have such a flawed way of looking at the world," he says.

"All I've ever known is what I've seen at the tavern—men slobbering over me, looking at me as nothing more than a sexual object. No one in there ever gave a shit about *me*. They only ever cared about the outside of me. They were only interested in Snow White."

"That's not true." He clears his throat. "At least, it's not true where I'm concerned."

"I know," I say with a soft nod. "That's why I got so scared that night, Herrick. I don't want to look at you the way I look at them, even Malvolo. I want you to be different."

"I am different."

I shake my head. "You're a man, Herrick. And men have only ever regarded me in one way—my body and my face. The inside of my body. They gape at me, they pay money to watch me but they never see the real me."

"No, that's not how all men are."

I shake my head. "I wish that were true," I start. "And I thought it was…"

"But I proved you wrong the other night. When I pushed myself against you."

I nod as he shakes his head, a bitter chuckle escaping him. "I wish there was a way to end Darius twice for giving you such a low opinion of my gender. Men of honor protect their women. Sex is a gift, given freely and for love. I would never be so callow, Neva."

He reaches down, cupping my chin in his calloused palms, splaying those long fingers along the soft line of my jaw. And he just stares down at me as I stare up at him. Slowly my eyes move to his mouth and I swallow hard.

Then he leans down and his full mouth slides over mine in a kiss that's a tender reprimand. My hands weave into the silky strands of his hair at once. Maybe it's the poppy juice, or maybe the tingle that starts in my toes and sweeps up the rest of my body is true affection. I can't tell. I can't think when he touches me, kisses me.

When he pulls away, his breath feathers enticingly over my lips. I want more. He leans his forehead against mine, preventing me from stealing another kiss.

"We're dragons, Neva. Dragons love treasure. Reve hasn't bothered to communicate in years, not until you came along. Malvolo didn't kill you when you entered his horde. And I can't keep my hands off you, even though I damn well should."

Fatigue makes me sway and my eyelids flutter closed before I force them open again.

"Enough talking for the day, Neva. You need sleep, and I need time to drag my brother from his cave so we can formulate a plan."

"Will you stay with me, Herrick? At least until I fall asleep?" I feel like a child when I murmur my request. Still, letting him go now feels impossible. I crave his kindness, though I don't deserve it. Reve will be waiting for me when I nod off, guarding my dreams. But I want Herrick here to shield my body.

"Of course. Whatever you ask."

There's not enough room for both of us in the bed, but I move as far back as I can and Herrick lays down beside me. Due to the limited space, I find myself laying half on top of him, our legs tangled together beneath the bedspread. I rest my head on his chest, the slow, steady beat of his heart a soothing rhythm that lulls me toward sleep.

I'm out in mere minutes.

SEVENTEEN
Neva

"We agreed we were through," Malvolo says through clenched teeth, glaring murder at his brother. "We'd cut all ties. We said we were never going back. Isn't that what you said to me after Nighburrow?"

I'm trapped between the two brothers and anger roils off each of them, saturating the air. I don't think I'm imagining the heat exuding from their skin. I'm afraid that one or both will explode into an enormous dragon at any moment, leaving the cottage a pile of straw and tinder and me trampled beneath them.

"I meant it when I said it, Malvolo. It's not as if we're enlisting again. These are extenuating circumstances. And something has to be done." Herrick takes a breath. "Even Reve agrees."

Malvolo's antagonistic stare shifts to me and I cringe back into my bed. "We only have *her* word as to what Reve believes. She could be lying."

"To what point or purpose?" Herrick demands. "The journey will be dangerous, especially with a Gryphus huntsman on her trail. If she were looking out for her own self-interest, she'd want to stay here."

Malvolo looks like he's swallowed something sour. "No. We're not doing this."

Herrick's hands ball into fists at his sides and he looks like he might take a swing at his brother. "You know your magical contacts are better than mine. You and Reve always seemed to charm the witches. Send a carrier pigeon to Hattie, Vasalisa, or fuck, even The Sea Witch! One of them is bound to know where Tenebris is hiding out these days."

Malvolo shakes his head before Herrick has even completed his request. "No. I won't do this again. Not for her, not for any human. Tenebris bound her for a good reason. You want to keep her safe? Find a witch in Ascor. Or Everreach. Or Midborn, I don't fucking care. But she's not my fucking problem."

He glares at me and I fucking hate him.

"We're not getting roped into Guild business again," Malvolo continues. "And I don't want to speak to that Tenebris bitch ever again."

"Be reasonable. You know she didn't mean…"

Malvolo stalks toward the door. "If you insist on going, then go. But know that if you die trying to defend her, I'm going to finish the job and rend her limb from limb."

I stare after him, dumbfounded. In the short time I've known him, Malvolo has always been hostile. But this hostility gives new meaning to the word *callous*. I can't reconcile the heartless man marching away from us with the man who'd hovered by my bedside, or the roguish man who'd first brought me pleasure. I don't recognize him.

Herrick doesn't seem to, either. He looks thunderstruck at Malvolo's words. "Malvolo, how can you say that, after…" he mutters.

"Do we need him?" I interrupt as I turn to face Herrick.

"Unfortunately, yes. This enchantment can only be undone by the sorceress who cast it, or someone with equal power. Reve might have been able to do it once upon a time, but he's not capable of much beyond the mindscape now. And until one of the ten champions comes to wake him, he won't be able to help us."

"Champions?" I echo.

"Yes."

"Ten of them?" I remember hearing this story from him before. "Remind me of the story again?"

He nods. "A prophecy foretold their coming, and one of them will wake Reve. But we don't know which one or when. We don't even know who all ten of them are."

He begins to recite a poem in a dry, clipped tone, as if the whole thing is entirely rote. "*When a pall is cast upon the land, despair not, mortals, for come forth heroes ten. One in oceans deep, One the flame shall keep, One a fae, One a cheat, One shall poison grow, One for death, One for chaos, One for control, One shall pay a magic toll...*"

"Interesting," I say.

Herrick trails off, rolling his eyes. "As with most prophecies, it's horribly vague and utterly unhelpful at picking out who's who. I'll spare you the rest of it. There are twelve more stanzas, and each is more confusing than the last."

My shoulders slump. "So, you're saying we don't stand much of a chance without Malvolo?"

"Exactly." He sighs. "We'll give him a day or two to calm down while we gather our supplies. If he's still not cooperating, we'll have to take our chances without him."

The fierce determination on his face makes me smile. It's easy to forget that behind the kind and handsome exterior, he's got the stubborn and proud soul of a dragon. The fierce possessiveness is comforting in its own way, and I'm surprisingly touched to be so treasured.

I push up onto my tiptoes, planting a soft kiss on his cheek and I trace the strong line of his jaw with my fingers. His arms wind around me at once, tugging me flush to his chest. It's getting easier to let him touch me. Unlike Malvolo, I'm convinced Herrick means me no harm. Not that he *can't* cause me harm. If his dragon form is as big and feral as Malvolo's, he could tear me to ribbons with his claws or turn me into a briquette with minimal effort. But I have faith he *won't*. Herrick's first instinct is to heal, not to harm.

I'm wearing something more sensible and form-fitting than his tunics now. In addition to purchasing the poppy juice, Herrick returned with a spun shirt, a pair of breeches, and soft leather boots that mold perfectly to my feet. I'll be willing to bet these had been meant for a sprightly young man and not a girl of my proportions, but I was still grateful not to be wearing a highly impractical slip and kirtle in the harsh mountain environment.

"Thank you, Herrick," I murmur as I pull away from him. "For everything."

"You're welcome," he says with a broad smile.

I take a deep breath. "Please don't be cross with me for what I'm about to do."

Then I duck beneath his arm and sprint for the door, leaping out into the chilly evening air before he can stop me.

"Neva! Where are you going?" he calls after me.

"I have to try to convince Malvolo to help us!" I call back and he doesn't argue. Good. Herrick knows the importance of Malvolo in this as much as I do.

***

This time, I snatch a lantern from one of the hooks hammered into the entrance of the cave. I hadn't spied them the last time I'd come here, probably too obsessed with my need to find my cocaine to really get a look at my surroundings. I won't be so reckless this time.

Malvolo may very well kill me for this intrusion, but at least I'll die trying. It's a nobler death than cowering in the cottage while my mind tries to suffocate me with memories I'm not equipped to handle.

I'm trembling and it takes me three tries to strike a match, light the candle, and shut the glass panel over it. Once I do, the lantern casts a circle of pale shivering light around me as I venture further into the tunnels. The path to Malvolo's horde is winding and treacherous. I'm not sure how long I wander before I finally reach one of the offshoot tunnels that deposit me into the shimmering sea of treasure that Malvolo uses for a bed. My calves are burning when I land with a clatter of sound on a hillock of coins.

I'm expecting to find the giant black dragon with its head bowed over its forelegs, snoring away, as I had the last time. Instead, I find Malvolo draped over his stolen throne, glaring moodily at an intricate bauble. He doesn't glance up as I approach. He doesn't need to see me in order to confirm my identity. According to Herrick, a dragon's sense of smell is superior to that of a bloodhound's.

139

Truly, dragons are the ultimate hunters and they sit at the top of the food chain. The only chance one has against a dragon is to blind it or to catch it unawares in human form.

"You know not to come here," Malvolo grinds out when he finally glances up from his treasure. "You disarmed me once, you won't do it again."

"Malvolo," I start and he looks up at me, eyes blazing.

"You can't sway me with a simple fuck, witchling."

"You're a coward."

He sits bolt upright in his chair, as though I've just shoved a cattle prod right up his ass. His eyes are completely inhuman when his glare fixes on my face, smoke curls from his nostrils, and his voice comes out garbled when he tries to speak.

"What the fuck did you just call me, little girl?"

"A coward," I shoot back, locking my knees so they don't give out from under me.

The rational part of my brain screams at me to run. If I continue to poke this beast, my life is going to end with the crunch of bone and a spurt of blood. This cave will be my tomb.

Malvolo towers over me only a few seconds later, his face a rictus of terrifying, inhuman rage. I continue, though it feels like spitting in the face of a god.

"You think you're the only one who's had a wretched life? Well, you're not! And hiding in this cave isn't going to undo what's already been done."

"I care not for your thoughts."

"Fine! Don't!" I yell back at him. "If I had a brother like Herrick, I'd go for his sake, not for mine. You claim to want to protect your family, but you won't lift a finger to

140

help them when it really matters. So, yes, I'm calling you a coward."

"Humans are the cowards. I laid everything on the line during the war, witchling! *Everything!* Four brothers dead, one enspelled. I lost count of how many friends fell in battle. I became a cripple. A joke. And what did the humans do? They bowed to Morningstar's will, because they were weak! And even the kings who fought, gave up in the end. That seal on Morningstar?" he asks with a laugh. "It won't hold. The world is going to end within another human lifetime or two. Do they give a damn? No. It's a problem for a future generation to solve." He snickers and it's an ugly sound. "But, if that's the way they want it, fine. It's not my problem, either."

I shake my head, immense sadness settling over me. "You had to have been a good man once, Malvolo. Herrick wouldn't love you if you weren't." I pause. "You could be that man again, if you didn't hold onto your bitterness like a stubborn child."

He turns around, facing the wall as though he doesn't want to look at the truth in my eyes. It's then that I see the immense scar on his shoulder blade. I take the steps that separate us and reach out a trembling hand, sliding it up his back to cup his right shoulder blade. He flinches, like I've just prodded the wounded nub that remains beneath his skin. I stroke it gently.

"I'm sorry this happened to you, Malvolo. I wish I had the power to change things."

"No one can change it," he mutters. "And if you think you can manipulate me, you've got another think coming. Just leave; your pleas fall on deaf ears."

"Look me in the eyes when you say that."

He pauses for a moment but then turns around. I stand there mutely, staring up at him as he faces me. He holds my gaze but neither of us says anything. I nod mutely because I see the stubbornness in his eyes.

"I had to try," I say as I tilt my face up, offering him my lips.

"What are you doing?" he demands, sounding irritated.

"Offering you a kiss goodbye," I whisper. We're so close, my lips brush his, and it sends electric tingles down my spine. I may not like him, but my body wants him. It always has.

"A goodbye kiss?" he asks, his breath fanning against my mouth.

I nod. "We'll probably die since you won't help us." I try not to smile, but my lips curl up anyway. "This is probably the last time I'll ever be able to vex you again and I'm fairly sure you're going to miss it… and me."

He flinches. "Stop taunting me, witch."

"It's not a taunt. It's fact," I say as the smile dies and my mood turns serious. "Without you, Herrick and I *will* probably die."

"Don't say that."

I close the distance between us, pressing my lips against his in a kiss that seems to have no beginning and no end. Finally, I pull away. "Why shouldn't I say it? I know you don't like me."

"I don't dislike you," he starts.

"But you don't like me."

"True."

I smile, I can't help it. But it's a bittersweet smile because this feels like goodbye. And the fact that it most probably is goodbye suddenly hits me and I feel a weight descend on me. We don't like each other, so why does this hurt so much?

"Neva..." he breathes when I pull away. Those ember eyes sizzle with unspoken emotion. It gives me a thrill to hear my name on his lips for the first time. He doesn't call me witchling, human or witch.

"Goodbye, Malvolo," I whisper.

I don't wait for a reply. I seize my lantern, turn on my heel, and start toward one of the exits that spills out into the network of tunnels, blinded by the haze of tears that suddenly start in my eyes.

It's a long time before I reach the surface.

EIGHTEEN
Malvolo

Damn her. Damn her straight to Avernus. Though I can't see it, I can sense the sun creeping over the eastern horizon. The witchling has cost me a full night's sleep.

This whole business is doomed to failure. If Tenebris doesn't want to be found, it doesn't matter if Mim and the others pour out a veritable ocean of magic. She'll remain hidden until the end of time, if that's what she desires.

At least, that's what you keep rationalizing to yourself, I think.

Regardless, someone needs to stay behind to watch over Reve. He's as defenseless as a babe and dragging him out would only put him in more danger.

But it sounds like a flimsy excuse, even to me. Though Herrick and I are nowhere as skilled in sorcery as Reve, we're decent with wards and potions. There are defenses we could put in place that would protect him during an extended journey.

"You had to be a good man once, Malvolo. Herrick wouldn't love you if you weren't. You could be that man again, if you didn't hold onto your bitterness like a stubborn child."

I gnash my teeth. Insolent witch! What in the name of Avernus does she know about suffering? She thinks she suffered in her laughably abbreviated existence. She doesn't know the half of what we've endured! And the trials we endured were the reason she's even alive! I have a right to be bitter.

So, why am I spinning in furious circles, trying to figure out if she's right? Cowardice is an appellation I've shunned for over a century.

General Malvolo of the Southern Dragon Clan runs from nothing and no one!

At least... he didn't used to.

What if she's right about everything? Would inaction truly end Herrick's life?

It's a thought I can't stand. I'll trade everything in my horde, my other wing, even my life to preserve Herrick and Reve.

With regard to preserving Herrick, it's not as though Herrick isn't strong and capable. He wouldn't have survived the war if such were true. But there's a Gryphus huntsman after Neva which means there's a Gryphus huntsman after Herrick.

They are both walking targets.

With a snarl, I push up from the floor of my cave and stalk toward the exit. Herrick will get himself killed trying to protect her. Someone has to stop the fool from perishing in an act of lethal gallantry. And if he won't stop trying to protect her (which it appears he won't), someone has to protect him.

Fucking fuck.

I'm greeted by the infuriatingly chipper call of a whippoorwill as I emerge from the mines. The sky is a stunning lapis lazuli, with only the barest of clouds to taint the perfection of the day. The frost has melted away, leaving the ground soft. The wind is still cool, but bearable. It's a good day for a journey.

I lope down into the valley, convinced I'm already too late. For all I know, they stole away in the night and are halfway to wherever the hell they're going by now. The cottage is already warded when I reach it, and the horses have been freed from the small stable we maintain. Even my roan mare is missing.

A soft chuckle sounds from behind me and I whirl, a half-snarl already on my face, to find Herrick standing there. He's dressed for travel, trading his tunic and buckskin for a heavy woolen cloak, shirt, jerkin, and breeches. Gone are any of the small trappings of wealth he keeps on his person. Now he truly looks the part of a golden-haired highwayman. His dapple gray nickers and nips his hand, tossing its magnificent head impatiently. Herrick pats her nose reassuringly.

"Well, I'll be damned," he says. "A woman actually swayed you. Now I've seen absolutely everything."

The dirty look I shoot him would have any mere mortal in the vicinity scurrying for cover. Not my brother, though. He actually smirks. For a moment that seems to stretch longer, I consider laying him out with a punch. It's been years since he and I had a brawl, and the anticipatory glimmer in his eyes eggs me on. He knows I want a fight. He'll give me one, if I instigate.

I hate being so thoroughly predictable.

"Where's my fucking horse?" I growl.

"Saddled and ready for you, at Neva's insistence. If you hadn't shown up by midday, we'd planned to set off without

146

you." Herrick's eyes soften. "I'm glad you're with us, Mal. It means a lot."

"Yeah, yeah," I grumble. "Let's get on the bloody road. We're wasting precious daylight."

My brother throws his arms around me, pulling me into a tight embrace. I stiffen, unused to such affection after years of tending to our own solitary pursuits. I don't know what the girl is doing to us, but it's beginning to feel like it used to again. I'm unsure if that's a good thing.

Neva waits for us at the edge of the wood. A braid of golden chain is draped around her neck, and a large ruby is settled between the swell of her breasts. A warding stone. I hadn't known Herrick still possessed one.

I slide a foot into the stirrup and hoist myself onto the back of Virago. She makes a contented sound and canters forward without prompting. Neva looks nervous balanced atop Reve's gelding, Eidolon.

"Hold on tight," I warn her. "The forest spooks them and they'll be liable to buck."

Her trepidation prompts an unwilling smile to curl my lips. What a strange woman. Bold enough to call the scourge of the Southern Dragon Clan a coward to his face and emerge living, but timid atop a horse.

"This doesn't seem safe," she mutters as she glances down at the grand beast with nervous eyes.

"This journey will be dangerous. If you want safety, don't seek out Tenebris," I answer. "We could always end it now."

Her jaw sets and those amber-gold eyes harden into steely resolve. "I don't really have a choice, do I?"

No, I do not. So I spur my horse forward, leading our procession into the Forest of No Return, ready to hunt down the sorceress I fucking loathe.

"Keep your eyes sharp, and stay behind Herrick or me, Neva," I toss over my shoulder. "It's the only thing that's going to keep you alive."

NINETEEN
Herrick

Watching the interest between Malvolo and Neva is a bittersweet blessing.

How long have I prayed the Gods would send my brother someone or something to care about? How long have I wanted him to emerge from that hard, cynical shell he's resided in for over a decade?

So, why am I now wishing he'd go back to the disinterested and isolated prick he's been for the last decade or so?

I can answer my own question. It's because I'm an inherently selfish creature, and because dragons so rarely share. My beast has desired Neva from the moment I first laid eyes on her in that tavern in Ascor. My instinct to protect her had lurched into overdrive when I observed the abuse and neglect to which she was subjected. And that protective instinct was the reason I stole her away from the Gryphus huntsman.

I've touched her, I've slept beside her, I've kissed her, I've marked her with my scent.

To my beast, there's no clearer indication she's mine. But, she's not mine.

It grates to watch her lean in close to Mal and snatch a bite from his bowl and dance away with a wide grin on her face. Mal flings a forkful at her for good measure as he curses her but beneath the faux anger, he wears a smile. And Neva's pealing laughter echoes through the clearing where we've set up for the night. We're a week's journey from the Enchanted Forest, and beyond that, a small hamlet named The Hollows where Tenebris is rumored to be staying.

Even with that daunting confrontation on the horizon, my brother is still in high spirits. I can see desire for her dancing in his eyes. He's come much closer to having her once already (although, as I understand it, she slipped into the dreamworld at the point at which she orgasmed which disallowed him from actually penetrating her), which technically makes his claim to her is more valid than mine.

I regret being so damn respectable all the time. If I'd been a brute like Malvolo, I'd already know what that gorgeous face looks like when she climaxes. I'd know the chorus of throaty sounds she makes when she finds her pleasure and have the satisfaction of knowing I was the one who caused it.

***

It hurts less to keep my eyes fixed on the surrounding forest, watching for threats. The Enchanted Forest is prettier than the one we've just left. The silver oaks shimmer in the moonlight, slanting through the trees as glittering orbs of light dance through them—pixies. The hot springs are numerous here, warming the air so it feels like we're traveling through a land of perpetual summer. Light fog drifts between the trunks and I focus on what might be hiding in the swirling vapor, rather than the sounds of Malvolo striking up a card game with Neva.

I snort. Never bet with a dragon when treasure is on the line. Fortune favors the greedy.

I should warn her, but I hold my tongue. It's too good to see Mal's face animated again. More than that, he seems carefree—an emotion I haven't seen him enjoy in over one hundred years. Surely, I can step aside in order to allow him his happiness?

Apparently not.

When he wins, there's a round of laughter from them both and I wish I could thrust the nearest branch through one ear and out the other. I push up from my perch: a fallen silver oak coated in clinging vines and a fair amount of moss, and turn so my back is facing them.

"I'm going to bathe," I announce, keeping my voice as level as I can.

I don't trust my eyes. They burn like fire and I just know they're showing the white-gold of my dragon's form. Neva is still frightened by unprovoked anger and I don't wish to make her feel as if this is somehow her fault. This jealousy is my own damn problem. I'll solve it alone in a hot spring, as nature intended.

Malvolo doesn't even bother to comment. Neva calls after me breathlessly, but too late. I'm already feet into the underbrush and her words are quickly swallowed by the woods.

I keep up a sprint until I reach a hot spring that's almost out of earshot of the campsite. If something or someone should attack, I want to be able to reach them quickly. But I don't want to be so close that I continue to listen to their flirtations that could and most probably will lead to more.

I strip out of my jerkin and shirt quickly; doffing the trousers is a little more difficult. My cock is semi-hard already—owing to the fact that Neva bent over in front of me and I could see the outline of her tight and round ass through her trousers. Ugh, I've got it bad and then some. The kiss we'd shared only whet my appetite, leaving me hungry for more. Abstaining is physically painful at this point.

It's a relief to slip into the steaming pool. The water rises to chest-level when I take a seat on the natural rock shelf that rings the pool. I give myself a cursory scrub, removing the grime that comes from a few days of hard riding. I don't want to look like some rogue when we ride into The Hollows in a week's time. Tenebris might mistake us for huntsmen if we come in sporting weapons and a layer of caked-on dirt.

I've just finished rising my hair and pleating it behind my head, when there's a rustle in the underbrush. I freeze, trying to determine where the snap of twigs is coming from. Zeroing in on a point to my right, I lean over to retrieve one of my abandoned knives and ready it to throw.

Neva comes through the brush a few moments later and I relax back onto my perch, feeling abruptly foolish for the overreaction. With the exception of the wildlife—a few bears about to settle in for hibernation and a wolf pack with more daring than sense—we haven't been attacked by anything. It feels somehow like we're being lulled into a false sense of security. I'm tensed and ready, waiting for the other boot to drop.

Neva's look of concern melts away and is replaced by an almost impish grin when she spies the pile of my clothing

152

on the shore. She takes in my state of undress and seems to like what she sees as she smiles broadly.

"I didn't think you were actually bathing."

I raise an eyebrow at her. "Why? I said I was."

"I know."

"So, what did you think I was doing?"

"I wasn't sure, so I thought I'd come and find out."

"I already told you, Neva. You don't owe me anything. I understand if you want to pursue Malvolo."

Her brow furrows as she unlatches the silver fastenings of her cloak, letting it fall to the ground and puddle at her feet like a pool of navy ink. She undoes her hair as well, letting the perfumed fall of it spill around her shoulders as she makes a thoughtful sound in her throat. I finally understand what she's up to when she reaches for the hem of her shirt and tugs it over her head.

I really ought to look away from her, but I can't. I've seen her almost nude before, watched her scintillating dances on stage every night at the tavern. I carried her unconscious body through the woods and bandaged her when she was injured. So I don't know why it feels like a fucking revelation when her breasts spill free of the simple cloth shirt, dusky pink nipples puckering at the contact with the air. My mouth goes dry when she reaches for the waistband of the breeches.

"Neva, don't," I croak. If she takes them off, I'll never unsee this. It will torment me for weeks to come.

Her smile falters and she seems confused. "You don't want me?"

"I *do*. Gods, Neva. It's all I can think about sometimes. But that doesn't mean…"

153

She undoes the series of small buttons and squirms free of the tight fabric. I've imagined what her ass looks like for weeks as we traveled. The breeches gave me a good idea of just how round and firm it is, how good it would feel in my hands.

She tugs the trousers down and steps out of them, kicking them to the side to join the rapidly growing pile of clothing. Vapor swirls around her pale, lithe body and I wonder idly if this is a dream. She's too beautiful to be real. Too innocent to be meant for me. But when I blink, she's still there, still standing shyly before me, blushing like a maid.

She dips a toe into the water and sighs at the temperature. "Do you mind if I join you?"

"You ask this *after* you've already gotten undressed?"

A surprised punch of laughter escapes her chest and it does very interesting things to her exposed body—sexy interesting things. Her grin is bright and infectious. I can't help but smile in response when she wades into the pool, the majority of that lush body disappearing beneath the steaming water. I don't know what she's after—she's made it clear that she wants only a platonic relationship with me and minutes earlier, I would have sworn she had set her sights on my brother. Yet, here she is… with me and not him.

Her slender shoulders and pale, swan-like neck are still on display. The scent of her hair saturates the warm air between us and calls to my beast in a way nothing has in years.

Neva, Neva, Neva. You're going to be the death of me.

The water moves, forming ripples and eddies as she slinks toward me, trying to put off an aura of calm. A useless deception, when facing a dragon. The face can lie, but the body always betrays one in the end. I can hear her heart ricocheting off her ribs with a beat like a snare drum. Her spicy scent becomes a touch acrid as trepidation settles onto her slim shoulders. But there's arousal there, too—and fuck, it's intoxicating.

She steps between my legs, nudging them apart so she can lean over me, placing those delicate hands on my shoulders. Now it's my turn to feel like my heart's going to burrow its way out of my chest.

The vixen is starting a game I can't play with her. If I take selfishly and hurt her, I'll never forgive myself. I want her to think of me in a different way than she thinks of the other men she's known—even Malvolo. I want her to know that I care about what's inside her, rather than just what she can do to my cock.

And this isn't the way.

"Neva…"

"Shh." She presses a slender finger to my lips and I fall silent, though I know I should argue. Then she continues as if I hadn't interrupted her, sliding the slick, soft skin of her outer thigh against my groin. My hips buck in surprise. I've been painfully hard for a while and the contact is enough to draw a strangled sound of want from me.

"You never ask for anything, Herrick," she whispers to me. "You've always given everything to others without ever considering yourself. Praise, treasure, women. You're willing to let Reve or Malvolo have them, so long as it makes *them* happy. You deny your dragon's base nature. You never prioritize what *you* want."

I can't argue with her because what she says is true.

She trails one finger down my chest and then dips her hand beneath the warm water, continuing her path until her hand rests just outside where I need it, nestled on my hip. My hips jerk up of their own accord, trying to make the contact I've been craving for weeks.

"So, tell me," she continues. "What do *you* want, Herrick?"

"You," I groan. "I want you. I've wanted you since I first saw you, Neva."

"Then be a dragon," she murmurs, dipping her head so our lips barely touch. "And take what you want."

It's as though I've been waiting for those words for a lifetime, but then, as is my wont, I think of her. "Neva, no," I say and shake my head. "I can't... do this with you until I know for sure that you won't think I'm... the same as all the others—that I'm using you."

She smiles and the view is the most beautiful I've ever seen. "I know I can trust you, Herrick. I trust you the most... of anyone."

"You trust me?" I repeat, wanting to be entirely certain this is what she wants.

"I have had much time to think about our conversation after our... kiss," she explains. "And in that time, I've realized you are different. You care for me in a way no one else has." She pauses for a moment and weighs her words. "Actually, I believe Reve cares for me in a similar way as well."

"Let's omit Reve from this discussion please," I say with a smile.

She returns it. "Anyway, I believe you."

"You believe me?"

156

She nods. "I believe you that good men don't just use a woman for her body. That they care about what's in her heart and her head. And I believe you are a good man." She takes a deep breath. "And I made the choice that I want to understand what it means to make love," she continues. "I was hoping you would show me."

The moment the words fall from her lips, I'm in motion.

I slide two hands around her to cup that pert ass and lift her off her feet, hauling her as close as I can manage. My cock brushes her inner thigh and it takes all I have not to slide into her slick heat at once. I'm beastly, but not *that* beastly.

"I will never hurt you, Neva," I whisper as I pull away from her and stare down into those lovely eyes.

She smiles up at me. "I know, Herrick."

I claim her lips and they part at the slightest flick of my tongue. She tastes fucking delicious and I plunder her mouth, trying to take in as much of her as possible. She tries to kiss back inexpertly. She makes a fuss about not being a virgin, but she might as well be. One partner in her whole life, and one so onerous, he'd never bothered to do more than dip his wick and leave. She is a novice, engaging in intimacy with the first man who's ever given a damn.

It excites my dragon. The golden dragon of the south is oft described as a gentle creature in the stories and legends. It isn't. It craves dominance and control, just like any other. And if she's inexperienced, it means I can teach her.

She gives my mouth a hard nip and I struggle not to push into her then and there. A languid smirk tugs up my lips. She has no idea that biting any sort of shifter is always a bold move. It's a challenge, a power play. The little dove wants to play? I'll play. I bite back harder, tugging her scarlet lip between my teeth until she whimpers and rakes her nails over my shoulders and back. Her hips move in little rolls, nudging my cock.

"Herrick, please..."

No. I want to take my fucking time with her. Let her ride my fingers to a noisy climax before I lay her out on the shore and coax another with my tongue. *Then,* I'll join her.

But Neva doesn't give me time to think or object. She hoists herself further up my slick chest, lacing her fingers behind my head, teasing my scalp gently with her nails. The sensation is so fucking delicious, I groan.

Her eyes burn with determination and amber fire when she straddles my waist and sinks slowly down onto me, thrusting my entire length into her body with one languid stroke. Her entire body bows, her breasts bouncing from the water in one of the most beautiful displays I've ever seen. Her mouth opens and breathes out a shaky sound of pleasure.

Fuck, she's so damn tight. That barkeep must have been particularly unimpressive, because I could swear I've just claimed a maiden. Dragons are always larger than humans, and must be double what she's used to. I roll my hips once, slowly, trying to get her used to the sensation. I drag another moan from her throat and the sound is so beautiful, I almost climax then and there.

"Does it hurt?" I murmur, lavishing her neck with a dozen fluttering kisses. "Do you want me to stop?"

"Stop and I'll murder you... right here," she pants.

I can't help my smile as I thrust shallowly into her and her body clamps down on me, erasing all thought from my head except how good she feels. I want to take her hard and fast and write a claim into her skin so all dragons—especially Malvolo—will know I've had her.

But I won't. I have to be careful with her.

I thread my fingers into her hair to keep her relatively still and drive my length into her again, growling softly against her throat as she squeezes me tight. So fucking ready for me. Her walls flutter in a tell-tale sign. It won't take long at all for her to find her pleasure. She squirms, making a desperate whine in the back of her throat.

I keep my pace slow but driving, settling my hands on her hips, coaxing her into a rhythm until she adopts the rhythm on her own. She meets me stroke for stroke, peppering my face with kisses. Everywhere our skin touches feels like lightning, our desire supercharging the air and building to something explosive.

When Neva comes, her magic flares white-hot and feels more scalding than the water we're submerged in. Holy mother of the Gods, there's so *much* of it. Reve was right. We need Tenebris for this. I'm only feeling a fraction of her strength. Too much magic escaping at one time will overload her and leave her as lifeless as my sleeping brother.

But I can't focus on that for long. She's here and she's lovely, and I still want her. Though my pleasure came and went with that explosion of power, I don't feel ready to release her.

I'm not imagining the soft golden glow that alights on her skin when she sags, boneless and sated against me. She rests her head on my shoulder with a contented sigh.

"I didn't know it could be like that," she says in awe. "Is it selfish to say I want more?" Looking over at me, she shrugs. "Not that we can, since you've uh…"

I chuckle.

Oh, sweet, lovely woman. You have no idea what I'm going to do to you.

"Lay back on the bank," I instruct in a throaty purr. "We'll see what I have left."

TWENTY
Neva

The bank is icy compared to the steaming water, but I haul myself up anyway, too eager for more of Herrick. His fingers skim my thigh, and a squeal gets caught in my throat. I'm oversensitive; every touch feels like it might send me spinning headfirst into ecstasy once more. A warm chuckle escapes him and the sound curls around me like warm down covers. In his arms I feel treasured, protected, maybe even loved.

He nudges my legs slightly apart before his golden head disappears between my thighs and he places a soft nip very near the apex of my thigh. My entire body trembles in response, going weak beneath his hands, his teeth, his lips.

He reaches between my legs and his fingers glide between my folds, the roughness of his hands adding extra sensation as he finds the swollen piece of flesh that's begging for his attention and strokes it with his thumb. My legs twist desperately around him, trying to hold him in place.

"Please," I pant.

I'm not even sure what I'm begging for, but he seems to understand. His fingers trace a ticklish path between the backs of my thighs and my ass and I arch upward, hips coming almost level with his face. He doesn't release me, his hold tightening on my ass cheeks while his other hand pushes two fingers into me. His fingers find that delicious spot inside me and begin to beckon me toward blinding pleasure.

What sorcery do these brothers possess? Only a few short weeks ago, I was ready to die rather than let myself be touched by another man. But with these dragons... there isn't a moment where I don't want them in some fashion or another. I've stopped flinching at sudden movements, stopped cringing away from the smallest scrap of desire because when I tell them what I need, they give it to me. Even if what I need is space.

Herrick's fingers slide out of me and I keen at the loss. I'm so close to finding that tantalizing edge again.

"Neva, try not to pull my hair out," he warns with a fiendish grin before he's back to lifting me up, slinging my legs around his broad shoulders. He spreads me as wide as he can and then his face delves between my legs. The rasp of his stubble against my bare skin has me crying out all over again, this time in shock and pleasure. His warm, exquisite mouth finds the bud between my legs and he latches onto me, making an utterly indecent sound of satisfaction in the back of his throat.

I'm sure Malvolo can hear my screams. But, I don't care.

Herrick's warning is apropos, because my hands immediately find their way into his hair and tug as his tongue does exquisite things to my body. I'm afraid I'll end up suffocating him at this rate, but he doesn't let up, his dexterous tongue making me writhe. Wave after wave of honeyed pleasure crashes into me, until my breathing is coming in gasps. My skin feels drawn taut and every beat of my heart feels like it might be my last. Is it possible to expire from pure bliss?

For a moment that stretches a euphoric eternity, I'm absolutely sure it will be the end of me. I can barely feel my body. My vision has gone white, tinged with the hint of gold as the power of Herrick's dragon strokes along my skin.

And then I'm slamming back down to earth, like Icarus, the stupid boy who melted his wax wings. The fall feels impossible, sure to be fatal. And a second later, I realize it's not just my frenzied imagination—I really am falling. The bracing strength of Herrick's arms is the only thing that keeps me from colliding hard into the ground.

When I can finally force my eyes open, he's pulled me to his naked chest and he's struggling to hold onto me. We're both still dripping water, after all. I almost slide from his grasp, but he manages to steady me at the last second.

"What happened?" I slur, choking back a giggle even though this isn't really all that funny. My body is still buzzing with energy, high on whatever he's just done to me.

Herrick's eyebrows draw together in concern over those enthralling tawny eyes. I realize belatedly they've bled to a new color. A pale ivory, marbled with gold and edged in a copper shade so light, it almost blends into the same color. The slit pupil of his eyes startles me out of my euphoric haze. His dragon eyes are showing. It's the first time I've seen them in his human face.

"I was hoping you could give me the answer to that question, actually," he murmurs quietly. "Do you normally hover in the air when you climax, Neva?"

"Erm... that's actually only the third time I ever have. So, I suppose you should congratulate yourself. I only had a seizure with Malvolo."

He takes a quick inhale at the mention of his brother's name.

"And the third time?"

I smile shyly. "Was with myself and all that happened then was… I felt good."

He doesn't crack a smile.

I drop my eyes and suddenly feel so guilty for mentioning Malvolo. I apologize.

Herrick lets out a rueful laugh. "You have nothing to be sorry for, Neva. I should have known that copulating would bring your magic to the fore, and I shouldn't have taken chances with your safety like that. It was selfish."

He misses the reason I apologized but I move on, figuring it's the best thing to do. "That was the first time I've actually even seen anything that might suggest I'm magical."

He nods. "Now do you believe me?"

"I guess so." I smile and twine my hands into his damp golden hair. I envy him the color and the texture. It's so incredibly fine beneath my fingers, and a childish part of me wants to braid it into a crown around his head and place flowers or shapely leaves into it. The proud dragon would probably react poorly to that, I suspect. Hmm, or maybe not?

"You shouldn't blame yourself. You were able to keep me from floating off somewhere," I finish with a laugh.

"Still, it was dangerous."

"An orgasm has never killed anyone."

He laughs. "You've clearly never met an incubus."

My curiosity is piqued and I open my mouth, about to ask him to elaborate, when a furious bellow sounds through the misty grove of trees and echoes to where we stand, naked and wet.

Herrick sets me on the ground at once and doesn't even bother to retrieve his abandoned clothing. He pelts through the woods toward the source of the ruckus.

I don't bother to dress either, but I retrieve our fallen clothes and trail after him, heart hammering. That sound can only mean one thing. Something's at our campsite.

And it's attacking Malvolo.

TWENTY-ONE
Kassidy

Motherfucking, cock-sucking, son of a troll whore.
What the blazes *is* he?

I pivot, planting one boot against the silver trunk of an
oak, using all my strength and momentum to launch myself
into the air, flying in a neat arc over his head.

At least, that's what's *supposed* to happen. Mere human
or slightly-above-average human opponents never fend that
one off. It's a special huntsman trick that Sabre taught me on
my ninth birthday, after I positively begged him to train me.
Of course, it's a lot more impressive when it's an inhuman
bird shifter who can transform into a hawk or a rook at the
height of their arc, but the point still stands. Humans can't
generally react fast enough to stop me, before I land. And
when I land, I'm always off like a fucking shot, gone before
they even know what's hit them, their pockets lighter than
when I first encountered them.

But this man is different. He must not be human.

Fuck fuck fuck.

The enormous man plucks me from the air like I'm an
errant fly buzzing around his head. He snags my ankle and
whips me to the ground so hard and fast, the air completely
leaves my lungs and I feel my head bang against the hard
ground. Blank shock creeps up my back and that, more than

166

the violent action or malevolent man towering over me, scares the life out of me. I've never gone into shock before.

He's hurt me. Hurt me bad.

I test my fingers cautiously, pleased when they wiggle in response. My toes follow suit. My muscles scream in agony, but they all seem functional as well. He hasn't paralyzed me. Yet.

His boot comes down hard and I manage to roll, avoiding the impact by mere seconds. He's fast. So fucking fast.

If only my head would clear of the stars currently plaguing my vision…

He's strong, too, it appears. His boot digs a deep furrow into the ground that tosses sod in every direction. With the approach of much colder weather, the earth is hard. Too hard for most shovels to pierce, and yet, he did it without much trouble. So that kick was probably meant to take my head off. Even the effort it takes to swallow is excruciating.

I stagger to my feet. My back throbs in time with my pulse and I know if I somehow manage to limp away from this battle, it'll be a sheet of purple-blue bruises by morning. That's a big if, though.

"You're a little small to be a huntsman," he says, idly reaching down to retrieve his weapon.

I eye it longingly. The scabbard of the sword is encrusted with jewels, and it alone would fetch a handsome price if I tried to sell it. But it's not the pretty exterior that made me decide to risk a little deviation from Sabre's original plan. It's the magic rolling off the bloody thing like heat. The lattice of spells is incredibly complex. It's not quite as good as a Tenebris weapon, but it's damn close.

167

Which means it's almost priceless. Which means it's price just went way way way up.

It's exactly the sort of thing I can use to finally sway Captain Hook into negotiating with Sabre and me. Hook is a collector of the highest order, and this sword is sure to make the knave's cock hard. At the very least, it should buy me passage to and from Delorood as often as I need it.

But back to the big, strong jerk. He'd been asleep. Well, clearly not. Okay, I could have sworn he'd been asleep when I *entered the clearing*. Then, a loud cry issued from the surrounding woods, and I'd made a rookie mistake and reacted. And now, here we were.

"I'm not a huntsman," I reply, taking a small step to my side and giving him my most winning smile I can muster, given the headache that's pounding through me and the fact that I feel lightheaded. But the point still stands: Have the face of an angel, and no one really watches where your feet are going. Another trick Sabre taught me.

But the canny man's eyes flick down for a half-second and catch sight of what I'm doing. He adjusts his position ever so slightly to compensate and lifts his sword. It glints dangerously in the amber glow of the fire.

"Like I'm going to believe that load of toss," he growls. "Where's your signet ring, Gryphus?"

I stiffen, lip curling in disgust. I'm not a huntsman. I'm truly not. But being raised by three of them does make one a little defensive. And to be called a Gryphus is about the most insulting thing he could have lobbed at me. My adoptive brothers were from the Order of Corvid, and I take it upon myself to be offended on their behalf.

I reach into my belt and draw the twin daggers I have strapped there. Draven gave them to me for my last birthday. They aren't good for this sort of melee, given how truly enormous my foe is. I swear he's got to be the better part of seven feet tall, and his reach is insane. My bow is out. I can't leap up into the trees to get to higher ground. But I have to do something. I won't let this insult stand.

"Take that back. Or I'll…"

I'll do what? Let him step on me?

The man actually cuts off my threat with a laugh. "Sting me with your little knives?"

"Oh, shut up!" I don't have anything better left to say.

"Drop the knives and you can die painlessly. Force me to put you down, and it'll hurt."

I bristle. What an arrogant prick, condescending before we've even done serious battle.

"I'm not a fucking huntsman, you cock!" I snap. "And I'd certainly not be a Gryphus hunstman, even if I was one!"

He lunges forward, almost too fast to track, and it's only my finely-honed reflexes that keep his swing from parting my head from my neck. I'm as flexible and fast as any gymnast or carnival tumbler. The blade whistles in the air above my head, shearing several golden ringlets off my head. The fuck. It's not a huge loss, in the grand scheme of things, but I still like my fucking hair, okay? They don't call me Goldilocks for nothing.

I drop to my knees, roll once, coming halfway to my feet, inside his guard this time. I shove his trouser leg up and get a death-grip on his ankle, easing my power forward. My magic crackles on contact with his skin and then sinks in, burrowing in fast and deep like a vole, searching to find what can be leached from him.

There's a veritable ocean of power to draw from. I seize what I can, though I don't know how much it will weaken him. He's something far beyond human, if what I'm feeling is only his magic. I haven't even reached for his life force yet. By the time I reach my limit, I'm punch drunk with power and the headache and dizziness is long gone. I feel gloriously strong and supple. Strong enough to finally do some damage to this prick.

Without pausing to think, I balance, take aim, and put all my weight behind a kick at the leg he planted for the swing. His knee comes out of its socket with a satisfying pop and then he issues a bellow that shakes the leaves on the surrounding oaks.

For most men, I'd expect that to be the end of the fight. The pain of a dislocated limb can be enough to cause a blackout. Certainly enough to take them to their knees. But not this motherfucker.

He staggers, shifting his weight to the uninjured leg to compensate, but he doesn't fall. He doesn't even lose his grip on his sword. He lets out a shaky exhale, sizing me up again.

"Not a huntsman, my ass."

"Then your ass!" I say with a shrug. "I'm a thief, and nothing more," I pant, worn out from even the short exchange. Even injured, this man will probably still beat me. Sabre, Draven, or Titus might have been able to take their chances with this beast. But they'd all advise me that discretion is the better part of valor in this case. I'll have to find something else to sway Hook's decision. The mission of the Guild is too important for me to die so pointlessly.

Just about the time I've decided to flee, my attention is drawn away from my adversary. It sounds like an elephant is crashing through the underbrush. I toss the dagger lightly in the air, allowing it to smack down into my palm with the weighted blade at my fingertips. If something comes charging at me full tilt, it'll be slowed when my steel buries itself into its eye.

I'm ready to let it fly when a pale blur streaks into the clearing. It skids to a stop a foot away from my original opponent and, as it stops moving, I can tell it's another man. As tall as the first, but much paler, with hair almost as gold as my own, cascading loose around his shoulders. His very bare shoulders that connect to a bare torso and a bare... all of him. The man isn't wearing a stitch of clothing.

And his body is quite happy to be nude, apparently. A monstrous cock is still semi-hard between pale, muscular thighs. I need to stop staring at him, because the angry one will take the opportunity to cleave my head open if he's given the chance.

But there's just so much of this new one to look at! And it's not like I've seen many naked men at all actually. This chiseled, muscular physique is certainly worth admiring, along with his beautiful, sharply-carved face, and eyes that almost appear to belong to a bird of prey. Are these men huntsmen? Order of Accipitrine? That would explain their strength and resilience.

"It took you fucking long enough!" the beastly one yells. "And where the fuck are your trousers?" he demands, appearing almost as flustered by the arrival of his nude companion as I am.

The blonde's eyes narrow. "You just shouted loud enough for half the forest to hear and you're worried about my clothes?" He pauses. "What the fuck happened?"

"I've got this under control," the big one says and looks at me with a frown, like he's embarrassed I'm so small and… girly.

"It's just a huntress."

"I'm not a huntress, dipshit!" I snap.

The new arrival eyes his friend's misshapen leg and grimaces. "Your knee is dislocated, Mal, possibly even broken. You clearly don't have this under control."

It's at this point that the naked guy looks over at me, like I'm the one at fault… hmm, I guess I am the one at fault. I shrug. "I wouldn't have had to attack if he hadn't tried to lop my head off!"

"You tried to take my sword!" the big one yells. "I've killed for less."

"Well," I hesitate. "I needed it."

"You needed it?" the big one glares at me.

I nod. "You have no idea what its sale could do for our cause." I adopt an almost wheedling tone. I hate to beg, but I don't see many other choices. I'm outnumbered and, if this new man is as strong as his companion, I'm hopelessly outclassed as well.

I hastily untuck my shirt and jerkin from my trousers, pulling it up to reveal the raised golden edges of my tattoo. The sigil twinkles in the light of the fire like a dozen gleaming stars. "You may not know what this is, but," I start.

"It's a fucking Guild tattoo," the grumpy one barks. "And I've had mine a lot longer than you've had yours, little girl."

He tugs up the spun cloth of his shirt to reveal a tattoo that's identical to mine, though less refulgent, worn down by time and years of washings. And, um, I can't help but notice his abs which look like mountains.

Jeez.

My eyes dart to his naked companion, eyes dipping down to his hips. It's a struggle not to focus lower, where his cock hangs loose and distractingly large. I've never actually had one inside me before, but if all men are this large, it assures me that the act of sexual congress is not something I'm designed for.

Sure enough, a Guild tattoo gleams subtly from his skin, almost disappearing against all that golden flesh.

"Why are you naked?" I ask.

He glares at me. "We'll do the question asking."

I just shrug.

More crashing through the underbrush draws my gaze up and another figure darts into the clearing, this one much smaller than either of the men.

It's a woman, and she's also wearing little or nothing. She holds a bundle of clothing against her front, obscuring most of a generously-proportioned chest. Her hair is so dark, it shines blue in the light, making shadow pale in comparison. I can't tear my eyes away from her because, impossibly, she's even more attractive than either of her traveling companions. I've never been a lover of women, but even I'm a little curious to see how those scarlet lips might feel on mine.

She's absolutely stunning. Leggy and pale, with soft curves and a dramatically cut waist to keep her from looking like some sort of wraith. Her eyes are the oddest color I've ever seen—an indecisive shade that hovers between amber and gold—and are utterly compelling. My mouth goes dry and I try to tear my eyes away. Thankfully, I'm not the only one staring at her.

The angry one's eyes narrow. "And you're missing your clothes, as well. Three guesses what the pair of you were up to."

"Uh oh!" I call out with a big laugh.

All three of them glare at me.

"Do you really think this is the time to discuss it, Malvolo?" the woman asks weakly.

My eyes bug. "Malvolo?" I repeat, my mouth dropping open. "As in *General* Malvolo? The Scourge of the Southern Dragon clan? *That* Malvolo?"

Everyone ignores me.

Even with the buzz of his power riding me, my knees threaten to buckle as I realize just who I tried to square off against. Circe's teats, I'm lucky to be alive!

And this strange woman is staring at him reproachfully, like some sort of scolding fishwife. What strange parallel land have I staggered into?

"Put down your sword," the blonde one says to the bigger man. Studying him closely, I can just catch the gleam of golden dragon's eyes in the low light of the fire. That must mean he's the Golden Dragon of the South. The healer, Herrick.

"We can talk this through," Herrick continues.

174

General Malvolo glares at me again. "I'll drop my sword when she drops her knives."

I realize I still have a white-knuckled grip on my daggers and so I hastily uncurl my fingers. I let my daggers drop to the ground with dull thunks, and Herrick nods his approval with a gentle smile. It eases my nerves somewhat.

For a tense second, I'm sure Malvolo won't back down. Then, with a look from Herrick, he grudgingly shoves the magnificent blade back into its glittering scabbard.

Herrick settles all six-something-gloriously-nude feet of himself down onto a fallen oak and pats the space next to him.

"Now, it's time for us all to talk."

"Sure, but," I start, looking at him. "You think you could put some clothes on?"

TWENTY-TWO
Neva

After Herrick and I excuse ourselves to dress hastily in the bushes, we return and I fold myself onto Herrick's lap and wrap my arms firmly around his neck. His hands slide around my waist automatically and he pulls me closer, tucking me into one broad shoulder. It doesn't escape my notice that he's kept his dominant hand free, in case he has to draw his sword.

Our visitor doesn't look like much of a threat, at first glance. She's at least a head shorter than me, though she makes up for several inches with a thick mass of blonde, corkscrew curls. She's a thin, little thing in clothing that seems too large.

But once I get a good look at her face, I realize how beautiful she is. Her eyes are currently spitting fire and they're the most unique shade of green. Almost like an Emerald.

She sits across from the three of us and I notice she can't seem to keep her eyes from dropping to Herrick's lap every so often, as if she can still spy his assets through his trousers. It's hard to blame her—Herrick is beautiful. Any woman with a healthy libido would be interested.

I keep repeating that fact over and over to myself, but it doesn't seem to do much to quell the seething jealousy that rises up within me. She's younger than I am, I'm fairly sure and with that wild hair, that's the color of spun gold, I'm sure the men find her attractive. They'd be blind not to.

Herrick divorces himself from my tight hold and stands up, walking over to her to tend to the minor cuts and bruises she's sustained while Malvolo glowers at him disapprovingly.

"Healing the enemy?" Malvolo asks.

"I'm not your fucking enemy," the girl responds.

"Could have fucking fooled me," Malvolo grumbles.

Herrick faces him. "You didn't have to hurl her down so hard, Mal. She's just a tiny thing and she's going to have bruises for weeks."

A growl rumbles in Malvolo's chest. "That little wench dislocated my fucking knee."

"You had it coming," she argues as I try to suppress a laugh. She's got a lot of fire.

Malvolo glares at her. "She's not a harmless little dove. Lash her to a nearby tree, at least. And I'm still waiting for an explanation on what the fuck she did to me."

"What she did to you?" Herrick repeats, glancing over at his brother.

"Yeah, she pulled some witch magic on me!" Malvolo insists.

He turns a fierce glare on the newcomer and she cringes, moving the wounded arm Herrick is tending out of reach.

"I can heal myself!" she grumbles at him.

He tsks impatiently, shooting his brother an annoyed look before scooting closer to remove more grit from her wound. "You can also use all the help you can get," Herrick answers.

She doesn't argue with that but faces Malvolo. "What you saw was just my ability," she mutters. "The reason the Guild saved me from my deadbeat father, Odale, years back."

"And what is that ability?" Herrick asks.

She shrugs. "My magic is to steal. Power, life force, magic, objects—you name it. If it can be taken, I'm the best at taking it."

"I wasn't aware the Guild regularly employed thieves," Malvolo spits acidly. "Good to see their moral fiber is still intact."

The newcomer shoots to her feet, every inch of her vibrating with furious indignation. "Who the fuck are you to judge our tactics, oh venerable General? You haven't been with us for over *ten* years. When the seals were erected, you turned your back, just like everyone else did. Meanwhile, *we've* been trying to do something about it."

Malvolo half-rises to his feet. "Watch your tone, girl. I can still crush your skull into powder."

"Stop the theatrics," Herrick says as he frowns at his brother. "The girl's not our enemy."

"Tell that to my fucking knee," Malvolo responds.

I'm amazed at the courage it takes to keep her sneer fixed firmly in place. "Stop with all the 'girl' bullshit," she says. "I have a name."

"Nobody fucking cares," Malvolo says.

"What's your name?" I ask, frowning at him. He frowns right back at me. He's in an even more sour mood than usual.

The girl faces me and gives me a brief smile. "It's Kassidy Aurelian, but my friends call me Goldy." Then she motions to her hair, as if any of us had failed to see it.

"Nice to meet you," I say.

She nods to me and then glares at Malvolo. "And you'll forgive me, *General,* but while you've been missing, many of my comrades have died trying to contain the threat."

"The threat?" I repeat.

She faces me. "The Great Evil." Then she faces Malvolo again. "The seals have been breaking down. More things slip through every year, and at the rate they're deteriorating, we'll be on the brink of all-out war within the next five years. So, you'll have to excuse the less-than-ethical means we're using to prepare. We're probably the only thing standing between Fantasia and total annihilation."

Malvolo stiffens and I can see his anger increasing. When I'm absolutely certain he's going to burst out of his skin and become a massive onyx dragon, he finally relaxes, taking in a deep breath. His voice adopts a clipped, impatient tone I'm unfamiliar with, like a general demanding a report.

"What exactly has come through?"

Kassidy shrugs one well-muscled shoulder. "It's hard to say. At least a few hellhounds. Some of the lesser imps, wairua, and some of Bacchu' oreads."

I shudder at the mention of hellhounds. A brief, terrifying fragment of memory plays behind my eyelids. *Enormous shaggy dogs with sparks flying off their backs. Breath like choking sulfur and a desire to consume like fire. I'll trade what little value I have to my name to never meet one ever again.*

179

Malvolo hisses a breath in through his teeth, and even Herrick, unrelentingly focused on Kassidy's wounds, looks a bit pale beneath the golden cast of his skin.

"Why didn't someone contact us? We would have come, had we known," Malvolo says.

Kassidy barks a bitter laugh. "As if anyone knew where to find you! We weren't even sure you were still living. I don't suppose that's why you're on the road now? We could use the allies, now more than ever."

We all exchange an uneasy glance. Kassidy hasn't done further harm since we arrived, but that doesn't necessarily mean she's trustworthy. It's Herrick who finally speaks.

"We're not certain yet. We're looking for Tenebris. We heard she's staying in The Hollows."

"She's not," Kassidy says with a dismissive flick of her wrist as she sits down again and Herrick continues cleaning her wounds. "She left The Hollows months ago, when it looked like a huntsman might be on her trail."

"A huntsman still on her trail?" Malvolo snorts a laugh. "So Gatz is as much a lovesick fool as ever?"

Kassidy's face breaks into a reluctant smile. "So it would seem. I can take you to Tenebris, if you'd like. But I'm going to need something in return."

She eyes the jewel-encrusted scabbard strapped to Malvolo's waist.

"No fucking way," he says as he flexes a hand over his weapon at once.

Kassidy jerks her thumb toward the west. "You know the woods that straddle the line between Sweetland and Neverland, just before Delorood?"

"Yes," says Malvolo.

180

"Well, there's a compound of werebears there. They make Ambrosia. I'm aiming to steal some of that Ambrosia so I can get it into the hands of Prince Aric. Delorood is the only kingdom with a standing army and the prince has agreed to side with us if war breaks out. And, as you know, we need them. But, I need something worth trading to Captain Hook to barter unlimited passage." She pauses to look at Malvolo. "So, I need your sword."

Herrick stares at her like she's gone completely mad. "Those werebears will kill you! Next to dragons and hellhounds, bears are the strongest shifters alive. They'll tear you to shreds for daring to lay a hand on that Ambrosia."

Her smile is beatific and glitters in the firelight. She looks like a little imp, up to no good. "They'll have to catch me, first. And trust me, that's not as easy as it seems."

"Wasn't that difficult," Malvolo mutters.

"Yeah, for a fucking dragon!" Kassidy says and glares at him before facing Herrick again. "He's such a cock."

Herrick just smiles and nods.

Malvolo lapses into silence, staring into the fire so long, I'm convinced he's forgotten all of us. He strokes the raised surface of the jewels on the scabbard almost reverentially.

"You'll take us safely to Tenebris?" he asks at last.

Kassidy leans forward eagerly. "Yes. And I'll escort you safely back, as far as my next destination. I just need that sword."

Malvolo appears to be chewing the inside of his cheek. Then, he nods slowly to himself. "We need a cure more than I need a sword. You may have it upon the successful completion of our journey."

My eyes prick in the strangest way and my throat closes off so tightly, I can barely breathe. Immense gratitude and a sense of deep unworthiness war inside me. Malvolo is giving up a weapon he clearly treasures. *For me. For our safe passage to Tenebris.*

"Here," Kassidy says. "I know it's customary to give a dragon a token treasure to seal agreements. This is what I have on me. Sixty gold pieces and a stone I stole off a Shepherd on the way."

Kassidy reaches for a pouch at her side and unlatches it, tossing it lightly across the clearing. I snatch it from the air before Malvolo can. He glares at me but I just give him a self-impressed smile. It was a good catch.

"A stone?" I wonder aloud as I untie the strings of the satchel. "What would Shepherds be doing, carrying one of those around?"

She looks at me. "It's a soul stone. It's used to trap unwilling spirits and anchor them to the bearer during their journey to the afterlife."

"What the hell were you going to do with it?" Malvolo asks her.

She shrugs. "Thought I might be able to sell it for more gold on the way to the werebears. It's yours now."

Curious, I reach inside the pouch and withdraw what looks like a turquoise river stone. It's worn as smooth as glass and I rub my finger across it once, wonderingly. The second I do, the stone begins to glow like backlit jewels and emits a shower of blinding golden sparks.

"What's happening?" I cry.

182

Kassidy sounds as panicked as I feel. "I don't know! Only Shepherds or powerful mages are supposed to be able to activate them. Are you either?"

Truthfully, I don't know. The stone glows so red-hot, I'm forced to let it tumble to the ground. I'm afraid it will burst into flame, but instead, when it impacts the hard earth, a brilliant blue light spears the night. When the light dims, there's a figure standing in the middle of the clearing.

Nearly seven feet tall. Leaner than either male shape in the clearing, with almost pearlescent skin. Burgundy hair threatens to spill into his eyes as he squints around at the rest of us, as though he too was just exposed to bright light.

"Gods," I breathe. "Reve!"

TWENTY-THREE
Reve

I'm jerked forcibly from my 6,086, 043 game of chess by a sensation of gripping force and a bright, strobing light.

When I blink the stars from my eyes, my surroundings have changed drastically. Gone is the bloody red backdrop of the Battle of Nighburrow that has been my constant companion for a little over a decade. Instead, the world appears almost drained of color after the garish hues of my hellish prison.

I'm standing in the middle of a decently-sized clearing, surrounded by pale silver oaks drenched in moonlight. The ground is hard beneath my feet, as though winter is creeping on the land. Still, the air is almost muggy, draped in gauzy mist that smells of the forest, clean water, and the subtle scent of Neva's skin.

I turn my head, looking for her. If I've somehow slipped from eternal sleep into death, this has to be an eternal reward. I scour every inch of the clearing.

But instead of locking eyes with Neva, I come face to face with a small woman with hair as gold as gold itself. The tendrils blossom out of her head in sausage curls that reach her shoulders and frame a heart-shaped face with tanned skin, a batch of freckles atop the bridge of her pixie nose, and full pink lips. Her bright green eyes widen noticeably as she stares at me with an open mouth, as though she's spotted a ghost. She's quite lovely.

"Reve!"

Neva's exclamation comes from behind me and I turn to find her arms half outstretched toward me. She looks more solid than I've ever seen her, and in the moonlight, she's even more breathtaking than I remember.

What is this? What's going on?

At my feet is a luminous blue river stone. It appears to still be sparking with magic, but before I can reach down to pick the curiosity up, a solid weight comes crashing in from my right. I'm slow on the uptake, after so many years in sedentary sleep and relative mental silence. I feel about as nimble as a tortoise. If my attacker means to kill me, I'm about to meet the end of my very brief respite.

But after a second, the contours of the body against mine become familiar. We've spent too many summer nights wrestling in the middle of the valley for me not to recognize Herrick's weight. His broad hands clap down on my back and he draws me to his chest as though I'm as fragile as a child.

A laugh bubbles out of me.

Fuck, but I'm glad to see him in the corporeal realm. Because that's what this must be, isn't it? Unless… unless they've all died, along with my sleeping body, and we are now in the realm of the afterlife?

"Am I dead?" I ask, my voice sounding odd to my ears. Of course, I haven't used it in… so long.

"No, you're not dead," Neva says with a broader grin.

Then what? My mental abilities have atrophied over the years, so there's no way I could be sharing a collective

185

dream with both Neva and my brother, let alone with the stranger who's staring gobsmacked at the sight of me.

I wrap my arms around Herrick as tightly as I can manage, seeing with dismay that my touch still goes part of the way through him. I'm not fully corporeal, then. But I'll take whatever I am, all the same. I'll take anything that allows me to set eyes on my brother again.

"Reve," another familiar voice croaks from just behind Neva.

Malvolo steps into the light still emitted by the rock, face uncharacteristically open and vulnerable as he stares at me. I don't think I've seen him wear an expression like that since we were both children. I extend a hand to him over Herrick's shoulder, beckoning him forward.

"Embrace me, brother."

His first step is shaky, but the following are sure and steady. He crosses the clearing in mere moments and throws his arms wide, enveloping both Herrick and I in a monstrous hug that threatens to snap our ribs into splinters. Herrick wheezes but doesn't release me.

"Is it really you?" Malvolo demands, gruff, even in his urgency. I smile. Some things never change…

"It's me. But how I'm here, I can't say."

It must have something to do with Neva, of that much I'm certain. The spell is still in effect, or I'd have woken in my body, with full use of both it and my magic. But this temporary solution is more than I could have ever imagined. At least I'm now aware.

Neva bends to retrieve the river stone. "You came out of this," she explains as she holds it up for me to view. "Kassidy gave it to us."

"Kassidy?" he repeats.

"Er, Goldy," Neva says as the slip of a woman I first spied, steps into my line of sight.

"That would be me," she says, her green gem eyes glowing with a sense of pride.

"And what is this stone?" I ask as I look down at it.

"It's used by Shepherds to house unwilling spirits," Kassidy responds. Then she glances at Neva in doubt. "I've never seen the stone work before until she touched it." Then she shrugs. "She must be a witch or something?"

Neva is certainly that because she's bewitched me from the start. I look over at her and smile as I take in all the loveliness of her face. Then I glance down at the stone again.

A temporary conduit to anchor the dead… I suppose my half-state must be close enough to qualify. Perhaps that should alarm me more than it does. But, no, it doesn't. I'm just grateful. Grateful for Neva and the salvation she offers. She's only just starting to come into her power, and she's already given me so much. If I could just get that kiss in person...

Kissing her now wouldn't produce the same results as it would were I asleep, but it would still be damn satisfying.

I shake free of my brothers, squeezing from Herrick's grasp and ducking Malvolo's beefy arms. In three long strides, I cross the clearing and I go to Neva. Her eyes go wide when I sling an arm around her, sweeping her into me. I'm only half-formed, my control over the mortal world limited. But I can still do this.

Her lips part invitingly when I slide my hands up the smooth column of her throat and tangle them into the fall of her ebony hair. Her lips are soft when I press them to mine, hungry and urgent. Gods, she tastes good. I close my eyes, shutting out the silver wood temporarily so I can fully appreciate the sensation of her here in my arms.

The kiss stretches for an indeterminate amount of time and we only break apart after I hear the sounds of throat clearing several times over. When I release Neva, her eyelashes flutter open in a very comely way. I crane my neck to see who has rudely interrupted us.

"You need to teach me your tricks," Kassidy says to Neva. "You've got more men than I'd know what to do with!

Neva laughs as the girl continues and faces me with a frown.

"Hey ghosty, can you save all that kissy crap for your own time?" she demands. Then she faces Neva. "What in blazes just happened?" she asks pointedly, gesturing broadly at me before facing my brothers. "Where'd the ghost come from? And who is he?"

"This is Reve," Herrick answers, watching my hands fall away from Neva with a frown.

"Yeah, I got that much," Kassidy answers. "You all repeated his name like he'd forgotten it."

"I didn't forget it and I'm not a fucking ghost," I ground out at her with a frown. What does she take me for? A fool?

No, a ghost.

"He's our brother," Herrick continues.

"Also known as the Midnight Dragon of the South," Malvolo adds.

I almost wince at the formal title. I never did like it much. Only father used to call me *Midnight Dragon*; even the soldiers I led called me Reve.

"But how is that possible?" Kassidy asks. "I was told by my brothers that the Midnight Dragon was dead."

"Close," I mutter. "But not quite." Then I take a deep inhale and exhale just as deeply. I bring my gaze from Neva to my brothers. "I wouldn't mind an explanation myself, if someone has one handy. Where are we?"

"We're in the Enchanted Forest, about a week's journey to The Hollows, where Tenebris was rumored to be staying," Malvolo answers.

"I already told you," Kassidy interrupts. "Tenebris isn't there!"

"This girl," Malvolo continues and gestures toward the blonde who now has her hands on her hips and regards him with undisguised irritation, "Kassidy apparently knows where Tenebris is currently hiding."

"No 'apparently' about it!" Kassidy barks. Then she faces me. "Which is why we need to get on the road now," she continues with a firm nod. "There's no telling how long Tenebris will stay in The City of Secrets, with Gatz still searching for her."

"You're sure she's in The City of Secrets?" Herrick questions.

Kassidy nods quickly and her curls bounce in response.

"Fuck," Malvolo says as he shakes his head.

I understand his lament—the City of Secrets, if it's anything like it was before I fell into my forever sleep, is full of the sludge of society—the thieves, murderers, and con-artists, just to name a few.

189

"The City of Secrets is only a week's journey away," Kassidy continues. "If we hurry, we should be able to make it there long before"—she waves a hand—"*this* wears off. And besides, the sooner we get on the road, the sooner I can report back to Draven." Then she sighs and shakes her head. "He's going to be pissed I'm taking this detour. But, what the fuck am I supposed to do about it?" she asks rhetorically, shrugging.

"Draven?" Neva echoes, doubt lacing her voice.

Herrick and Mal's heads swivel to her in surprise. Having witnessed the unraveling nightmares that are her hidden memories, I'm unsurprised. But my brothers must be wondering just how Neva knows the name of the elder Corvid Huntsman. Most only know him by the name Middiean, or as the bodyguard to Princess Carmine of Ascor. Which means the newcomer, Kassidy, must be closer to him than most.

Kassidy arches a brow at Neva. "You know Draven?"

"Yes... no?" Neva responds as she shakes her head and sighs. "I'm not sure."

"Um," Kassidy says as she frowns at the taller woman. "What do you mean, you don't know?"

Neva kneads her forehead with the tips of her fingers, grimacing. "It's all so confusing. Reve says the memory charm is Tenebris' work. If that's the case, I need to find her quickly."

"The memory charm?" Kassidy asks.

"Not that it's any of your fucking business," Malvolo barks at the little blonde. "But, Neva has a spell that disallows her access to her memory."

190

"Well excuse the fuck out of me for asking!" Kassidy says, frowning up at my immense brother.

I like this little tow-head, I decide. She has fire and spunk and has the potential to be annoying as all hell, but for the time-being, she knows where Tenebris is and that makes her valuable.

Kassidy nods again after a moment. "Then, at the risk of sounding repetitive, we really do need to go. Tenebris doesn't stay put these days. Her skills are needed more with every passing year and she doesn't remain idle."

Neva nods. "Kassidy is right. We should go."

Herrick doesn't argue. Malvolo puts up only token protest but begins to dismantle the campsite, dousing the small crackling fire when everything is loaded onto the horses. Kassidy doesn't have a horse, so Neva gives up her mount—which used to be *my* horse. I find it strangely gratifying to know she's been riding Eidolon.

I smack Neva lightly on the ass as she passes me on her way to Herrick's steed and Malvolo grunts.

"Control yourselves, both of you," he grumbles as Neva giggles and stumbles the last step or two toward Herrick.

He catches her with an easy smile and tugs her a little closer, his own hands slipping down to cup her ass. It's such a bold and unexpected move for my brother, I just stare at him in disbelief for a moment.

Well, I'll be damned! They're fucking!

Of the three of us, I didn't think mild-mannered Herrick would be the first to bed her.

I've been able to infer from Neva's dreams that she has feelings for both Malvolo and Herrick (and for me, of course) and, clearly, they both have feelings for her. But those feelings are problematic as it's not in a dragon's nature to share. We are hoarders and when we find a treasure, we hoard that treasure, disallowing anyone else to ever find it again.

And if anyone is territorial and protective of his treasure, it's Malvolo. Yet, I see the way he catches sidelong glances at Neva whenever he believes she and the rest of us aren't looking. Yes, my brother wants her, but he's going to have to learn how to share. Because Neva isn't just any treasure. She's proving to be the most valuable treasure each of us has ever come across.

Though I feel my own instincts telling me to mark her with my scent and take her for my own, I know I can't do that. Herrick's scent is already all over her and clearly, he's the only one who has actually copulated with her. I'm jealous of course, but I'm also willing to share. Only with my brothers though.

And as that thought leaves my head, Herrick looks over at me, his eyebrows drawn in a silent question I immediately understand. I incline my head to him, answering the questioning look he shoots me.

Yes, I will share.

The question is, can Malvolo? In our centuries upon this earth and the countless women we've bedded, the only time any of us have shared a woman, it was the female huntress Peregrine, and it was all seven of us then. Choro had taken it the worst when she'd died, and all our ardors cooled in the wake of her death. Broken as we were, I didn't think we'd ever find a woman we could share again. But, now I wonder…

When I sneak a glance at Mal in my periphery, he's only got eyes for Neva, watching with a slight frown as Herrick lifts her onto the saddle of his dapple gray, Heilwig. Malvolo gives me a sour look when I offer him a smirk and my hand.

There are a limited number of mounts and Kassidy doesn't seem eager to share with a "ghost" so I'll have to ride with Malvolo. "Aren't you going to help me into the saddle?" I ask innocently, batting my eyelashes. It feels good to taunt my brother again. It's been far too long since someone gave him a hard time.

Mal's scowl just deepens and he eyes my hand for a few extra seconds before taking it, slinging me roughly onto the back of the saddle. I weigh little in this half-corporeal state and I almost shoot off the other side of the horse. Mal catches me before I can fall to the ground, righting me in the saddle as he assumes his position at the reins.

"I'd rather be riding with the witchling," Malvolo grunts.

I just smile into his shoulder.

"You and me both, brother. You and me both."

TWENTY-FOUR
Malvolo

Thirteen days have passed and we're in the middle of the most dangerous part of the journey to The City of Secrets, and Herrick can barely manage to keep his damn trousers on, even as he and Neva ride up ahead of us.

I grind my teeth, trying to block out the soft sounds of Neva's pleasure. He's not inside her—yet—but it's simply a matter of fucking time. The next stop we make, I'm sure he's going to fuck her.

Luckily our guide, Kassidy, is far ahead of them, otherwise I'd be embarrassed for them—at having someone witness their inability to keep away from one another. It's bad enough Reve and I have to witness it.

Yet, Reve doesn't appear as put out as I am, clearly too happy to explore the bounds of his semi-corporeality to worry about what Herrick's doing with his cock. And why should Reve worry? He's had more intimate contact with Neva than either of us, being able to meet her in the dreamworld and dive deep into her psyche in a way Herrick and I could only wish. Magic like that takes place soul to soul, and it's more intimate than Herrick and I will ever hope to be with her.

And damn it all, but I *do* want her. As much as I've fought the connection between us, the connection has won. And I can see the desire that burns in her eyes whenever she

194

looks at me. I know it's there. Yet, it's Herrick she disappears with into the woods to fuck. And it's Reve upon whom she depends—Reve who has mastered a connection with her so intimate, neither Herrick nor I will ever be able to fully understand it.

And that begs the question: Just what am I to Neva, except a brute who argues with her?

Of course, I already know what the answer is—Neva wants me as much as I want her. But if I decide to give into my longing, I also know what that will mean—I'll have to share her with Herrick and Reve.

I know how to share.

I've done it once before, with more brothers than are left now. But times were different then—*I* was different then. And I can say, without hesitation, that I didn't care for Peregrine the way I do for Neva. I wanted Peregrine, yes, but the want only extended to the thrill my cock experienced when it was my turn to have her. And it's different with Neva.

I want Neva. But, I want more than just her body. I want her caring, nurturing… I want her love.

And that's absurd because I was convinced I'd turned that need off within myself long ago. Yet, here it is— surfacing again. Fuck me! I want to turn into my dragon shape and burn all these fucking beautiful trees down to charcoaled stumps, I'm so fucking frustrated and pissed off.

When Neva's posture goes rock hard from where she sits in front of Herrick and he turns her face and swallows her moans with a kiss, I want to beat his face in. Fuck! What is fucking wrong with me?

It's not that I begrudge Herrick for having her. It's that I'm not sure how to go about having Neva for myself, at least once. The sexual frustration is beginning to drive me to distraction.

It's not like I couldn't dip my wick, were I so inclined. After her initial fear wore off, Kassidy has begun to regard me with a puppyish sort of hero worship and asks for stories of the war as often as she can. She's a very beautiful woman, once she shrugs off her male clothing.

I've seen her naked already—when we camped two nights ago and she disappeared in the forest in order to bathe. I wasn't going to just let her go alone—there are many animals and creatures of magic in this forest and Kassidy would make a quick and easy morsel.

Neva was off fucking Herrick at the time, and thus unable to accompany Kassidy, so I followed the little blonde, unbeknownst to her. And when she dropped her clothing and stepped into the hot spring, I saw her naked form. Young. Toned. Breasts that were pert and an ass that was shapely. Kassidy is a maid still, if my senses don't deceive me. It would be easy to coax her into my bed.

But I don't. And I won't. Because it would be a cheap, hollow way to distract myself, and unfair to the girl to boot. The man who claims her virginity should care, not use her as a stand-in for another woman.

***

We take a break to water the horses and rest them. And, just as I expect, Neva and Herrick disappear into the forest. And I'm livid inside—jealousy the likes of which I've never before experienced plows through me.

"Mal," Reve asks as I turn to face him. "Are you well, brother?"

"Yes, I'm fucking fine," I answer as his eyes go wide and a smile lights on his lips.

"Could have fooled me."

"We need to press on. I want to make it to the castle before nightfall."

'The Castle' is the abandoned ruins of Chimera Palace that borders the City of Secrets on its west side. We'll bed there tonight and we'll be in The City of Secrets by morning.

"Hopefully Neva and Herrick won't be much longer," Reve says.

I turn to face him. "They've been gone twenty minutes already."

"You've been watching the clock."

"As I said, I want to arrive at the castle before nightfall."

Reve nods and by his expression, I can tell he wants to say more.

"The cat's got your tongue," I say.

He nods again. "Can you share her, Mal?"

I'm surprised by his question but I'm not given the opportunity to reply because Kassidy emerges from the trees, heading towards us.

"She's quite beautiful," Reve whispers to me as he faces Kassidy.

"She is," I grumble. *But she's not Neva.* The comment goes unsaid by both of us.

"Where are the others?" Kassidy asks.

I take a deep breath. "I will go find them, so we can be on our way."

"Sounds good!" Kassidy says as she turns to Reve's mount and feeds him a handful of grass.

"I'll be back," I grumble to Reve as I leave the dirt of the road and venture into the forest, where I watched Neva and Herrick disappear earlier.

Hearing Neva's giggles, I rap my knuckles against one of the nearby spruce trees and call loudly enough for both to hear.

"Break is over!" I grumble. "The horses are fed and rested, so we're moving on. I'll give you two minutes to dress before I come in after you and drag you back."

The giggling abruptly ceases and Neva stage-whispers, "Later, I promise."

I bite back a growl. Herrick is the luckiest fucker alive. My hands carve divots into the trunk as I wait.

I know Herrick's sexcapades aren't the only subject that has me on edge. My sixth sense has been on alert for days, insisting we're being followed. But when I search the surrounding woods, I find next to nothing. Only the heavy tread of boots and the lingering scent of ozone, which is quickly whipped away by the icy aroma of the woods.

I grip the hilt of my sword tighter and feel as though the blade warns me of worse things to come. It's probably the fucking Gryphus huntsman. Not a glaring threat, with our superior numbers and two and a half dragons to face him. But I'm still twitchy. I will remain twitchy until Herrick gets his ass onto his horse and spurs us on toward Castle Chimera. The sooner we're behind stone walls, the better.

I return to Kassidy and Reve, figuring Neva and Herrick heard me and they'll make their way back to us shortly. When I arrive, Kassidy taps her foot impatiently, seconding my irritation. I feel a mite warmer toward her for that, even if she is a thieving little reprobate. I mount my horse and watch as Reve makes no motion to mount behind me.

When Neva and Herrick finally emerge, they're flushed and their clothing thoroughly rumpled. Herrick's got a bruise blooming on his collarbone and his cock strains the front of his trousers as he walks past me. He gives me an unrepentant wink when he reaches his mount and offers a hand to Neva.

I seize her around the waist before Herrick can and lift her onto the back of Virago, surprising all three of us.

"I'll feel safer if she travels with me the rest of the way," I say by way of explanation.

"Safer?" Herrick asks with a frown.

I nod abruptly. "There's something after us. I can feel it."

"This is the first time you've mentioned it," Herrick argues.

"That doesn't mean it isn't true," I argue in return.

Herrick frowns at me. "And even if there is a threat, Neva is safe with me, Mal."

"She's safer with me," I insist.

Herrick's eyes narrow. "How do you figure?"

I glare right back at him. "*You* haven't been going through drills I have every day for the last decade." He cocks his head to the side to acknowledge my comment as true. I take the reins to Virago and tighten my hold around Neva. "Do us a favor, and trust me this once, Herrick."

Herrick shrugs after a second of thought and allows it. Neva, for her part, looks startled and a bit put out, but doesn't argue with me as I settle back into the saddle behind her.

"What the fuck am I then?" Kassidy says, glaring at all of us. "I don't see anyone jumping in with concern for me over the fact that there could be something out there!"

I shoot Kassidy a warning glare over Virago's head. "You're a capable and magically-trained Guild member who can take care of herself."

Kassidy's gaze goes flat at once and she gives me a one-fingered salute. I smirk, in spite of myself. Yes, I'm definitely warming to the little bandit.

"Oh, and I'm not capable of taking care of myself?" Neva demands.

"Bloody hell," I grumble as Reeve laughs from below me, where he still stands on the ground.

"You brought it on yourself, brother," he says as he bypasses Herrick who is already mounted and ready to go. "I'd prefer to ride with the reprobate, brother," he says with a smile as he approaches Kassidy.

"May I ride with you?" he asks as he looks up at her.

"I guess," she grumbles as Reve helps himself up into the saddle and settles behind her.

I take off at a brisk pace. Perhaps too brisk, given the maze of gnarled tree roots that dominate the landscape here. Half of them are covered in snow, making a treacherous path for a horse to travel. One wrong move could lame Virago, Heirwig, or Eidolon, and then we'd really be up the creek.

I've learned not to doubt my instincts, though, and my instincts tell me something is closing in, getting nearer with each moment we dally. I should have dragged both of those love-addled fools out of the bushes ten minutes ago.

I urge Virago still faster, leaving Herrick, Reve, and Kassidy far behind as urgency grips me. This castle, though derelict and shabby, will do for our purposes. Any castle worth its salt will have wards we can activate with blood magic. My own blood should have enough magical power to charge the wards for at least a week without repeat application.

Our surroundings blur into charcoal grays, blacks, and whites as Virago finally adopts a gallop. It still doesn't feel fast enough. I'm about to bring the horse to a halt and take my chances with flight when we come to a break in the trees that opens onto a high stone wall. The archway that leads inside has been blown to cinders, and I have to bring Virago to a complete stop before we reach the debris.

I'd heard Tenebris did her worst here, cursing the prince, who owned the castle, and his two mages to live half-lives as things that were utterly inhuman. One became a monstrous chimera, a beast that terrorized The Hollows as often as it could manage. The other two seemed to keep to themselves, so I wasn't quite certain what Tenebris might have turned them into.

I dismount and then seize Neva around the waist, chivvying her toward the archway. "Go. Get inside and find a place to lock yourself in. I'll come for you when it's safe."

"But, Herrick and the…"

"Go!"

She remains stubbornly put, arms crossed over her ample chest. Damn it. She shouldn't be so damn desirable, even while furious with me. I open my mouth to order her inside again but I'm cut off by a deep, chilling growl. I whirl back to face the way we've just come and before I can even think, I clear my sword of its scabbard with nary a sound.

They're difficult to see at first, emerging from the deep shadows that pool between the trees. But when they stride into the open, it's easier to make out the great shaggy beasts. They're at least five feet long and easily as tall.

Shorter than me, even in my human form, but the height difference doesn't give me much of an edge. Hellhounds can't actually breathe fire, like dragons, but they can superheat the air, using all the oxygen in a place, rendering one dead as effectively as fire could. And the suffocation is a kinder death than being cooked slowly, layer by layer.

The stench of sulfur coats my nose. Now I remember why I fucking hate these things. Smelly, smart, and incredibly savage. A trifecta of bad news.

I don't regret racing ahead of the others, though their help would be invaluable at this point. Trapped in the confines of the narrow path, it will be impossible to shift to my dragon form.

Neva finally reacts with some sense and scurries back a step with a whimper. I adjust my position, putting my body between hers and the oncoming hellhounds. They want to get to her, they'll have to tear through me first.

They pause about three feet away from us, as if listening to a signal I can't detect. I don't relax my guard, waiting for the other boot to slam down with crushing force.

It comes seconds later, when two shapes come striding out of the shadowy forest behind the line of mutts. The first has got a plain face, icy blue eyes, and a thin mouth. He's decked out in the trappings of a huntsman: dark clothing with silver buttons, and a heavy cloak that's charmed to act as a tent during bad weather. The spells are worked in at the hem by skilled Aves sorceresses. It's the signet ring on his pinkie that gives him away, though. This is the Gryphus huntsman that's been after Neva—the one who attacked Herrick and Neva in Ascor.

But it's the second shape that diverts my attention. I believe he and I are acquainted, and ice slips into my stomach as I drink in the profile of a very familiar, very hated enemy. He's just as grizzled as I remember, with more skin shredded than left whole. Claw marks drag one eyelid most of the way down, and the sclera of that eye is milky white and blind. He wears a monocle over it most of the time, a stolen Tenebris trinket that can provide extrasensory information to the sightless—meant for much more philanthropic ventures than those to which he puts it to use. His other eye is the luminous blue-gray of a timber wolf's. His mangled mouth lifts into a jovial smile when he spies me.

"Ah, General Malvolo. It's been some time. I haven't seen you since the day you maimed me."

He waves airily at his ruined face. He might have been good-looking at one point, had I not destroyed his face.

"Forever is not long enough, Lycaon," I snarl. "How did you escape the ass-end of the nether realm, by the way?"

Lycaon laughs in my face, and my entire body shudders with the need to explode into my dragon form. I can't. Not with Neva here. There'll be a minute-long lag while I shift, which is ample time for Lycaon's hounds to rip Neva apart. Fuck, fuck, fuck. And the others are still around the bend, completely unaware of Lycaon and his hellhounds. This isn't good.

"You expected that pathetic gambit to work? The seals don't hold shit, old boy."

"Apparently not," I grumble.

He smiles, as best he can. "Our servants have been wandering Fantasia since day one. We've been amongst you, building our forces slowly. And when we're all the way through, you'll rue the day you tried to banish us."

"Are we going to quibble over technicalities, or are we going to fight?" I bark, bluffing with every ounce of bravado I have. The hellhounds I could fend off with effort, even in my human form. In my dragon form, it would take an army of them to even inconvenience me. The Gryphus Huntsman might be a greater challenge, but only just. Huntsmen can withstand beatings that would kill other mortals. But again, the huntsman is no match for my dragon.

Lycaon is another beast entirely. He's a figure from antiquity, one who became the first and most powerful wolf-shifter after he fed the gods his own son as a meal. A master of beasts, but with a particular affinity for hellhounds, he could bring almost anything to bear against me. All threats combined, it's almost impossible to defend Neva from all of them without shifting into the dragon.

Why hadn't she run when I'd told her to, damn it?

A smirk slithers like a trail of slime across Lycaon's face, his thoughts clearly mirroring my own. I'm backed into a corner, about to be fucked from every conceivable angle.

"This doesn't have to end in violence, General," Lycaon drawls. "Morningstar can be gracious."

"Morningstar and gracious don't belong in the same sentence," I manage.

Lycaon laughs, a deep and ugly sound. "Regardless, my statement still stands."

"How can Morningstar be gracious?" I demand.

"Simply hand over the girl, and we'll walk away to leave you and your brothers in perpetuity."

I stall for time, mind spinning wildly as I try to come up with a battle strategy. If Neva runs, the hounds will follow. I'll have to defeat them first and somehow keep the huntsman and Lycaon off my back.

I allow my mouth to run, while my brain is otherwise occupied. "And what does Morningstar need with a tavern dancer, I wonder?"

Lycaon's smile is sunny, and that flash of pure joy scares the life out of me.

"You truly don't know what she is? Still?"

"Aside from a great fuck, no," I answer, hoping Neva won't hold my lie against me later. But, I want Lycaon to think she's nothing to me. That I would just as soon turn her over to preserve myself. But, even if such were the case, I know Morningstar and his ilk well enough to know I can't trust him—turn Neva over to them and Lycaon would still come after me. Old grudges die slowly.

"My, I never thought you brothers were slow. I suppose all the gasses in those tunnels must have addled your brains," Lycaon says.

"Speak plainly, Lycaon. What do you want with the girl?"

I motion behind my back for her to flee. She takes a few more steps back before stumbling over the keystone of the arch.

Lycaon's eyes follow her form before they return to me. "She must die. For the greater good, of course."

"Why?"

Lycaon shrugs. "Can't have her mucking about with our plans. Goodness knows it took us long enough to track her down. Tenebris' spellwork is still something, is it not?"

"I suppose."

He shrugs. "I've never seen a cloaking spell so ingenious. The girl would have remained hidden forever without that blessed little barkeep bringing her notoriety."

Damn Darius to a hell worse than the one he's already inhabiting! I'm going to find him in whatever sordid little afterlife he's reached and I'll rip his entrails out his nose.

"So? Do we have a deal?" Lycaon continues. "You pass over the girl and I allow you and the others to leave without incident?" he asks casually but I know he's perched on my response.

"I'm afraid I can't take that deal."

"Don't be a fool, General."

"Send my regards to Morningstar when I finish you. Give him a great big fuck you from General Malvolo."

Lycaon hums his disappointment. "Very well, then." He turns to face the hellhounds. "Vash, Klaus, and Lucius—kill him."

The hellhounds leap forward, crossing the distance in the time it takes to blink. One tries to bypass me and get to Neva. I lunge, digging my boot into its soft underbelly. The contact burns through the leather of my boot and singes my toes, but I ignore it, using my momentum to send the creature hurtling into the trunk of a nearby spruce. It yelps in surprise and then goes quiet, sliding to the ground in a limp pile.

When the fucking hell are Herrick and Kassidy going to catch the fuck up? I could use their help right about now. I'd include Reve in that thought but I'm not sure what he can do in his current incorporeal form.

One of the hellhounds leaps onto me, sharp claws digging searing furrows into my bicep. I fling it off with a roar of pain, but it doesn't travel as far as the last one. It digs its claws into the hard earth and comes to a stop just before the feet of the huntsman, who's leveling a crossbow at me. I barely have time to twist out of the way as he looses a bolt in my direction. The shot meant for my heart sticks in my already much abused arm.

I roar out my pain.

I definitely can't hold them all. Lycaon hasn't even entered the fray yet.

"Run up to the castle!" I shout at Neva even though I don't turn to face her. I have to keep my attention on my enemies who are currently surrounding me.

From the corner of my eye, I see her climb shakily to her feet. Fear rolls off her like acrid smoke, clogging my nose. She's like a fucking gazelle, prey ripe for the picking.

The nearest hellhound darts past me, and I turn my back to the remaining three attackers to catch it, spearing it through one of its meaty haunches. It's the stupidest thing I can do, under the circumstances, leaving my back open. The next bolt will find my heart, my liver, or my kidneys—and in my current human shape, it will be as good as a killing blow. But I can't let the hounds get to Neva.

Can't let them touch her.

She's mine. Mine to protect, mine to love. And I won't let Lycaon or his minions lay a hand on her while I still breathe.

I screw my eyes shut, prepared for pain.

And open them once more when a brassy, ear-splitting shriek splits the night air. I turn my head just in time to see a hulking golden shape twice as large as any war elephant sail over our heads. My heart lifts, hopeful in spite of our dire situation.

"About fucking time," I grumble.

Herrick's dragon settles in the clearing between Lycaon, the Huntsman, and myself, crushing a few spruce trees flat with the weight of his tail. Reve and Kassidy cling to his back. As I watch, the thief slides down his armored flank and springs nimbly to her feet, jogging to reach my side.

"Neva. Tell Herrick to get Neva," I pant when Kassidy reaches me.

"He's got Neva in a safe place already,' she assures me, slinging an arm around my waist. "And I've got you."

"I'm not badly hurt," I argue as I pull away from her. "Get into the castle and raise the wards. I can hold them off."

"Don't be a fucking martyr, General. And don't be a fucking idiot either."

"Gods, but you are vexing!"

"So are you, asshole," Kassidy seethes at me. "Now, limp behind the walls with the rest of us, you idiot."

I don't have the energy to argue with her at this point. The furrows in my bicep are deep and pouring blood. Not enough to kill me, but enough to weaken me and throw my balance off.

Herrick releases a gout of flame that makes every hair on my body curl in response. It must singe at least one of our attackers, because I smell burning flesh. I hope it's Lycaon.

Kassidy helps me behind the walls of Castle Chimera, and after a few minutes of frantic searching, I find the crest of blood magic on the dusty flagstone. I slap my hand onto it, focusing all my will into erecting the barrier between Herrick and our enemies. The warded barrier springs up seconds later, a humming wall of power that saps still more energy from me.

I sag into the thief's arms, black spots dancing over my vision. The last thing I hear before I'm dragged under is the flap of enormous wings and the tinny sound of Neva calling my name.

TWENTY-FIVE
Neva

I flinch as Malvolo releases another long string of expletives as I remind myself not to feel too hurt by it. After all, I could have just let Herrick clean his wounds. But, Herrick, Kassidy and Reve are currently checking the perimeter of the Castle Chimera to make sure all the wards are in place and protecting us.

It probably would be kinder to Malvolo if I bowed out gracefully and waited for his trained brother take my place. It just feels like I *have* to do this. After all, Malvolo received these wounds for my sake. It seems only right that I try to patch him up.

Those few minutes when Malvolo faced our enemies down were the scariest in my life. And when he'd turned his back on them to tell me to seek shelter, I'd thought for sure he was a dead man. Terror locked me into absolute stillness. I couldn't have run much further than I had. Malvolo had nearly died for me.

"I'm sorry," I murmur, a runaway tear escaping my control. I'm just so incredibly scared for him—he risked his life for me and if he loses his fight and succumbs to his injury, I don't know what I'll do!

The tear streaks down my face and drips onto his wound, and I wipe it away quickly with my cloth. Great. Now I'm literally rubbing salt into his wounds.

Malvolo stills and sucks in several deep breaths. "Stop apologizing," he manages in between grimaces. "I'm a lousy patient, no matter who's doing the nursing. Ask Herrick."

All the grit appears to be out of his slashes, now all that's left is to remove the arrow and stitch him up. Herrick says I'm to push the arrow through until the arrowhead sticks out the other side of his arm, and then snap the shaft off. Ripping it out with the head still on, he told me, will destroy Malvolo's muscle. I'm also not to get the fletching into the wound, either, lest we risk infection.

Malvolo grips onto the table as I begin, gritting his teeth so hard, I fear he'll shatter them.

"Do it quickly!" he orders.

The wooden tabletop creaks ominously, threatening to crack. It's one of the only pieces of furniture left intact in this room, aside from the candlestick on the mantle of the fireplace and the battered grandfather clock in the corner. The table comes apart in splinters by the time the arrow is out.

Malvolo relaxes somewhat when that's through, wincing only occasionally when I pull the thread through his skin, sealing his gashes. Each is about six inches long, and it's going to take most of the thread Herrick packed to close them up. I can only hope none of us are injured on the journey to or from The City of Secrets tomorrow. If Malvolo is strong enough to travel, that is.

"I really am sorry," I murmur.

"For what?" he huffs. "You didn't injure me."

"Maybe I didn't shoot the arrow but I put you in the position that allowed you to be wounded."

"What do you mean?"

"You risked your life to defend a lousy human," I say in a soft voice, willing myself not to start crying again. "I know you think very little of us."

Malvolo turns his head and regards me with those serious ember eyes. "Do you truly believe I'd do all this for someone I disliked?"

"I... I don't know."

"I think all indicators up to this point show I definitely don't dislike you. Did you think I kissed you back in my cave for the sport of it?"

"But Herrick said..."

"I do hate most humans," he concedes with a shrug and then a wince. "Or I *did.* Between you and the little reprobate, Kassidy, I'm beginning to remember why I ever thought humans worthwhile at all. And some are definitely worth laying down my life for."

He slides his hand onto mine. It's feverishly hot, which is good. Herrick says I'm only to be concerned if Malvolo's skin starts turning clammy. Malvolo uses his grip on my hand to tug me closer and I fall forward, finding myself pillowed against his bare chest. The contours of him are delicious beneath my hands. He's more muscled than either Herrick or Reve, and neither are anything to sniff at. I doubt there's an ounce of fat on Malvolo anywhere.

His breath ruffles my hair as he presses a searing kiss to my forehead. "You're worth it, Neva."

My throat constricts and I shake my head, even as fresh tears spring to my eyes. "I'm not. I'm really not."

"How can you say that?"

"Because I'm a liability. And now I'm a danger to you all." I pause as I wrestle with myself to control my tears. I don't want to cry in front of Malvolo. He only appears to respect strength. "You heard that man, Lycaon. If you'd just turned me over, you, Herrick and Reve would be safe, forever."

Malvolo snorts. "Yes, because Morningstar is a bastion of honesty. I trust him about as far as I can throw him."

"But…"

Tucking me close to his chest, he rolls us so that we're resting near the fire. The golden light traces every feature of his handsome face, and all I can read is earnestness in his expression. "I decide what's worth risking my life, Neva. And you're worth it." He pauses for a few moments and traces the line of my right cheek, down to my jaw. "I just wish you believed that too."

"I love you, Mal," I confess on a shaking exhale and his eyes widen. I'm surprised by the admission as well, but I won't take it back because it's true. And it's something I realized when his life was threatened. "I love all of you. And it's not fair for any of you."

"Yet you can hardly help it," he says.

I shake my head as I realize how completely unfair I'm being to all three of them. But now that the words are out, I see how true they are. I do love all of them and what's more, I want all of them. "I'm a selfish girl."

"The heart wants what it wants," Mal says in the most understanding voice I've ever heard him use.

"I should be so lucky to have just one of you. Me, a lowly little whore."

And that's when he reaches forward and smacks me across the cheek. It's isn't hard enough to truly hurt, but it smarts all the same. I feel my eyes go wide as I bring my hand to my face and cradle the tender cheek. Malvolo's expression is hard.

"Never refer to yourself as a whore again in my presence," he seethes. "Any other person who ever called you the same in front of me would be dead by my bare hands," he continues and his eyes are steel. "You are the most kind, thoughtful and beautiful woman I've ever met."

The tears come freely now and I shake my head as I close my eyes against them. How can he say these things about me? What does he see that I don't?

He brushes my hair behind my ear and I open my eyes as he shakes his head. "We have no idea what you are, Neva. But you're certainly more than your past, if Lycaon wants to end you. If I hadn't thought you the most important woman before, I know now."

He bends down, covering his mouth with mine, swallowing my arguments. Once the kiss starts, I don't have the will to argue, anyway. Besides, he was so offended to hear me speak so negatively about myself, I definitely learned my lesson.

The truth is, I can't think of anything other than the relief I feel at knowing he's alive and mostly whole in my arms. They wind around his shoulders, my hands sliding into all that touchable dark hair as he grinds his evident arousal into my thigh.

But then I pull away.

"Herrick," I start as I shake my head.

"Will share," Malvolo finishes. "We all will."

I cock my head to the side as I study his expression. "Are you sure?"

He nods. "Herrick and Reve know they're already sharing you," he explains. "I was the wild card and I've had enough time to decide this is what I want as well." His grin broadens. "Now, the question is, witchling, can you handle three dragons?"

"I can try," I say as I swallow hard. We just stare at one another for a few seconds before I speak again. "Make love to me, Malvolo."

"Unfortunately or fortunately, from my position, it will have to be *you* making love to *me*," he says with a chuckle and motions to his injured arm.

I laugh in response as he rolls us so I'm straddling him, hands braced on his chest. I pause, unsure of myself. Where do I start? Malvolo is so much different to Herrick and the truth of the matter is that he intimidates me. What if I displease him? What if he realizes I'm really not knowledgeable of a man's body?

What if. What if. What if.

Herrick seems to enjoy our trysts enough, but I don't think my usual tricks are going to impress this forceful man. I bend cautiously and tease one of his nipples with my teeth. He groans in response, head rolling back.

I reach for the waistband of his trousers. He's hard beneath them, almost alarmingly large. Even after these weeks of feeling Herrick deep inside me, I'm only just accustomed to the size of these men.

Malvolo reaches for the front of my shirt and tears it open without even bothering with my buttons. I squeal in protest, but the squeal is soon lost in a moan as he lifts himself into a half-upright position, descending on my breasts with an animalistic sound of satisfaction. I know

Malvolo will be dominant and maybe even rough with me. He won't be the tender lover Herrick is. I know this and I've prepared myself for it. I trust Malvolo and after seeing him risk his life for me, I know he cares for me. Deeply.

And that's why I can give myself to him. I can allow him to dominate me, to do things to me that might scare or intimidate me. Because I trust him.

His mouth latches onto me, teasing and tasting every inch of exposed skin. His hands hold my hips firm against him, even as the rest of me writhes.

"I need to be inside you," he groans against my skin. "I've waited for this fucking moment for ages, it feels like."

At this point, I can't think of anything I want more. I fumble with the fasteners, almost laughing to myself at the absurdity of it all. I'm in love with dragons. Three dragons, to be precise. And I'm about to fuck the most ill-tempered, contrary, and daring of them all. I'm already embarrassingly wet, the slickness soaking my underlinens.

Malvolo pushes urgently at his trousers when I've gotten them loose, pushing the material down until his cock springs free. I have to climb off him for an instant to undo my own. I never thought I'd miss skirts, but at this moment, they'd be much more convenient. Malvolo hauls my hips down the second I'm bare, sliding his length inside me in one smooth stroke.

I arch my head back and scream out at the invasion. But there's no pain. Only a pleasure that feels so good, I almost climax from that alone. Malvolo isn't through, though. With his grip on my hips, he lifts me almost off him before slamming me back down again. The contours of his rock-hard cock drag across that spot inside me and I let out a small, mewling cry of pleasure. If he keeps this up, I'm going to find my release in mere seconds.

Sure enough, I find bone-melting ecstasy a minute or so later. I don't become aware that Malvolo has paused until I come down into my panting, sweaty reality. He's still hard and thick inside me, so he's not finished. But I follow his gaze to the doorway and spy Reve and Herrick watching us, twin smiles on their faces.

I try to find any hint of disgust or jealousy on their faces, but find none. They're both… excited at watching us?

"Perverts," Malvolo scolds with a grin. "Stop peeping."

"And do what instead?" Reve asks.

"Join us or fuck off," Malvolo answers.

Herrick's tawny eyes search my face. "What do *you* want, Neva?"

"You," I breathe. "And Reve. I want all of you." As soon as the words are out of my mouth, I drop my gaze to the bedlinens. I'm ashamed at my own selfishness, no matter how true it might be.

"Neva?" Herrick asks as he and Reve enter the room, closing the door behind them.

"I'm selfish," I answer their questioning glances.

Reve smirks and gives a little shrug. "Maybe. But we're dragons. We're the very definition of selfish."

Herrick nods. "Think you can live with that?"

"I think I could love it," I confess, tears stinging my eyes. Three gorgeous dragons who all want me. It seems like too much for one amnesiac peasant girl to hope for.

Herrick sheds his clothing as he approaches and I watch, mouth going dry with nerves and anticipation. Reve doesn't undress, just circles us all with predatory grace, pressing kisses all over my body at odd moments, sending jolts of pleasure straight to my clit with each brush of his magic.

I feel bad for him and myself because he can't join me the way the other two can. Hopefully this will be enough for him. For now anyway.

For the next few hours, I'm aware of only three things: The glide of their bodies over mine, the sound of our cries as they bounce back from the walls of the room, and the guilty but amused realization that Kassidy will be getting absolutely no sleep tonight.

TWENTY-SIX
Neva

As we enter The City of Secrets, I'm amazed by the filth that surrounds me. Trash lines the sides of the road and the stench of feces and rot is thick in the air. Rats and larger animals roam the streets, difficult to spot in the darkness of the sky. Only the moonlight reveals our path.

Growing up in Ascor probably spoiled me, I realize as I look back on it. The streets were almost always lit, even at dusk. So many torches and lanterns illuminated the streets, night never felt as truly dark as it is. The streets were cobblestone and the filth was kept to certain areas.

The City of Secrets looks like a jumble of buildings arranged around a crossroads, the roads little more than mud and filth. The homes are more like shacks: small and modest and most reveal peeling paint, chipped clay or broken boards. A few of them have wood nailed across the windows and doors. I'm briefly struck with a wave of nostalgia for the Vorst cottage back in the dragons' valley.

What few people there are out and about at this hour of the night, pause in mid-motion as we ride into town. I can't say I blame them—we make quite the motley crew: two beautiful women, two men who are nigh seven feet tall and clearly inhuman, and a third who is just as large and flickers like a phantom every few minutes or so. Needless to say, I doubt we're the average visitors to this city.

"You're sure she's here?" I ask in an undertone to
Kassidy.

She's riding with me today, to save the squabble of
which brother I'll be accompanying. Herrick has Reve, and
Malvolo is, as always, grumpy and alone on Vigaro.

"Yes, I'm sure," she grumbles.

"You seem to be in a bad mood," I continue.

She turns around and glares at me. "You fuckers have
kept me up for the last three fucking nights so yeah, I'm in a
bad mood."

I can't help but laugh. "I'm sorry," I say when she
thrusts another glare at me.

Spotting a tavern at the end of the road, with a sign that
proclaims it to be 'The Ol' Witch's Tit', we tie the horses
and make a beeline for it. It's quite small compared to the
Wicked Lyre. The entire building is roughly the size of one
of the Lyre's back rooms. If Tenebris is here, this is where
she'll be staying.

Malvolo pushes through the tavern doors first, hand on
the hilt of his sword, ready to strike down anyone who
comes for us. When he doesn't immediately fly into action,
the rest of us push forward, assuming enough safety to enter.
Herrick goes in next, followed by Kassidy, with Reve and
me taking up the rear.

I seize Reve's hand as much as I'm able and squeeze it
with all my might. After traveling so long, we've almost
reached our goal. I'm having trouble believing this is truly
real. Perhaps I've dreamed up this whole scenario. Perhaps
Darius actually beat me to death in a fit of rage and this is
my afterlife.

"Inside, Neva," Reve prompts gently. "We won't get answers out here."

"Answers?" I repeat.

He nods. "To many questions we all have."

I squint at him suspiciously. Reve has always struck me as being the wisest of the three of the brothers—wise in that he's always a step ahead of everyone else. "You know something about all of this, don't you? And you won't tell us."

He raises my hand to his lips and brushes a kiss across my knuckles, a glint of puckish mischief in his eye. "It's not a matter of won't tell you, love. It's a matter of can't. Give us a kiss when we get home and I'll sing like a lark. Now, in with you, wench."

He swats me lightly on the ass and I stumble through the doors with a laugh.

The interior is dingy, with only five occupants at present, besides our party. Two are slumped over the bar, so deep in their cups, they're paying mind to nothing else. The bartender barely looks up from cleaning a glass, except to nod when Reve asks for a round of beers. The fourth man is asleep in a back corner. Which leaves only the figure at a small round table in the middle of the room.

A woman.

"Tenebris," Kassidy whispers to me.

It's hard to believe this is the famed sorceress. I don't know what I was expecting to find, but this woman isn't it. Yes, she is most assuredly beautiful. It's just... from the tales the brothers spin, I expected her to be as large as life itself, with magic shooting like lightning from her fingertips.

221

I can barely see her around Herrick's elbow. The brothers have formed a sort of blockade around me, hiding me from her view.

But I can make out that her hair is a dark caramel brown and falls loose around her shoulders, offset by wide almond-shaped eyes of the same shade. She's slim and petite, and she looks barely older than I am, though she has to be at least twenty to thirty years my senior to have fought in the last war.

Her eyes fly open wide when she takes in Herrick and Malvolo. But her surprise only lasts a second or so.

"I didn't think I'd ever see you two again."

"Was hoping to avoid it myself," Malvolo grunts, not bothering to disguise the utter contempt he feels for the sorceress. "But sometimes, things can't be helped."

She nods. "Why have you come?" she asks, facing Herrick.

"We need your help, Tenebris," he answers.

"We demand your help," Malvolo corrects.

The woman shushes him automatically, eyes darting around the tavern. I don't see why she bothers. No one here is paying us any mind.

"I've told you a million times, General," she starts, spearing him with an angry expression. "Call me Belle when in… uncertain circumstances."

"I'll call you whatever I damn well feel like," Malvolo grunts. "We've traveled halfway across Fantasia to find you, and I *will* wring your scrawny neck if you don't help us... *Tenebris*."

Herrick lets out an almost inaudible sigh. "Do we need to have that discussion on honey versus vinegar again, Mal?"

"Doesn't really matter what I slather her body in," Malvolo continues as he glares down at the small woman who glares right back up at him. "The vermin will pick her apart regardless."

"That's not what I..." Herrick pinches the bridge of his nose and then exhales. "I don't know why I fucking bother." Then he turns an apologetic half-smile to the sorceress. "I apologize, Belle. Clearly, we're all a little on edge."

She continues to stare down Malvolo. "Some a little more than others, it would seem."

Herrick nods. "We were attacked a few days back by hellhounds and Lycaon. Unsurprising to you, I'm sure, since you've been active all these years. But it shocked the piss out of us, as you can imagine."

"What did they want?" Belle asks.

"They were after our traveling companion and we thought *you* might be able to tell us why."

As if they've orchestrated it, both brothers step back to reveal Kassidy, Reve, and me. Kassidy flashes the sorceress a jaunty grin. Reve waves, and just the sight of him seems to completely stagger Tenebris... or Belle, as she seems to prefer to be called. It's a moment or two before she turns those penetrating eyes to me.

Recognition flits through them for an instant before she schools her expression. Still, I catch it, and so does Herrick.

"I knew it," he crows.

"You knew what?" she demands as she looks up at him.

223

"I knew it was *your* spellwork the moment I found Neva in Ascor."

Tenebris shushes him at once. "Don't speak so loudly, you idiot!" she says as she glances around herself, but no one in the tavern seems even the slightest bit interested in us or our conversation. "There are ears for hire everywhere. Do you want everyone knowing we're here?"

Herrick's enthusiasm dims at once and he slumps into the chair next to her, appropriately chastised.

Tenebris steeples her fingers in front of her face, barely acknowledging the barkeep when he sets the foaming mugs of beer on the table. Everyone but Malvolo and Reve gather around the table, the former because he seems to prefer to pace, and the latter because his corporeality has been slipping every so often. Less embarrassing to stand than to sink through a chair.

"What has happened?" Tenebris breathes at last. "I don't think I've seen such a mismatched band in... well, ever, if I'm honest."

"Which you aren't!" Malvolo spits at her.

She just frowns at him and faces Herrick.

So Herrick begins the tale where it started. It hardly seems possible that it was only a month and a half ago that I met these three beautiful men. He recounts finding me in Ascor, the abuse I suffered at the hands of Darius, and our flight from the Gryphus huntsman. Then he goes on to detail my first disastrous meeting with Malvolo, the memory dust I'd been snorting, and finishes with the skirmish with Lycaon and the hellhounds.

By the time he's through, Tenebris looks as though she might throw up. She shoves her half-consumed beer away with a grimace.

"That wasn't how it was supposed to happen," she mutters and scans the room once more, before turning her eyes back to Herrick. "Gregory was supposed to move Neva from Ascor after the sack of the city. Then she was supposed to be delivered to a secure location where Draven and the others could watch over her. When she didn't turn up, we assumed..."

"You assumed what?" Malvolo demands.

The sorceress blows out a breath. "Foolish to assume, I know. And now all of these mistakes have set into motion a chain of events we cannot change. That spell was set to be broken years from now by a dead man's kiss. And *only* by his kiss. This is a disaster..."

"No, it's not," I whisper, leaning forward to stretch an imploring hand across the table toward her. "You cast the spell, right?" She nods so I continue. "Then you can undo it, right?"

Her plump pink lips thin and she arches an imperious brow at me. "Weren't you listening to a word I said?"

"Yes," I narrow my eyes as I answer.

"Then you would have realized the answer to your question already." She lets out a breath of irritation when it becomes obvious we all expect her to explain. "I set the spell to be broken by one catalyst and one catalyst only, specifically so that I couldn't be captured and forced to unravel it under torture."

"Why?" I ask.

"I promised your father I would protect you, and I did it to the best of my ability. I had intended to have you grow up alongside Prince Payne or one of the vampires from Grimm to make the process easier, but clearly that didn't happen."

"So... this...coming here was a waste?" I demand. "You can't do anything for me?"

Her eyes soften with pity and I want to spit in her drink. "No, I'm afraid not."

"You can't tell me what I'm supposed to have forgotten?" I ask, grasping desperately at straws at this point.

She shakes her head. "You can't even tell me who my father was?"

"I'm sorry. I made an oath to your father."

"What the fuck does that mean?" Malvolo demands.

She looks at him. "It means that to break the oath, I would be destroyed. I can't do that, even for you."

"This is your fault," I hiss, hating the tremor that shakes the surety of my voice. "It's your fault I was beaten and raped for years! It's your fault I was an addict! It's all your fault! You left me alone and defenseless without my memory! And all you can fucking say is you're sorry?"

"Neva," Kassidy starts as she puts a hand on my shoulder. I shrug her care away and I take a step closer to Tenebris.

Her eyes seem a little glassy and she glances down at her hands where they're folded in her lap.

"The least you can do is fucking look me in the eyes," I seethe.

She looks up and I can see her eyes are swimming with tears, but they don't fall. "What else would you like me to say?"

"That you can fix this!"

"I cannot."

I seize my mostly full mug of beer and fling its contents into her face in a burst of white-hot anger. She barely has time to blink before it hits her, dousing all that wavy dark brown hair, staining the blue smock she wears, trickling off the end of her perfect nose into her lap.

"Thanks for nothing," I mutter and stalk toward the tavern door as I feel like I'm about to lose it and collapse into a pile of my own tears. Kassidy is right behind me.

I duck out into the weak morning sunlight and slam the door before the stinging tears begin to fall.

***

"Throwing that drink at Tenebris was badass," Kassidy confides with a wink and conspiratorial laugh. Then she mimics me holding my mug and throwing it. "Take that, you stupid bitch!" she yells and I can't help but think Kassidy is the strangest person I've ever met. I can hear Reve and Herrick chuckling at her antics from behind me.

"She could have turned you into a frog or something," Kassidy continues as she faces me with eyebrows drawn.

I can tell she's trying to lighten my mood, the way that everyone has been for days while we travel to the City of Bridgeport, located south, on the Sea of Delorood.

The journey is a long one, especially on horseback, and made even longer now that we've been forced to take a circuitous route to avoid the dragnet of still more hellhounds, their spectral leader, and the Gryphus huntsman.

When I don't crack a smile, Kassidy deflates a little. I feel bad for disappointing her. Despite having only known each other for a short time, Kassidy has grown on me quickly. I like her coarse sense of humor, the way she likes to heckle Malvolo, and her steadfast determination to complete her mission, no matter how suicidal.

We're set to part ways just outside Wonderland. And then Kassidy will be moving on toward the compound of werebears she's still determined to rob. And that's all the way near Bridgeport on the Sea of Delorood. She'll have to travel ten miles or so into thickly wooded forest, and I don't envy her the journey with that thick mass of curly hair. She's going to be snagging it on every tree branch she passes.

She shoves her hands into her pockets and rocks awkwardly from the balls of her feet to her toes. "I suppose this is where we go our separate ways," she says, finally as I slow the horse and she jumps down from behind me. I follow suit and the others do as well. Even Malvolo.

"Thank you for doing what you could, Kassidy," I say with a small smile.

She nods. "I'm sorry things didn't go well with Tenebris, Neva. I really am." Then she sighs. "I hope you can find a dead man to smooch soon…"

That does draw just a tiny smile from me, but it withers and dies a second later. I can't maintain a good humor for long, under the current circumstances. I'd thought Tenebris would have been the answer—to my missing memories and to unleashing whatever power I actually possess. But now knowing there's not a damn thing she can do to help me, I feel like a sitting duck.

It's only a matter of time before Lycaon, the huntsman and the hellhounds are back on my trail and I'm scared the next time they attack us, one of the brothers might be hurt.

Herrick wraps his arms around Kassidy and lifts her from the ground in a hug. Kassidy splutters for air and pounds his back a few times before he sets her down.

"Thank you for your help, Miss Aurelian," he says. "We won't forget this."

"No, we won't," Reve adds. "Come to us if you ever need aid."

"You'll find it's helpful to have dragons at your back," Herrick adds.

"Thanks, guys," Kassidy says with a smile as she pretends there's something in her eye.

"Well, leave me out of it. I've had enough bullshit to last me a lifetime," Malvolo sniffs, but the acerbic tone of his voice is softened by the smirk ghosting the corners of his mouth.

Kassidy just sneers at him. "You're going to miss me, you big pile of reptile."

"In your fucking dreams, reprobate."

Kassidy turns to me, arms half-extended. I don't have the heart to deny her, so I step into them, allowing her to wrap her arms around my neck, which she has to do while on tip-toes. She really is a tiny little thing, it's half a wonder how she's managed to survive so long since I'm sure she pisses people off on a daily basis. She kisses my cheek in an almost sisterly fashion.

"Be safe, Neva," she whispers. "And don't let your men give you any shit."

"Hey!" Herrick says.

I just smile. "I hope this isn't goodbye forever."

"It's not," she says with a shrug. "Just for now." Kassidy releases me and shoots Malvolo a guilty look. "I feel horrible for even asking to take your sword. I didn't do much to help." Then she sighs. "I'm only bringing it up because the Guild needs all the help, and riches, we can get."

Malvolo nods and removes the sword, scabbard, and belt he's wearing and tosses it lightly to her. The jewels catch the light, sending rainbows dancing across the trunks of trees before Kassidy's hands shoot out to catch the weapon.

If Kassidy feels guilty, it's nothing compared to how I feel. The treasure was given on my behalf and it paid for so little. We're no better off now than when we started.

"I gave my word. You upheld your end of the bargain. And besides," Malvolo adds, shooting a glance at Reve, who's watching me from the corner of his eye, concern plain on his face, "you gave me the answer to keeping my brother on this plane. I'd say that's more than worth one sword, no matter how fine its craftsmanship."

"Yeah, you've got a point there," Kassidy says with a shrug.

"Go in peace, Kassidy Aurelian."

"I think you all have earned the right to call me Goldy," she says with a smile. "I mean, I consider you all friends now."

"Best of luck on your mission," Malvolo continues. "Goldy."

Malvolo snaps her a military salute and, I swear to all the Gods, tears gleam in Goldy's beautiful green eyes for a second before she turns and sprints into the woods. Another ghost of a smile alights on my lips for a mere second.

I enjoy the rare moments I can see Malvolo's sweet side. It's buried deep down under a mountain of choleric temper and years of disappointment, but the fact it still exists is astounding.

When the smile fades and Goldy is truly gone, I feel even colder and emptier than before.

"Where to now?" Herrick asks, coming to stand at my shoulder, eyeing the place where Goldy just disappeared.

"Home to the mountain, please," I whisper. "I made a promise I plan to keep."

TWENTY-SEVEN
Reve

"My keen dragon's intuition tells me you're upset," I drawl, coming to sit beside Neva at the edge of the wood. Herrick and Malvolo have gone ahead to situate Virago, Heirwig, and Eidolon in the stables, as well as to try their experiment with the soul stone.

Their prevailing theory is that if I wear the stone on my person, perhaps my mind and body could be reunited, unraveling the spell that's held me immobile for a decade.

I know it won't work, but I don't try to dissuade them. I've wanted time alone with Neva for a while now. Neva snorts once in bleak amusement, though her spirits don't truly lift. She's been trying so hard to project an air of calm acceptance, it actually hurts to watch her. She's not fooling any of us. Even infuriatingly tactless Malvolo can sense she's not doing well.

"I think it was my pathetic display of tears that clued you in, oh wise dragon," Neva retorts on a sigh.

"Disappointment is perfectly natural, Neva. But we're not through yet."

Neva shakes her head, fresh tears stinging her eyes. "That's just *it*! I'm causing nothing for you three but grief. You were all living peaceful lives before I came along and wrecked things. Now you're under threat again from hellhounds, the Gryphus huntsman, and Lycaon and it's my fault."

A growl spills from between my teeth. "It's not your fault, Neva. We love you, and we'll fight to the bitter end to protect you."

She raises a hand, but continues shaking her head. "I know, I know. Dragons love treasure and you all think I'm something special."

"You *are* something special," I insist. Damn this curse for stilling my tongue. This would be so much easier if she knew—if I could tell her everything I want to. And damn my brothers for being so dense. How can they still not see it? "Suffice to say, you are far more than you could ever dream, Neva."

"I'm glad you think so."

"I know so," I nearly interrupt her. I push off the hard ground and gesture for her to follow me. "Come. I'll show you."

"Where are we going?"

"Someplace that won't echo quite so much and somewhere we'll have privacy."

Neva's cheeks color prettily. Gods above, I'll never get over just how beautiful she is. It's like she was crafted to be the perfect temptation. Sweet, beautiful, stunningly naïve at times, and kissed by magic.

"How can we, um...?" She gestures vaguely between us, letting the statement hang, misinterpreting my meaning entirely. I'm not corporeal enough to bed her, which is a damn shame because watching her find pleasure in the arms of my brothers has been maddening, knowing I can't have her, myself.

"We're not going to have sex." I tack on a mental *yet* and cross my fingers in a silent entreaty for good luck.

"Oh," she sounds disappointed. "What are we doing then?"

"I think I may be able to help you." I take a deep breath. "But it will be dangerous." And that's the exact reason I haven't attempted this with her already—the reason why I remained quiet as we ventured to find Tenebris. Because it would have been better if Tenebris had been able to help Neva. Better because it would have been less dangerous.

But desperate times call for desperate measures.

True animation flits across her face for the first time in days and she climbs to her feet. "What are we going to do?"

"I'll tell you when we reach the caves," I offer with a shrug. "I don't want my brothers to overhear, lest they try to stop us. Overprotective clods, the both of them."

Neva dutifully falls into step behind me and we trudge silently up the mountainside to the mouth of the caves. She retrieves and lights a lantern, following my lead towards a section of the cave she managed to traipse right past in her search for Malvolo.

My cave is the smallest of the three, because I use it so rarely. It's also glaringly lacking gold or precious gems. Instead, I've lined the dome-like space with shelves, stacking them high with tools, books, and various magical artefacts. Not all treasure is material wealth and to me, knowledge and magical talent have always held more worth than gold or jewels.

It is a little sparse, quite dusty, and not really outfitted for visitors. But it's as good a place as any to try this, and I'm confident Herrick and Malvolo won't come looking for us here.

Neva cocks her head at me, lifting a brow in silent inquiry.

"I'm not Tenebris," I begin cautiously.

"I should hope not!" she says on a laugh.

"I'm not Tenebris in as much as I don't have her level of power," I correct myself. "But I think I may have a way to lift the spell. But, like I said, it's dangerous, Neva. I can't stress that enough."

"If we don't try to break the spell, I'm simply a sitting duck, right?" she asks. "Simply waiting for Lycaon or the Gryphus huntsman to return."

"I suppose so."

"What are you proposing, exactly?"

"I was particularly good at memory retrieval during the war, when exposure to Bacchus could drive men completely out of their minds," I explain.

"Okay."

"I think… I can draw out your memories."

"Really?"

I nod, trying to dampen her sudden interest. "But the second you're aware of who and what you are, you'll only have twenty minutes or so before the spell completely unravels and then you'll be in danger."

"Unravels? What does that mean?"

"It means if you aren't fast enough to return, the spell could kill you…"

Neva's brow furrows, and I can tell she doesn't understand. But I don't have time or the ability to explain further, either.

"What do we do?"

"I need to enter your mind again, Neva."

"Okay."

"It will hurt, but you'll have to ride out the pain. And when I'm finished, you need to run, all right?"

"Run?" she asks, frowning.

"Yes, you'll need to run and leave this cave as quickly as you can."

She steps closer to me as she shakes her head. "Run from what?"

I reach forward and she rests her head against my chest as I thread my fingers through the heavy curtain of her hair. I can feel the weight but not the texture of the hair I thread through my fingers, feel, distantly, the press of her lips, but can't taste their sweetness. The magic of the soul stone is wearing thin, as I suspected it might. It's a stop-gap measure to transport the unwilling dead, not a bridge to full consciousness. I only have a day or two left to try this, which is why this must be done now.

And it's also the reason I don't have time to explain.

"You will understand as soon as I leave your mind. All I need to know at this point is whether you're willing to risk the danger and the pain in order to retrieve your memories, and thus, release yourself from the spell of ignorance that's been holding you hostage."

"Yes, I'm willing to risk whatever I need to."

"Even your life?"

"Yes."

She'll also be risking my life but I keep that information to myself because I know she won't accept the odds if my life is placed on the table.

Neva's eyes flutter closed and I splay my fingers on her temples, sinking into that vast sea of magic that Tenebris' spell barely contains. The magic has worn so thin, it's little more than a gate by this point. Neva's magic will bowl it over in mere days, which is worse than I feared. There's no time to find Prince Payne or any of his blood drinkers. This has to be done now. Improperly integrated, it will kill her.

I'm darkly amused when I ease my magic into her and a small moan builds in her throat. It's so easy to imagine easing something else into her, as well.

Focus, Reve. Focus.

I take her hand and together we step onto that ethereal plane that exists outside corporeal form, and I show her what I've been privy to since the day we met.

The shapeless, shadowy mass is more distinct now, with a vague female shape, becoming less amorphous as the days go on and it, little by little, merges with Neva's consciousness. I can't imagine what hell it's going to be—to deal with her inner monster when she finally combines with it.

Now, it tracks us both with amber-gold eyes, snarling softly.

"What is that?" Neva whispers, horrified.

"It's you," I tell her with a small smile.

"It's me?" she echoes disbelievingly.

"Or, at least, it's part of you. Formed of your magic and your forgotten memories."

"It's an angry beast!" she says, aghast.

I nod. "I can't blame it for being angry, with what memories it has to inform its consciousness."

The thing snarls its dissention and wordlessly offers a clawed hand to Neva. She shrinks into my side.

"You have to embrace it, Neva," I tell her. "If you don't, it will kill you."

Her eyes are huge in her face and she's never looked younger than she does now. It's easy to forget, given what she is, that she's still a sapling, just beginning her life. Easier still to forget when you're an ancient jaded being like a dragon, with centuries of life beneath your scales.

"Don't you want to know what's been kept from you?" I ask.

"I do, but..."

"Take its hand," I urge. "I will help to ease the pain as much as I can when the two of you become one and the same."

With one last nervous glance in my direction, she takes two staggering steps forward and places her hand in the outstretched palm of the shadow.

The transfer begins instantaneously, memories sliding past so thick and fast and in such sharp, painful clarity that it even slices my mind.

Neva's spine arches and I have to steady her before her legs fold. I haul her against my chest, one arm around her waist, as I use my magic as a brace, keeping her from breaking in two under the strain. I barely catch all her

memories, and I'm only experiencing them second-hand.
The flurry must be unbearable for Neva.

Memories of her childhood flash by at lightning speed.

A childhood spent within castle walls, wearing fine
gowns and wandering only within the gardens, watched over
by a hawk-eyed huntsman. The life of a princess was far
from glamorous. It becomes slightly easier for Neva when
her father remarries and she at last has a half-sister, borne by
the night hag that King Leon married against all warnings.

Princess Carmine Resia is one of the few things that
makes Neva's life bearable. Since Neva's been born, Leon
has been hiding her secret and chaining her power, knowing
it would make Neva an instant target.

But Neva shares the secret with Carmine when she is
twelve. She tells Carmine how she can change shapes. And
not in the way that their dutiful huntsman can change—Neva
is not limited to one form.

Neva is an omnifarious. A being able to completely
subvert the laws of nature. Imagination is the only inhibitor
on her abilities. She's been born for one purpose and one
purpose only—to defeat Morningstar's general, the djinn
named Hassan.

Neva is also a hero, heralded by the prophecy, designed
to be the end of Morningstar. She's one of the chosen ten.

Neva trusts Carmine not to tell anyone. But, in her
childish excitement, Carmine entrusts her mother, Queen
Salome, with the information. And that is the beginning of
the end. When Neva witnesses her father's death, she's
unable to draw on her own power to stop it, owing to the
charms Tenebris has used to chain Neva's power. All Neva
can do is run.

She's brought to Gregory's tavern, the Wicked Lyre, to
meet Tenebris, and Neva's consciousness is buried right
along with her power—leaving her tabula rasa, a blank slate.

Neva's screams echo through her mindscape, clawing at my eardrums and sanity as she merges with her angry other half, the wild, untamable omnifarious. Neva absorbs the memory of a repressed, betrayed little girl and becomes something new.

Something strong. Something fierce. Something dangerous.

Something real.

Tenebris' magic feels like a thousand knives as the spell begins to unravel and I jerk us both from the maelstrom of memory.

It's enough. It might even be too much. Neva has to go. Now.

Her eyes snap open, wide and full of tears.

"I'm a princess?" she asks, full of quiet wonderment. "I wasn't abandoned?"

"Not intentionally," I reassure her. "Now go. Keep your promise to me, Neva. Don't forget what it was." I can't name the promise now. I've already said and done too much against the magic that curses me. Now it will be up to Neva to remember.

"My promise?"

"Go," I say, shoving her lightly toward the door. "And hurry. There's not much time left."

"Time left for what?"

I can't explain. I don't have time. "You'll know what to do. And you have… perhaps twenty minutes. Go!"

Neva doesn't hesitate. She turns on one heel, hair fanning out behind her in a lustrous, sweetly-scented wave, and pelts for the exit.

"One kiss," I whisper to myself. "And set us both free."

TWENTY-EIGHT
Neva

I fly through the tunnels, moving back toward the light with a speed I'd hitherto believed impossible.

Fly. The word almost draws an elated giggle from me. Flying isn't an impossible feat for me, I know now. And though the drag of Tenebris' power still stings me like a thousand knives with each passing second as her spell unravels, I'm still impossibly giddy.

Finally, I have my answers!

After years of struggling against a blank white wall, with the lies that Darius fed me about being alone and unwanted, I now know better. My father never abandoned me. Not of his own volition, anyway. His life had been brutally extinguished by the man hunting us. He'd prepared failsafe after failsafe to keep me from the clutches of Lycaon and Hassan, the two greatest threats to my life.

There's the niggling question of Carmine still to deal with, though. Is my beloved sister still alive? Is she safe? Draven had always been sweet to her, always watched over her with particular care, though I was supposed to be his main charge. Does the Corvid Huntsman protect her still? Or has Queen Salome indulged in a little old-fashioned filicide during my long mental lapse?

I hope not. Gods above, I hope not.

It's not a matter I can brood over for long. Reve's estimate is off. I don't have twenty minutes. The monster that merged with me has intimate knowledge of itself and the magic that's caged it for years. I have five minutes at most. Maybe less. And the last tethers of Belle Tenebris'

powers keep me from shifting form. Damn her. I wish I'd
thrown more than a drink at her now.

Arrogant sorceress, to presume to dictate when and how
the curse would be broken.

When I catapult myself through the entrance of the
caves, I bowl Malvolo over, tumbling with him in a painful
jumble of limbs all the way to the base of the mountain. It
costs several crucial seconds for the stars to clear and when
they do, I see Herrick loping back down towards us with a
pinched look of concern on his face.

"Are you all right?" Herrick asks.

"What's going on, Neva?" Malvolo demands. "What
are you running from?"

I don't have time to explain it to them, so I yank myself
free of Malvolo and sprint for the cabin. Three minutes now.

Herrick and Malvolo's boots slap the hard earth behind
me, quickly closing the distance between us. I might be fast,
but they're still faster than me, chained as I am by this
limited shape. I'd trade just about anything for access to
wings or the speed of a large, exotic cat. Anything to get me
to Reve sooner.

Malvolo tries to yank me to a stop, turning me to half-
face him. "Neva, what's wrong?"

"Reve!" I shout.

"Reve?" he questions, shaking his head.

"I can't explain! I don't have time!"

Malvolo assesses my face for a portion of a second that
feels much longer before nodding. He scoops my legs from
beneath me easily and clutches me to his chest, charging
forward with a speed that whips the wind against my face
and draws strained tears from the corners of my eyes.

We reach the cottage with sixty seconds to spare. By
the time Malvolo disarms the wards and wrenches the door
open, it's only thirty seconds.

I run through the dim, dusty house, tripping twice in my haste. My legs feel watery and threaten to give out from beneath me. My vision pulses in and out in bursts of white light and alarming shadow. I fall again and Malvolo has to dive to catch me before my head can hit the floor. When I'm stable enough to move, I don't risk standing up. I crawl the last few feet to Reve's bed on my hands and knees.

Ten seconds.

Five.

I clutch Reve's bedsheets and use them to haul myself up. The pain is blinding, the desperation cloying, the joy at seeing him in the flesh palpable even so. I cup his face gingerly. I stoop and, ignoring Malvolo's shocked grunt, I press my lips to Reve's.

For one painful squeeze of my heart, I'm sure this won't work and that we're both doomed. Reve's warm, slightly chapped lips are utterly still beneath mine, just as I'd felt them last time, when I'd been seized by the absurd desire to kiss him awake. I should have acted on my instincts then, rousing him long before our ill-fated trip to find Tenebris. It might have saved us all time and grief.

But that's the funny thing about fate. She's a wily mistress; she knows just where you need to be and the time you need to be there. Without the journey, could I have loved these men? Perhaps, in time. But not the way I do now. And could they have loved me?

I draw back from Reve when the dizziness clears, the last of Tenebris' magic sloughing off my shoulders like a discarded skin that no longer fits. My curse is broken.

"Reve?" I say his name, hoping the spell has broken for him too.

But… nothing.

"What… what are you doing, Neva?" Malvolo asks.

241

"He was supposed to wake up!" I yell in response as I turn to look at Malvolo and then Herrick, as he bursts through the door.

"Look," Malvolo says and points at his sleeping brother.

Only now Reve isn't sleeping. Now his eyes are open.

"Reve?" I say as I look down at him.

He suddenly comes alive, arms coming up to hold my face, hands fisting into my hair. He draws me down with a desperate sound, rolling me beneath him. Then his lips are on mine, no longer warm and placid, but alive and full of profound hunger. He makes quick work of my buttons, parting the shirt before I even have time to do more than respond to his kiss. He touches everywhere he can reach, baring the skin that's obstructed by clothing as quickly as he can.

There's an answering hunger in my monster. Caged for so long, she also craves touch more than water, food, or air. My monster hasn't seen the light of day in nine years. Reve hasn't eaten, drank, or been inside a woman for ten. Trapped in an endless hellscape without human contact and human touch, it's a wonder he's not insane. So, I can't blame him when he divests us of our clothing and pushes himself inside me the second he can.

"What the fuck?" Malvolo manages to splutter. "He just... you... but that's impossible! Unless...?"

"She's the one who was meant to break the spell," Herrick says in an awed tone as they both watch us. "It was Neva all along."

"Neva is one of the chosen," Malvolo echoes.

Reve grunts, then moans aloud as he begins to set a rhythm. "Please, do me a favor, both of you..."

"Anything," Malvolo answers.

"Fuck off for the next few hours!"

242

TWENTY-NINE
Neva

Forget a few hours. Reve doesn't let me go until sundown.

This is the second time in as many weeks that a dragon has taken me so hard and often that I'm bow-legged afterwards. But I can't complain about the creeping sense of exhaustion that's threatening to drag my eyelids closed. I'm half out of my mind every second Reve touches me.

The ache between my legs is a pleasant one when he's finally through spending a decade's worth of passion on my body. Reve's eyes are still alert, and I doubt he'll close them for another decade at least. He smiles down indulgently at me when he tucks me into his bed, wrapping me so snugly in the bedcovers that I feel like a caterpillar who'll emerge a stunning butterfly... after about two weeks of rest, that is.

I'm desperate for a break, for sleep. The recent release of the spell, compounded by weeks of subpar sleep and recent vigorous sexual activity, has me exhausted.

So, of course, Malvolo raps urgently on the door when I'm about to slide peacefully off to sleep in Reve's arms.

"Go away, Mal," Reve calls. "She needs rest."

"Not the time for it, brother," Malvolo responds. "Our friends from the forest are back and they've brought company."

"Those fuckers don't know when to quit," Reve responds and I'm not sure if he's talking about his brothers or the huntsman and the hellhounds.

I sit up in bed in an instant as the words penetrate my head. A second or so later, I'm on my feet and halfway to the door, moving in a sleepwalker's stumble.

If Lycaon is here, I have to face him. He's not the threat I'm designed to face, but face him I will. I refuse to be the passive waste I was outside Castle Chimera. Now that I know who and what I am, I'll fight.

Gladly.

I exit the room first, stalking past Malvolo, gathering up the dregs of my energy through sheer spite. If I can't sleep until after this bastard is felled, so be it. I'm going to smack him into the ground so hard, he'll still be spitting earthworms when he reaches Avernus.

Malvolo and Herrick watch me through half-lidded eyes, clearly torn between their desire to stand between me and what's coming, and the desire to see me in action. After all, it's not every day you learn you've been fucking a creature of legend. When neither moves to stop me, I lift one of the heavy wooden shutters and peer out through the gap.

My confidence wavers just a mite when my eyes rove the front line. Company indeed. Malvolo really has a talent for understatement. Lycaon has brought a fucking army.

There are at least thirteen hellhounds and other assorted nasty creatures waiting for us. Thirty infantryman stand behind them, lightly armored and armed with crossbows, should the overkill prove ineffective.

The charge is led by a woman. Fair-skinned, with a cap of dark auburn hair, dark, penetrating eyes, and a thin mouth painted with her signature blue gloss, she holds herself straight in the saddle, regal pride substituting for the inches she lacks in height.

She'll still be a head shorter than me, even in her riding boots. Her cloak, tight dress, and bustier are all tailored to disguise the fact that, like most night hags, she's fairly shapeless. I'll never understand what possessed my father to marry this vile woman—she must have bewitched him with her powerful magic. It certainly could not have been owing to her looks because Salome was always painfully plain, but for her fine locks, which she's now sheared short.

She looks even less appealing than usual, with Lycaon's phantom features overlaid onto hers. So, this is how he's been getting around without a soul stone. He's possessing bodies, leaching power from talented magical individuals. It's forbidden, arcane magic of the sort that only Morningstar and his generals would resort to. It shouldn't shock me that Salome has allowed this. After all, it was she who arranged the coup that killed my father, leaving her the queen regent of Ascor and Lycaon free to sack the city in search of me.

I shoulder open the front door.

"Neva," Malvolo warns.

"She's ready," Reve says from behind us.

I turn to face Malvolo and I smile, nodding to him to let him know Reve's right. I am ready. Malvolo swallows hard and returns my nod so I stride into the yard, bare as the day I was born. Clothes will only be a hindrance to me at this point.

Seconds later, I'm flanked on either side by Herrick and Malvolo, with Reve's comforting warmth protecting my back. Malvolo tries to step in front of me and take the lead, though he's armed only with a kitchen knife. I once again regret causing the loss of his sword. Herrick looks like he might follow suit, and he wields no weapon at all except his fists. I place my hands on their forearms, lowering them gently.

"Don't. This is my battle to fight."

"I don't care what the bloody fuck you are," Malvolo says, voice coming out a baleful hiss. "I'm not letting you go into battle alone. I'm taking these fuckers down with you."

I appreciate the sentiment and show it by leaning in to press a brief but fervent kiss to his lips. "Just follow my lead, General," I say with a flirty smile, before turning back to face Salome.

Her painted lips stretch into a wide, malevolent grin as I acknowledge her.

"My dear, Neva," she drawls, insincerity dripping from her words like poison from an apple. "How good to see you again."

"Cut the shit, Salome," I growl. "I know Lycaon has his hands shoved up your flat ass. So why don't we stop this idle chit-chat and get down to what you really came for?"

Salome's smile slips an inch, but she recovers it before the pleasant façade can drop completely. "It doesn't have to end like this, Neva. Morningstar is merciful. If you lay down your arms and come with us now, you could see Carmine again. Wouldn't you like that? A chance to be reunited with your dear sister?"

It gives me very brief pause to hear Carmine's name. I've only had my recovered memories for an hour or so, and already the ache to see her is unbearable. But even if I found Salome's offer acceptable, there's no way to know if Carmine is still alive. Salome seems the type to put ambition and personal gain before the well-being of her own blood. Carmine's corpse might have been a maggot's meal years ago, and I would never have known. There's only one person I'll trust to confirm my sister is living, and I'm not entirely sure he'll be present.

My eyes flick over the line, and I pick up Draven near the back with the archers, watching the proceedings with stiff-lipped disapproval. He's got one hand resting lightly on the pommel of his sword. He's in an untenable position, as a secret plant of my father's. To defect and fight by my side will be to abandon Carmine.

I shake my head once, hoping he can read the plea in my eyes.

Don't worry about me, Draven. Do what you have to do. Keep Carmine safe.

His answering nod is barely perceptible, and Salome doesn't pick him out of the crowd when she follows my gaze. I use the time to harden my expression and inject some steel into my tone. I won't let her use my sister as a weapon to wield against me.

"Carmine betrayed me!" I call out. "She can rot in Avernus for all I care!"

Salome's thin brows bounce up in surprise and her lips part ever so slightly. "How very callous of you, dear Neva. Time has made you a jaded thing."

"Time has made me wise, step-mother. Wise enough to learn the lessons my father didn't have the chance to teach me or to learn, himself. Wise enough to know I have to end you and your lover, before you end me."

She scoffs, and when she speaks again, her voice is layered with some of Lycaon's gravelly bass. "If you could have ended me, you would have already acted, mewling little girl. Bound, you are no threat to me."

My smile slashes across my face, growing wider by the second. Salome's face goes completely bloodless, lips pressed into a tight line of rage. She hisses a spitting word in a language I don't recognize and the assembled forces, which have been frozen until now, stir into furious motion.

The hellhounds move almost too quickly to track, their enormous forepaws digging into the hard earth and spraying chunks of debris behind them as they take several scorching steps forward, starting little fires in their wake. I'm a second and a half faster than the lead mutt, and I spring into the air with the muscled strength of a jackrabbit, body stretching and morphing, the sound of my joints popping, echoing like shots around the clearing, even above the growls and furious howls of the hellhounds.

I twist once in midair and come down, golden fur stretching taut over finely-honed muscles. The thick sable fall of my hair feathers out into a dark mane around my crown and I roar a defiant challenge at the oncoming hellhounds. They pause, a few backpedaling as they come snout-to-snout with a furious, overlarge lion.

The lion had unsurprisingly been my father's favorite form when he was alive. It had also been the first accidental shift I'd made when I was two years old, racing after him in the garden.

I brush past the first hellhound with a furious swipe of claws, spilling grayish entrails onto the ground as its underbelly splits. One of its fellows yelps and goes down in the slippery mess, and I leap onto its exposed throat, crushing its windpipe with a satisfying crunch and a wheeze. Two hellhounds down and eleven to go. Then, there are the archers to consider. And, of course, Salome and Lycaon.

Lycaon is retreating to the back of the line, sheltering behind the hellhounds he's brought, confident that if I come after him, I'll meet a prickly end at the hands of his archers.

I need something stronger than a lion, something that doesn't take damage easily. I smile when the answer comes to me. I bound back to my lovers, who have arrayed themselves around the cabin, using its walls to protect their backs and sides from being flanked. I shift rapidly back to my human shape, whipping Malvolo's knife from his grasp before offering it to Herrick.

"Hey!"

"Shift," I order Malvolo. "We're going to take out the archers."

"You need Herrick or Reve," he snaps back impatiently. "I'm a cripple, Neva. I can't fly with just one wing."

"I know. Now shift."

A growl actually builds in his chest. "Neva…"

"Mal," I say, capturing his attention. "Do you trust me?"

Those intense ember eyes meet mine and scrutinize me for a furious half-second before he nods. "Against all fucking logic and sanity, I *do* trust you."

"Then shift."

His back hunches and his body rapidly darkens, elongating into something far more reptilian. A tail whips from his back and casually flicks away an oncoming hellhound who'd been aiming to score up my back. Malvolo gains mass quickly, shifting even more swiftly than I can. The earth shakes as his massive legs impact the ground and fear roils through the air as he assumes his full dragon shape.

I clamber up one foreleg, using the edges of his massive onyx scales to hurriedly ascend his body. I study his intact wing for a few seconds, taking in the shape of it, the thick arching juts of bone and the membranous charcoal wing tissue stretched between them. I commit the shape to memory, climb onto the nub of bone, and begin to shift.

I'm used to assuming animal shape, but it's not the only use for my powers. I can become non-living tissue. Metals, tools, furniture. But this is the first time I've tried to become part of a whole.

I dig my fingers into the bone and hold on for dear life, stretching to mirror his other, remaining wing.

Reve actually laughs and claps his hands when he realizes what I'm up to. "That's my girl!" he cries.

Malvolo realizes what I've done seconds after Reve does, and bugles a triumphant sound into the evening sky before launching his weight into the air with a leap and a flap of wings, sending us both high above the battlefield in a matter of seconds. The hellhounds fade to mere dots on the ground far below. The human line of archers look like scrabbling ants as Malvolo brings us over their line.

I have a second to pray for Draven to flee before Malvolo is belching flame, scouring the tree line and everything in it in red-orange flame. I have to force myself to look at the carnage below. I don't want to see the twisted shapes that accompany the caustic smell of burning flesh and hair, but this is my legacy—what I'm born to do, played out on a smaller scale. So I look. I look at the fallen shapes, cracked and blackened and barely human looking. I look at the half-mile of pines that have gone up like matchsticks, watch the billowing smoke choke the life from any that remain.

Malvolo doesn't stay put for long, banking hard to come around and deal with the next threat.

There are still ten hellhounds remaining, though they seem to be losing their battle. Lycaon came woefully underprepared, when he thought he faced an earthbound cripple, a magically-spayed champion, a healer, and a phantom.

Instead, there are three dragons on the field of battle and an omnifarious with the ability to transform into damn near anything.

The hellhounds aren't falling as easily as the humans. Their immunity to fire means a dragon's most effective weapon is essentially useless. Malvolo understands this and lands, catching me around the waist with a giant foreclaw when I resume human shape. He nudges my face gently with his snout, his thermic breath ruffling my hair in silent thanks as I turn to face the oncoming danger.

I smile and pat the side of his face. "You're welcome, General."

He chuffs a laugh.

Salome or Lycaon look ready to spit fire themselves when I stride forward, shifting again. I'm leaning toward a little karmic justice for this bitch and her consort. She'd once ordered my death and the death of my father at the hands of these stinking dogs—it only seems right she meet her end the same way.

When I launch onto all fours again, my fur crackles with sparks. The blood in my veins burns hot and I feel like I might turn into cinder any second. Acidic saliva dribbles from my tongue as it lolls out of my mouth, taking sizzling chunks of the earth with it while it dissolves into impotency seconds later.

I hope every motherfucking bite burns like Avernus when I tear them to pieces.

Salome draws a dagger from her belt, the shiny blade flashing dangerously at me as I approach. I pay it little mind. One dagger can't save her from me. Her hand shakes, too late realizing she's entered a losing battle.

This ends here and now.

It's not until I'm a foot away that I realize Salome's not shaking from fear. Her body is heaving with... laughter? Genuinely delighted laughter tears itself from her chest, both bass and soprano, like the pealing of bells. They're both laughing.

Why? I have no idea.

"Oh, child," Lycaon coos. "Oh, sweet, sweet naïve thing. Your father never told you about me, did he?"

"He said you were cursed and that a champion would rise to defeat you." My voice sounds almost as bass as Lycaon's, warped as it is by a canine throat. I take another long step forward. Only half a foot stands between us now. I should just go for their throat and be done with this. "And I'm that champion."

Salome's eyes glitter with barely repressed glee. "Oh yes, I *am* cursed. You see, when the fickle gods of Yore paid a call on me without warning, I had nothing to feed them. But you can't turn away a god, nor deny them food when they're in your home. So I used the only thing I had left after my disastrous harvest. I slew my son and served him up. His flesh was young and sweet and tender, and they feasted on him. But upon learning what it was they'd so enjoyed, they grew enraged. They turned me into a baying hound, doomed to wander until something more monstrous than I could destroy me."

"Consider it here," I growl, disgusted.

Lycaon tsks. "You haven't heard the end of my story, child." He takes a breath. "You see, I bred and bred and bred for a time. And I could control every offshoot of my blood with a thought, including..."

He forks two of Salome's slim fingers at me and my entire body goes rigid. My steps falter and panic begins to bubble into my veins as his meaning hits me.

"*Hellhounds,*" he finishes with relish.

I try to shift, try to become anything but this blasted canine shape. But it feels like I've been trapped under a heavy stone as Lycaon's control presses painfully into me. I can't shift out from under the command, can barely think past the malice that burns through his thoughts.

He crosses over to me and lodges one of Salome's riding boots into my flank, toppling me off my feet with a kick that lands like a warhammer. Several of my ribs snap like dry kindling and a shocked yelp escapes my mouth, followed by a whine as he clambers on top of me, using the spiked heels of Salome's boots to press my bottom half into the ground. The verdant blade flashes once in the fading light as he brings it to bear.

"Now die," he hisses, driving it down. It sinks up to the hilt in my guts. Something sloughs off the blade and begins to spread through my abdomen, lining my veins with liquid fire.

THIRTY
Malvolo

The omnifarious.
And the one who was prophecied to waken Reve.
One of the Chosen Ten.
I still can't fucking believe it. All of it.

Months ago, Herrick happened upon a tavern by chance and discovered the fucking omnifarious that was foretold in the prophecy. It was all there. If I'd ever believed in such toss, maybe I would have seen it sooner.

Neva's not only a champion, but she's the daughter of Leon, as well. A princess. Heir apparent to Ascor, when Salome is deposed. Once Neva ends that bitch once and for all, perhaps she can lead her people to ally with Delorood and start preparing the kingdom for war.

My dragon form isn't as effective on the ground, but it's a damn sight better than my two-legged shape when it comes to battling hellhounds. It's child's play to bat them off when they try to scale my sides or bite through my armored hide.

There are perhaps eight of them left when I hear a horrible cracking noise and turn, doing an about-face in time to see Lycaon's possessed body leap onto Neva, pinning her beneath his weight.

My thundering heart stutters for a beat. It shouldn't be possible. Lycaon is hopelessly outclassed.

And then I see where Neva has made her crucial, fatal mistake. Because the creature Lycaon has pinned is a hellhound twice the size of any we've yet faced. It emits a shocked yelp as spikes dig painfully into its side.

253

Neva's turned into the one thing Lycaon can control with an iron fist. Stupid, stupid girl.

My dragon form is too bulky. Too slow.

"Now *die*," Lycaon hisses triumphantly.

The knife disappears into her underbelly with a neat little snick of sound. Neva lets out a pained yip and it feels like I'm the one who's been gutted.

Nooooo!

It can't end this way! Not when we've just found her! Not when she's one of the chosen! Not when the prophecy foretold her!

Another hellhound comes streaking toward me, trying to rake at my exposed eyes with his claws. I shove him off and crush him idly beneath one of my heels, ignoring the ripple of discomfort as he combusts and burns to a cinder beneath me. I shriek a shrill cry of defiance at Salome and Lycaon.

Even if Neva doesn't die, Salome and Lycaon will still pay for this—for what they've done to her. Lycaon's eyes go wide when he registers I'm near. With another swift hand gesture, he summons the remaining hellhounds to form a furry barricade between us. A cackle actually escapes the mad king.

"Too late, General Malvolo. You're far too late. She'll be dead in under an hour. Attack now and you only guarantee it happening that much sooner. But the choice is yours, of course. I'd personally put her out of her misery, if she were my lover."

My lips pull back from my teeth. Lycaon thinks he's won. That I can't hurt him or his host without hurting Neva. But he's forgotten something crucial.

Hellhounds are fireproof. The line of bodies in front of me can't be killed by a gout of flame. Nor can the shuddering form of Neva, crushed as she is beneath one of his heels.

But Salome is a night hag. Nigh mortal, but for the extended life span and enhanced dream manipulation. Which means she's completely flammable.

I release the fire in my chest with a furious bellow, raining death down on them both. Salome and Lycaon realize too late what I intend. Lycaon dives from her body before the flames lift Salome off the ground and fling her a half-mile away, into the surrounding trees. I'm not sure if it's my fire that ends her, or the impact with a pine. The force of it snaps bone and she sinks to the ground in a jumble of broken bits, white bone stabbing out of her pale skin at odd intervals.

Lycaon spits curses at me before disappearing into the ether. I don't even bother to track the fucker. I lumber forward, shedding my dragon form as quickly as possible so I can go to Neva.

She's still living, thank the Gods. As I watch, her hellhound shape slowly morphs back into her delicate human form. I can't even enjoy the sight of her bare flesh, because she's streaked with dirt and blood, blade jutting out of her gut like an ugly thorn.

"Get my kit," Herrick shouts at Reve as the pair approach.

Reve turns on his heel and runs back toward the house to get Herrick's medical bag. Herrick drops to his hands and knees at her side. He's gone completely bloodless—he, too, looks like he's been stabbed.

Neva's hand gropes weakly for the handle of the dagger. "Burns," she complains. "Take it… out."

"We can't," Herrick says quietly, stilling her hands before she can reach the blade. "Not until we know what we're dealing with."

Green pus begins to foam at the edges of Neva's wound, emitting a foul smell, like her innards are already rotting. She twists and gutters once, like a candle exposed to wind. Herrick stares at the stuff and blood drains away from his face, leaving him ghostly pale.

"Drecaine poison," he mutters. "Fuck. It's supposed to be impossible to grow outside of Wonderland. It can't be imported, either."

"Then how the fuck did she get it?" I ask. "And, more importantly, is there an antidote?"

"There is. But it's almost impossible for the average apothecary to mix in the proper equation."

"What must be mixed?"

He shrugs. "A tincture of blood of the beloved, wine, and a dragon's tooth, ground to powder," he begins to babble in his desperation.

"Blood, wine, and dragon's teeth. All of which we *have*," I growl. "Tell Reve to get wine and a mortar and pestle."

"Mal…"

I ignore his objection, reaching as far back as I can to grip a slippery molar. This is going to fucking hurt, but I've definitely sustained worse over the years. Compared to having my wing wrenched off, this will be a pinprick.

Once I've got a good grip on it, I pull with all my strength. The root sticks stubbornly and pure agony lances through the bones of my face, pulsing white behind my eyes. I don't release my grip.

It's one fucking tooth. One tooth to save her. I'd cut off my other wing, if the antidote called for it. I can sacrifice one godforsaken tooth.

My jaw creaks and threatens to buckle before the damn thing finally comes loose. I spit a mouthful of blood to the ground and offer the tooth to Herrick, eyes streaming. "Grind it."

"Reve, get a bandage out of the pack," he instructs Reve, who's returned with the kit, pestle and mortar, and a bottle of Sweetland port. "Pack the socket with gauze, Mal.

And put three droplets of poppy juice under your tongue for the pain."

I obediently take the gauze pads from Reve and stuff them into my mouth, but ignore the vial of shimmering orange painkiller he offers me. I'm not fainting dead away and missing what could be the last moments of Neva's life, should we fail her.

Once the tooth is white dust, I drip blood into the mortar as well, and Reve splashes in a draft of port. Herrick brings the mix up to Neva's lips. Her eyelids barely flutter when she sips it. Her skin's gone ashy gray, and her heart is just a soft murmur.

We're losing her.

"It should be working," Herrick mutters desperately. "It's potent. Her color should be improving. So why the fuck isn't it working?"

"It's just Mal's blood in there," Reve says after a moment.

"Yeah, so?" I bite out. "*Blood of the beloved.* She said she loved me; it should work."

"She said she loves all of us, Mal," Reve corrects me.

Herrick's eyes light with sudden hope and understanding. "Yes. Reve, you're right. Give me a scalpel, quickly."

Reve digs around in the creaky leather bag for half a second before producing the shining silver tool. Herrick slides the blade over the pad of his thumb and drips a stream of blood into the mix. Reve skips the blade and pricks the tip of his index finger with an elongated canine, letting his blood drip into the tincture, as well.

When Herrick tips the whole thing into Neva's mouth, we lean forward, holding our collective breath. If this doesn't work, I'm going to find Lycaon, wherever he's hiding, and drag him screaming from the nether world so I can end his putrid existence once and for all.

Herrick removes the knife, which comes loose with a sucking sound, and immediately begins to pack the wound.

And a split second later, Neva's eyes go wide.

"It worked!" I yell.

She jerks forward as she takes a deep breath. Another second passes before she sits up and glares at Herrick. "That fucking hurt!" she chastises him. "Warn a girl before you feed her whatever that horrible stuff was!"

Herrick's eyes soften into a deep molten gold and a playful smile twists his full lips. "Don't die on us next time, and we'll talk."

She smiles, but he shakes his head. He's still playing doctor. "Move your hands," he orders. "You're not out of the woods yet."

Neva sags to the ground again with a groan, one hand coming up to shield her eyes as her cheeks tinge with the palest rose shade, from either frustration or embarrassment.

"How did this happen?" she asks. "I'm supposed to be invincible, aren't I? One of the champions?"

"You're not, nor will you ever be, invincible," Herrick snaps.

"He's right," I add in a dopey voice, owing to the gauze packed in my jaw. "You shouldn't have gone after Salome without training or backup."

"Heroes only become heroes with hard work and dedication," Herrick continues to lecture her. "Your wound is very serious, Neva. I'm going to have to put you on bedrest and monitor you for at least the next two weeks." He turns a steely raptor glare at me next. "And *you,* put some goddamn poppy juice in your mouth and join her for a day, at least."

"Fuck off," I say. Or rather, try to say. I just end up spraying more blood onto the ground.

Neva smirks. "You heard him. Drink your juice, Malvolo."

258

She winces as Herrick wraps her abdomen, then she gives me another strained smirk.

Herrick offers a quiet, half-strangled laugh. "Ah, young love. Nothing quite like it."

EPILOGUE
Neva

I reach for the brass knocker with mounting trepidation.

In other circumstances, I might add a few inches onto my frame with magic, but I'm strictly forbidden to shift until the wound is fully closed—doctor's orders. I can feel the steely, disapproving stare of said doctor boring a hole into the side of my face as I stretch.

"You're going to pull your stitches," Herrick complains from beneath his cowl. "Just let Malvolo knock."

"Let her do the honors, Herrick," Reve drawls, squeezing my free hand tight.

Each brother is touching me in some fashion as we huddle near the oak door. Malvolo has his hand around mine. His body brushes against my shoulder blades, his breath tickling the nape of my neck and his arousal nudging the small of my back. Herrick's shoulder is pressed against mine, and the hand around my waist is there to keep me from toppling over. I'm still not steady, even after the weeks I've had to recover.

The Drecaine Salome dosed me with slows my healing to a fucking crawl. I may be laid out for a year or more, which is why we're here...

We've been on the run for the last four weeks, forced to flee the Vorst ancestral home after word of Salome's death reached the ears of the regent in Ascor. The murder of the queen...

There was no safe place for us to stay permanently, save for a Guild stronghold.

We've been unable to contact Goldy, which means she's either succeeded in her mission and is halfway to Delorood with her spoils, or she's died in the attempt. Hopefully not the latter...

Ever since, we've been chasing whispers of Guild activity, and we've finally found what we're looking for at the border between Wonderland and Grimm.

The vegetation grows thick and colorful here, and the door seems to stand completely alone, without a house to support it. It's one of the stranger things I've seen since leaving Ascor. But this *is* the border of Wonderland. Things are bound to get a little mad the longer we stay here.

"I still say we should have gone to the Sea Witch or Vasalisa. I could do with a bit less insanity. This bitch is almost as bad as Tenebris," Malvolo complains.

"Neva's magic is chaotic. She needs a chaotic teacher," Herrick explains patiently, repeating his point for the umpteenth time. "Now, be quiet, Mal. She's coming."

Herrick is right. Disembodied footsteps approach the door. It swings inward quickly, colliding with the wall beyond it in an enormous bang that sounds disproportionate to the action.

A slice of the room beyond is revealed in all its glorious upheaval. There's not a space left unoccupied by something, whether it be a desk or a strange bauble, or a squirming, curious creature.

The most curious person of all steps into the doorway, drawing our eyes immediately with her eccentric attire and odd-colored hair. I've never actually seen someone with heliotrope hair corkscrewing from beneath a velvet top hat before.

She's quite striking, even in her haberdashery, silver buttons glinting as the light from the fire catches them. She blinks at us, quite shocked, as if we, not she, threw open the door with such tremendous pomp.

"Goodness," she says in a fluttery whisper. "Is it six o'clock already?"

Herrick's face breaks into a wide grin. "It's good to see you looking well, Hattie. May we come in? We can explain ourselves over tea."

Mad Madam Harriet Trillby steps aside, graciously ushering us forward. "No, no! The adventures first, explanations take such a dreadfully long time."

I extend my hand to her once the door's shut firmly behind us. There's a cozy sense of claustrophobia about the place, which I'm beginning to like. The world outside is vast and cold, and I'm happy to be tucked safely into one small corner of it for now.

"I'm Neva," I say. "It's nice to meet you, Miss Trillby."

Hattie quickly shoves me into a chair and whips out a tea set seemingly from nowhere to pour me a steaming cup of ginger tea.

"A pleasure, a pleasure. But I must ask you something before we begin."

I glance at Herrick, who rolls his eyes good-naturedly. Reve smiles faintly, stroking a cat that's in the process of appearing stripe by stripe atop his shoulder.

Malvolo just sighs.

"Okay. What's the question?" I ask.

There's a frankly madcap look in her glinting gray eyes. She offers me a gleaming smile.

"How, exactly, is a raven like a writing desk?"

To Be Continued in…

GOLDY
NOW AVAILABLE!

Get FREE E-Books!
It's as easy as:

1. Go to my website: www.hpmallory.com
2. Sign up in the pop-up box or on the link at the top of the home page
3. Check your email!

About the Author:

HP Mallory is a New York Times and USA Today Bestselling author who started as a self-published author.

She lives in Southern California with her son and a cranky cat, where she's at work on her next book.

Printed in Great Britain
by Amazon

82801871R00159